Rising Tides

Book Five
The Irish End Game Series

Susan Kiernan-Lewis

Susan Kiernan-Lewis

Other books by Susan Kiernan-Lewis:

Free Falling
Going Gone
Heading Home
Blind Sided
Cold Comfort
Murder in the South of France
Murder à la Carte
Murder in Provence
Murder in Paris
Murder in Aix
Murder in Nice
A Grave Mistake
Walk Trot Die
Finding Infinity
A Trespass in Time
Journey to the Lost Tomb
Race to World's End
Reckless
Shameless
Breathless
Heartless

to John Patrick

Susan Kiernan-Lewis

Rising Tides
San Marco Press/Atlanta 2015

1

It is impossible to believe that this is the same vibrant city I first flew into four years ago.

Sarah sat in the front of the Jeep Wrangler, an uneaten sandwich on the console between her and her husband, Mike. She stared out over the panorama of the damaged city.

Dublin. Once the grand mecca for communications technology and creative invention. The phoenix that rose from its own ashes when the city recreated itself from hatred, bigotry and fear now hovered over it like a black harbinger of doom. Sarah didn't want to think of her first visit to Dublin...with David. It wouldn't help. In fact it would make everything worse.

Because John had been there, too.

"You all right, then, love?" Mike asked, his face knitted in worry as he watched her.

She attempted a smile. "Just letting memories get in the way."

He reached over and squeezed her hand firmly with his large, warm one.

"One night," he said. "And we'll be on our way."

It was always one more night. Always something standing between Sarah and the effort to get going, get out—and start searching. And how long had John been gone now? A week? How far could a child get in a week? Especially a child as inventive and intrepid as John?

But Mike was right. Surely to God, this had to be the end of the waiting.

After leaving their fortified compound in southern Ireland, they'd driven into the city late this afternoon on what was left of the M50 motorway, the semicircle road which intersected Dublin. Their two passengers—prisoners, really—were unceremoniously deposited with the New Dublin Garda

Sìochàna although not quickly. At least not as quickly as Sarah had hoped.

Why was she surprised? When they drove over the Father Matthew Bridge on their way to the government complex, it occurred to her that someone might have an issue with one of their prisoners—a Catholic priest. Would he get a fair trial? Would they be willing to imprison him?

In the end, she had to let it go—as Mike was always urging her to do. Let whatever *would* happen, happen. And if it turned out she couldn't live with it, well, she could always come back and deal with it later.

Sarah ran a hand over her face to quell the nausea building in her.

Trust me to get morning sickness now of all times. It was strange enough to be pregnant at forty-four. She passed a hand over her abdomen and watched Mike's eyes follow the movement.

At least this little one is safe and I know right where he is at all times.

"You're not hungry, Sarah?"

"Just a little queasy."

"Aye, well, we'll save it then." He wrapped a sandwich in paper and stowed it inside the console.

The United States embassy—or what was left of it—had offered them quarters for the night which Sarah and Mike were only too happy to take them up on. Surprisingly, Dublin didn't look like a ghost town. Far from it. If anything it looked like every person in the entire country had opted to move here after the bomb dropped.

Except for government vehicles, there were no cars on the streets. She and Mike had prompted more than a few curious stares when they drove into town. And because there were few working cars in Ireland—and most Dubliners wouldn't know the tail end of a horse—the city dwellers appeared to have latched on to the next smartest thing. There were bicycles everywhere. They were parked under trees, inside stairwells, and in the burgeoning greenscapes that seemed to be slowly taking over the city.

As Sarah watched the cyclists zip up and down the streets without benefit of traffic lights or any obvious road rules, she couldn't help but wonder where these people had to go in such a hurry. And what did it matter? Why not just walk? There was no job to get to, no late afternoon barista date to make, no classes to be late for. Was it just habit?

The light had nearly faded, reflected from the broken windows in the building opposite where they sat eating their supper. Although she hadn't known Dublin well before the bomb dropped, Sarah was pretty sure this section of town would have been the business district. Even now, four years later, the glass and stone buildings shot straight up into the sky. Without working elevators—or employers—she found herself wondering what the structures were used for.

Since there was no one to care where they went or what they did, she and Mike parked in the middle of Saint Stephen's Green. Sarah thought she saw glimpses of the city trying to right itself but possibly that was just the carry over from their long day spent in fairly modern environs processing the prisoners. The complex where the Garda Sìochàna and provisional government were housed had electricity to go with its red tape. It was hard to believe that just a few steps outside the government compound were weeds growing out of pavement cracks, graffiti-scrawled walls and streets full of tents, primitive food kiosks and abandoned vehicles.

"It's in better shape than I thought it'd be," Mike remarked. A large man, Mike had been a fisherman back before the Crisis. He looked wedged into the driver's seat of their Jeep Wrangler.

"All of these people," Sarah said in amazement. Even the park was crammed with tents and sleeping bags. Some people had piled the park benches with what appeared to be all their worldly belongings. "It's like a whole city of homeless people. Why don't they just go sleep in the abandoned buildings?"

"Maybe they do when it gets cold," Mike said, finishing off the last of the sandwich they'd bought with the food chits given to them by the Embassy to use as money on the street. The food sellers would then exchange the chits to pay for rent or other supplies they needed from the government.

"It's a hell of a way to live," she said softly as she watched a young mother holding the hand of a child as she wandered through the park.

"Now, don't be inviting all of Dublin to come live with us in Ameriland," Mike said. "We've got about all we can handle as it is."

Sarah turned and rubbed his arm. If she was exhausted, then Mike must be too. He'd driven the whole way up from the south.

"Let's go find our quarters," she said. "I want to be on the road early tomorrow."

*****

Liam O'Reilly stood in the window of the provisional government building and watched the streets below. The compound was encircled by tall stone walls, each topped with coiled barbed wire. Even after four years more people came pouring into Dublin every day. *It's a wonder the poor sods survived as long as they had out in the country.* Even so, most of them got a rude awakening in the city.

"It appears to be a hundred kilometers south of here," his assistant Shane Sullivan said as he leaned over O'Reilly's desk. O'Reilly turned from the scene outside the window. Sullivan had been a Junior Minister before the bomb dropped. Like O'Reilly, he had moved up considerably in the last few years. With no family to hinder or distract them, both O'Reilly and Sullivan had done well with the changes in the new world political scene.

And if this business with America carried forward, there might literally be no end to how far they could go.

"What was there before?" O'Reilly asked, walking back to the desk.

Sullivan was looking at a map of Ireland, his thick index finger sitting on a spot midway from both coasts where Donovan's compound was located.

"Nothing. A pasture maybe."

"Had to be owned by someone."

"Probably but whoever it was, he's likely dead now. That area had a blistering series of attacks from local gangs right after the bomb dropped."

"How long has his compound been there?"

Sullivan frowned. "Four years? Why?"

"Is it true they've got electricity there? And electronics? That it's a world unto itself?"

"I think so. Why?"

"We'll have to do something about it."

"She's an American national."

"She's whatever we say she is, Shane. Her passport, if she still has one, is bollocks. Besides, the US has its hands full right now."

O'Reilly's mobile phone rang. He picked it up from the desktop and answered it after a brief inspection of the screen.

"I wondered when I'd hear from you." He shook his head at Shane to indicate he needn't leave. He listened quietly for a few seconds and then interrupted the person on the other end of the line.

"I don't give a sod about any of that," he said. "As long as you hold up your end of the deal. You do still want the lithium, I assume?"

He watched Shane sit down at hearing O'Reilly's words, his face its usual study of worry and indecision.

"It's really very simple," O'Reilly said into the phone. "Either get the cure or promise me no one will get it." He disconnected and tossed the phone down on the desk. Shane's eyes stayed on the phone.

"Our man in London," O'Reilly said, enjoying Shane's confusion.

"Is everything all right there?"

"I've got it handled."

"You can't trust the British."

"He's Scots, as it happens."

Shane snorted and looked about to speak but stopped himself.

"Don't worry, me boyo," O'Reilly said, grinning at his aide. "The end goal is the only thing that matters and *that* is well in hand. Trust me."

Shane stood up and pointed to the map on the table in front of them.

"What about the compound? Are we taking it?"

"We'll see."

Shane let out a snort of impatience. "What do you want me to do with the two they brought in?"

"Bugger me, how is it these country mogs think it's still business as usual? It boggles the mind. Who do we have?"

Sullivan glanced at some pages on the desk.

"An elderly woman, Margaret Keenan, for suspected murder, and a Catholic priest, James Ryan, brought in for it looks like accessory to murder." He looked at his boss.

"Process the old woman through Mengert's bunch and show the good father the working end of a shovel."

"Will the Vatican give us a hard time?"

"How will they ever know? Go ahead and get it done. No sense in wasting a day's food on her."

Sullivan gathered up his papers.

"Something on your mind, Shane?"

"No. No, it's just…this part of…the new restructuring is…challenging."

"So do it quickly then."

2

John walked swiftly to the Royal Oak public house on High Street. It was midday and he didn't expect to see much in the way of clientele even though the Crisis seemed to have significantly altered standard drinking hours in Wales. He'd slept in a ditch half way between Fishguard and Goodwick—a mile from where the barge had dropped him off three days earlier.

Three days in Wales and so far no sign of Gavin. With the dire warnings of the barge pilot ringing in his ears about not being allowed to return to Ireland in his lifetime, John was feeling his first twinges of doubt since he'd slipped out of the front gate at the compound.

His mother must be going out of her mind. And Mike? It wouldn't matter if John brought Gavin back gift-wrapped with an apple in his mouth. Mike would hug the daylights out of John —just before he throttled him. Probably Gavin too. John grinned. Thinking of Mike and his mother made him feel a little better, until he felt the crushing guilt of what he knew his leaving had caused them.

Where was the bastard? The note Gavin left him had clearly said he was going to Fishguard. John would have loved to know *why* since as far as he could make out, Fishguard was a festering eyesore with a growing infection on the side.

Protected from waves generated by the prevailing westerly winds, Fishguard Bay was placid and calm with most of its forty odd fishing boats either moored close to the shore or not far off. It was easy to see the ban on travel to Ireland was killing the fishing trade. What was also clear from the moment John stepped into the village was the sickness and poverty.

Before the plague, this town had probably supported itself pretty comfortably during the Crisis. *If you had fish and decent land behind you for grazing and farming, what more did you need?*

John stood outside the pub and knocked on the window. Today, the man was waiting for him. He wrenched the door open and John slid through the gap. The arrangement wasn't great and it wasn't easy, but it covered the necessities. For nearly a day of cleaning the back bogs and what used to be the kitchen, John was given two meals—both fish. And he felt lucky to have them. He'd hoped for sleeping accommodations too but the proprietor was an untrusting man. He lived in the pub with his mother, his wife and two small children.

John wasn't even sure that the pub belonged to him. After the bomb, back in Ireland where John came from, people moved out and new people moved into vacant spaces and claimed as their own. There were no landlords anymore and even if there were, what would they be paid? Money had become worthless within days of the bright flash over the Irish Sea.

Mr. Quig was a middle-aged man not given to idle chat or smiles. John often heard Quig's children while he worked but had never seen them. The work wasn't pleasant but he knew it would sustain him while he spent his evenings searching for Gavin.

The first day he arrived, after walking the mile from Goodwick where the barge left him, he was spotted by a group of boys who chased him until he disappeared in the winding streets of the fishing village. There was no doubt in John's mind they meant to relieve him of his knapsack and there was no real assurance they wouldn't kill him while they were at it. Especially since John wasn't comfortable just handing over his stuff. He hadn't seen that gang of boys since then but made a point to carefully hide his knapsack in the woods between Goodwick and Fishguard when he travelled.

There was a train alongside the pathway that had literally been stopped in its tracks at the moment four years ago when the EMP exploded and stopped time for the Welsh. The passenger cars had long been stripped clean of anything of use or value. Weeds grew between the track rails and out of the windows. John considered stashing his bag there but decided the place was too obvious. Instead he opted for branches in the trees or wedged the bag into the thick tangle of rhododendron hedges that lined the road.

Quig jerked his head to indicate that John was to go to the kitchen but he needn't have bothered. John knew the drill. He walked past the bar—a cheap formica and wood construction that had bar stools jammed up to it, many of them broken. *Guess he's not too worried about lawsuits,* John thought as he went to the kitchen. There wasn't running water, of course, but rather than make a fire to heat up the water he needed, Quig insisted John wash the plates and glasses with cold water. With the disease that was on their doorstep, it amazed John that the man didn't see a problem with that. Worse, because John knew the dishes and pans weren't being cleaned properly, he was at risk himself for getting sick since all his meals were taken there. It didn't matter. In the end, he was always too hungry not to eat.

After cleaning the pots and pans in the kitchen—and wondering how Quig's patrons paid him for the food he obviously cooked for them—John took his fish sandwich out into the back alley to eat. Quig had already let a few people into the bar. There was no point in savoring his lunch. He had too much work to do. He wolfed it down and emerged from the alleyway.

His plan so far had been to create a grid that allowed him to systematically question at least one person a day from each quadrant. Gavin had red hair and while that wasn't that unusual in Wales, it was something to start with.

John walked down the main street of Fishguard which was what he used to reconnoiter the town. To the west and toward the harbor, he'd leave for last. It looked to be more residential to the east. John took the first street on his right and jogged until he came to a row of fishing cabins whose paint was long peeled from them. Some of the cabins had their windows broken out and the weeds were thick and tall around them.

A young man stood outside one of the houses, urinating against the side of it. John waited until he was done and then made a deliberate noise to announce himself. The man whirled around.

"Oy, ye gave me a fright!" he said. He had an Irish accent which wasn't much of a surprise this close to Ireland.

John had decided to mask the fact that he was American. He needed to blend in during this fact-finding mission.

"Oy, yourself," John said, giving a wave and approaching him. "I've lost me mate and was wondering if you'd seen him?"

The man, probably not long out of his teens himself, frowned and watched John approach with unconcealed suspicion.

"Whut's he look like?" the man asked.

"Tall, Irish, red hair."

"Sure, that's all of us!" the man said grinning and John laughed too although neither he nor the young man were tall or had red hair.

"What part of Ireland are ye from?" the man asked.

"Me friend is from the coast," John lied. "But I have reason to believe he's here in Fishguard."

"A fisherman, is he?"

Okay this is getting tiresome.

"Have ye seen anyone sounds like him, I wonder?" John said, forcing his voice to stay friendly.

"Naw. Sorry, boyo."

"No worries. If you do see someone like that, could you tell 'im John's looking for him?"

"Would that be you, then?"

"It would."

John waved and retreated. He knew the man was still standing there, watching him leave. That in itself wasn't unusual. Everybody was suspicious of everybody these days. He had just enough time to talk to one more person before he needed to get back to the pub. He'd prefer it to be someone older—and female, ideally, but they tended to stay hidden indoors. He trotted further down the street until he saw a woman sitting on a porch. She was wrapped in a blanket and held a metal water bottle in her hand. It seemed so strange to see evidence of athletic centers nowadays. The water bottle had been common a few years back—hikers and bikers had them mostly. To see it now looked as out of place as a pig pushing a shopping cart.

"Excuse me, Missus," John called to the woman, careful not to approach too closely or give any hint that he might be thinking of climbing the stairs.

"Jeremy!" the old woman shrieked in response. John stopped, his eyes on the door to the cottage behind her. Unless Jeremy was an Olympic track star, John had plenty of distance between them to spring safely away if he needed to. He held up his hands.

"I just wanted to ask if you'd seen someone, ma'am," he said.

"Feck me, you a Yank?"

Crap. He'd forgotten to fake an Irish accent.

"He's a good friend of mine, missing. Tall, red hair…"

The door behind the woman swung open and an old man came to stand next to the woman.

"What's this?" the old man said.

"Lad says he's looking for his friend. He's American."

"American?" The old man turned to scrutinize John. "I don't believe it."

"Say something, boy," the woman said to John, "in your American words, like."

"I'm looking for my friend," John said tiredly. It was starting to seem clear that these two didn't know anything. But at least he was pretty sure he could outrun the old geezer if he had to.

"Feck me, you're right. What the hell's an American doing in Fishguard?" the old man said, settling onto the top stair of the porch as if ready to watch his favorite TV program.

"Well, I'm looking for my friend," John said patiently. "Have you seen anyone new in town? Tall with red hair? His name's Gavin Donovan."

"Is he American, too?"

"No sir."

"Why would he be here in Fishguard?"

"I don't really know except his grandfather lives here. Maybe you know him? Archie Kelley?"

"Archie Kelley you say?"

"Yes sir."

"Feck me, ye hear how he talks? Just like those chaps on fecking CSI Miami."

Before John could ask his question again, the old woman began violently coughing and the old man jumped up to thump her on the back. Did she have the sickness? There weren't many people on the streets of Fishguard and some mornings when John came to the pub he'd see a body laying on the sidewalk. When he came out at midday it was always gone. He took that as a good sign. It was when people stopped collecting the dead that he figured things were going south pretty fast.

"I'm sorry you're sick, ma'am," John said. "Is it...the illness everyone's talking about?"

"Aye," the old man said, holding the woman's bottle and rubbing her back. "Doc says she's got a fifty-fifty chance of beating it. Plenty of sunshine and liquids he says, didn't he, Alice?"

The woman's coughing finally subsided and she beckoned John to approach them. He stood at the foot of the steps. He knew he needed to get back to the pub if he wanted to keep his arrangement, but if either of these two knew Archie or had heard of Archie's grandson Gavin being in the area, he needed to stay and hear it.

"Is this Archie fella Welsh, do ye ken, lad?"

"No, ma'am. He's Irish. We heard he was living in Fishguard."

"Sorry, lad," the old man said, rearranging the blanket over the woman's knees. "We don't know your friend or his grandfather. We don't get out much." He looked past John as if he could see into the heart of the little fishing village. "It's dangerous now and people are afraid."

The old woman cackled abruptly. "Only now it's me they're afraid of. Afraid of catching what I got."

"I'm sorry," John said. "Can you tell me where the doctor is you saw?" It occurred to John that with the sickness, there must be a decent infrastructure of healthcare set up. It might not be better than wandering around asking random people, but on the other hand, it couldn't hurt.

The old man pointed inland as if John could see the clinic from there. "It's in the main town," he said.

John frowned. "I thought this was the main town."

"No, lad, this is Lower Fishguard."

"The original village," the old lady rasped.

"It's a right jog over yonder hill but you look a strapping lad. You'll take it without stretching your leg."

"It took us near the whole day," the woman said. "And then it was for nothing."

"I imagine the clinic was pretty full?" John said. If the streets are averaging a body a day, the clinic was bound to be stuffed to the rafters with sick people.

"Aye," the old man said sadly. "And no medicine nor any knowledge of how to stop it or why." He shook his head.

John thanked them for their time and hurried back to the pub. He wasn't sure he'd gotten any helpful information. But he went back to work with a heart heavier than when he'd begun.

*****

Later that evening, John left the pub, exhausted and already cold. It was a good mile hike to where he'd hidden his pack. At one point he was tempted to go back to the old couple to see if they'd put him up for a night or two. He figured he could find something to do for them in trade. On the other hand, he couldn't help thinking about what the old man said about some people getting the sickness and others not and nobody knew why. Maybe the ditch was the safest place for him.

John didn't mind the dark because it hid him from anyone who might want to stop him. While he didn't travel with his valuables, sometimes the frustration of finding a traveler with nothing to steal would prompt a bandit to do worse. It made sense, the stories he'd been told. These were dangerous times.

Quig had been annoyed with John's late return and, as a result, John's dinner was smaller than usual so he walked back to his ditch hungry, bracing against the wind that whistled down through the tunnel of trees that led to Goodwick. He'd need a better shelter tonight. It was much colder and the sky had threatened rain all day. As if on cue, he felt the first drops before he was halfway to his backpack. Pushing up his collar to prevent the cold onslaught from pouring down his shirt, John quickened his steps though the bracken and dun-colored underbrush. Rather than go straight to his pack, he always crouched in a nearby bush to listen and wait. In his experience, people who wanted to ambush you didn't have the patience to be still for long.

Confident that there was no one out in this weather but himself, he walked the rest of the way to where he'd hidden his pack. It was still there. Without realizing he was going to do it, he pulled the gun out of the pack, tucked it in his waistband and slipped the pack onto his shoulder and headed back to Lower Fishguard. Although he'd slept worse in the last four days, he couldn't shake loose the idea that a warm dry place to rest his head could be had.

He walked back to the old couple's house. It looked dark and he thought he should be seeing at least the flicker of candles or a lantern. He tried to think of what he could offer the couple in exchange for a night's lodging.

He knocked on the front door. There seemed to be no activity in this neighborhood and he wondered if the other houses were even inhabited. That wouldn't surprise him. Life sucked everywhere these days and it was human nature to move on to see if it didn't suck a little less somewhere else.

"Go away, ye bastard!" the old man yelled, his voice wobbling with fear. "I've got a gun!"

"It's only me, sir. The American kid?"

John could hear conversation and footsteps from inside.

"Is that you, lad?" the old man said.

"Yes sir. I was wondering if I could sleep on your porch tonight because of the rain." Given the old guy's obvious terror, John didn't feel like he could ask to come inside.

No answer. John turned to look at the porch. It beat the hell out of the ditch with the one exception that he would be sitting on his pack and anyone could come and relieve him of it. Maybe this wasn't a good idea after all. Suddenly the door jerked open and the old man's face appeared. He looked like he was about to speak but then his eyes went to something behind John and he slammed the door again.

John turned to see three men standing in the drive in front of the porch, no more than twenty yards from him. They'd come in the dark and they'd come silently. That, combined with the old man's reaction to them, made John drop his backpack at his feet and turn to face them. The gun in his waistband gave him courage.

"There's sickness in there, boyo," one of the men said. "Reckon you probably caught it just standing on the porch." He wasn't a large man or very young. The only weapon he held in his hand was a cricket bat. The two men with him held rope and an axe.

"What's it to you?" John said,

The man's face glittered sweat in the dark. John couldn't make out his features but he could see the whites of his eyes shifting as the guy looked from him to the door of the house.

"Oy, lads, seems this gobshite wants to take us on!" Now John could see his teeth flashing in the dark.

John looked at all three men, wondering if they would try to rush him. At this distance, he could shoot all three if he had to. An image flashed into his mind of poor old Seamus and how he'd shot three gypsies intent on murdering him and John's mom —all because the gypsies hadn't thought he was a threat.

And if this was another world or another time, I'd lift my shirt to show you not to approach, John thought as he watched them take the measure of him. *I'd give you a chance to walk away rather than take your chances with the young punk with a gun.*

But these were not normal times and so John waited for someone to make the first move. No matter how things went down, he figured he could live with that.

It was the loudmouth with the bat. Because John was expecting it to be him, he had his gun drawn and aimed before the man lifted the weapon fully over his head.

John shot him. Not waiting to see the strangled look of surprise on the man's face, not waiting for him to fall John swiveled on his foot and pointed the gun at the other two. They didn't wait either but dropped the rope and axe and fled into the night. John watched them go. The pounding of his heart was loud in his ears. He could hear the last gurgling groans of the man on the ground. He vaguely heard the door open behind him and the grating shuffle of the old man coming out onto the porch.

"Lad?" the old man said.

When the man on the ground was finally, blessedly, quiet and John had lowered his arm to his side, the old man touched him lightly on the shoulder.

"Come inside, lad," he said. "And rest. We'll be fine for tonight."

Susan Kiernan-Lewis

3

The morning Mike and Sarah left Dublin, the rain was pouring in torrential sheets but neither of them cared. Painted in hues of grey, especially through the wall of rain, the city felt like a wounded animal stripped of its pride and capable of doing whatever was necessary to survive. They were anxious to leave.

At what had once been the American embassy, breakfast was sausages and eggs with surprising amounts of good coffee. The American ambassador and his staff still hadn't returned since weeks before the bomb dropped four years earlier. Besides office support staff, cooks and waitstaff, there were no diplomat representatives, American or otherwise, in residence.

"Don't you think it was weird that there was no American presence at all in the capital?" Sarah asked.

"Nothing's normal any more," Mike said.

He looked tired to Sarah. His handsome face was still ruddy with color from the sun but the gunshot graze to his shoulder he'd received less than a week ago must be paining him. She detected a paleness beneath his tan.

"Does your arm hurt?"

Mike had refused to let the medics at the Irish Provisional Government building take a look at it.

"Nay," he said, wincing, belying his words. "I'm grand. And yourself?"

Sarah knew he was referring to her pregnancy. It had been a surprise for both of them—especially at her age.

"I'm good," she said, dropping her hand to her abdomen. "Just really anxious to finally be on the road to finding our boys. "I just can't get over that there were no Americans at the American embassy."

"Aye, it was odd. Odder still was the reception from me own lads."

"I know! I thought so too. Is that the new provisional government? Because it looked a whole lot like nobody knew what they were doing."

"Well, you'd better hope that's not true since they've got their finger on the trigger. What with the Garda Sìochàna and all."

"It was a little scary. Almost like there were no more rules."

"Well, we've been isolated down there in the south," Mike said as he drove down Abbey Street. "All we've heard are rumors. Nothing like seeing it for yourself."

"It's no wonder the ambassador hasn't returned yet. It's almost like Ireland's a third world country now."

"Well, in fact, isn't it?"

Sarah shivered.

"I just want to collect our boys and go back to Ameriland," she said. "Where everything's in place and there's a sense of community."

They passed a thin man in rags standing with his bicycle on the curb eyeing them warily. Sarah wasn't sure he wouldn't try to jump onto their Jeep.

"Can you go faster?" she asked quietly.

"Aye. I'll feel better when we're past the city limits," Mike said, accelerating and maneuvering around an abandoned car in the road.

"Why are we the only one's driving I wonder?" Sarah asked. "The soldiers at the Provisional Government compound implied that there were still working vehicles in Dublin."

They passed a bicycle attached to a small trailer. Sarah could see two legs sticking out of it—whether sleeping or dead, she couldn't tell.

"I suppose the definition of *working vehicles* is the key there. But you're right. After four years, I'd expect the capital to be in better shape. It's almost like they're not even trying."

Sarah gripped the ceiling handle above the passenger's seat as they made their way painstakingly out of the city. As soon as she saw the sign for the M50, she let out a breath she hadn't realized she was holding.

"What do you think they'll do with Margaret and Father Riley?" she asked. "I mean, here we've been thinking if we ever get in really bad trouble we can always call the Garda and honestly, did it even look like they had a holding cell? Are they even set up to do trials and due process?"

"I don't know, love."

"Should we...should we have looked into that before we handed them over?"

Mike glanced at her. "They wouldn't have taken them if they didn't have a way to deal with them. I'm sure the one thing they're set up for in post-apocalyptic Ireland is lawbreakers."

"Assuming there are still recognized laws to be broken."

"Are ye in a mood, then, Sarah? Because either there are law or there aren't and, except for Ameriland, there's damn little we can do about it. Don't we have enough on our plate?"

"You're right," she said nodding. But the feeling wouldn't go away. The feeling that both Margaret and Father Ryan had somehow fallen outside the system.

"But next time—"

"Aye," Mike said, his eyes on the road. "Next time, we take care of it ourselves." He drove to the crest of the next hill and stopped so they could look down on the city for a moment. The blue expanse of sea stretched out to their right behind the once great city. From this distance and because there were no cars or trucks to distract them, they could see subtle movement below as the city struggled to begin its day.

Mike reached over and squeezed Sarah's hand. "Ready, love?"

She leaned across the gearshift to kiss him.

"Let's go find them," she whispered.

The plan was simple and Sarah took a great deal of comfort from that fact. Because they were carrying prisoners from Ameriland, they'd had to go straight to Dublin without stopping. Gavin had been gone for nearly two weeks and John one.

Their only hope was to meet people who'd met the boys or, if either of them was being held against his will, find clues deliberately left by Gavin or John for whoever might be trying to find them. Mike and Sarah would drive south from Dublin along the coast to Rosslare and then cleave the southern half of Ireland at Waterford, stop back in at Ameriland to refuel and then continue west and north depending on what information they were able to gather.

It was December and already quite cold but so far, no snow. Sarah wasn't sure whether to pray that the roads stayed clear or just jump to the end and pray that the first person they spoke with had seen one of the boys. She decided to pray for both.

An hour south of Dublin, they found a cottage on the country road they were on. While it had obviously been someone's home before the bomb, it was a waystation and pub now. Two bicycles and a pony trap were parked out front.

Mike let the Jeep idle in the middle of the road and glanced at Sarah.

"Hungry?"

"Not really. Do you think they have lager?"

"Doubt it. Likely they have something someone whipped up in the back dunney."

Sarah made a face.

"Where's your gun?" Mike asked, his eyes still watching the door of the makeshift pub.

Sarah twisted around and pulled a Glock from the back seat. She checked the clip and looked at him. "Are we both going in?"

He took the gun from her and got out.

"Slide over and get behind the wheel. If I need to leave in a hurry, be watching the front door for me."

Sarah felt a spasm of anxiety as she watched him stand outside the Jeep and tuck the gun into his back waistband before striding toward the front door. She climbed over the gearshift. When she put her hand on the throttle, she saw her hand was shaking. She didn't wait long. When the door opened up, Mike strode to the car. His gun wasn't in his hand, so that was a good sign. He walked around and hopped in the passenger's side.

"Feel like driving?" he asked.

"What did they say? Have they seen them?"

"Yes and no. Drive on, Sarah. I'll tell you as we go."

She put the vehicle in gear and popped the clutch, making the Jeep jerk forward but it didn't stall out. She could smell the alcohol on him. Again, another good sign.

"Three old boggers in there," Mike said. "Friendly enough—at least after I bought rounds. They hadn't seen Gav or John but they did say there's been a lot of activity down toward Rosslaire."

Rosslaire was the main ferry crossing to Wales.

"Oh, Mike, you don't think they've gone to the UK, do you?"

"I don't know, darlin', and let's don't panic until we know for sure. The lads in the pub were all about the sickness they've been hearing about."

"Has it made its way to Ireland?"

"They didn't know about that. The good news is that taking the coastal road south seems to be a solid plan." Mike eased back into his seat and closed his eyes for a moment and Sarah had to smile.

"The bad news," she said, "is at this rate you'll be thoroughly hammered before we get to Wicklow."

*****

Mike and Sarah spent that first night on the road sleeping in the Jeep. They'd made it just north of Arklow on the coast. Forty-four miles south of Dublin. In a normal world, just under an hour's drive. With them stopping any time they saw life and driving slowly around roads with debris and abandoned vehicles, it took nearly eight hours. There were two other waystations that served as publican houses that they stopped at. At each one, Mike heard the same story: there was a plague offshore and the rumors were that the Garda would shoot on sight anyone trying to leave or come across the channel.

Nobody had seen anyone fitting either Gavin or John's description.

Mike knew Sarah was uncomfortable although she wouldn't say why. Whether it was the pregnancy or just the low-grade terror she'd nursed ever since John slipped away from the compound to go in search of Gavin didn't really matter. In any case he was powerless to comfort her. Even so, the fact that they were moving, actively searching, had to help. It helped him, God knows. Even though it was likely a waste of time and effort.

He shook the thoughts out of his head as he pulled the Jeep onto a crest along the side of the road overlooking the sea. There were tall trees that would shield them from the cold winds coming off the water—especially this time of year.

He looked over at Sarah. She had her eyes closed, her hands folded across her belly. She was just beginning to show. Her face, even in semi-repose showed the strain of her grief and worry.

What they now knew was that Gavin had left the compound with a trusted adult—the village priest—and was taken to the band of druids in the outlying woods. There, he'd been attacked and prepared for sacrifice but had—by some miracle—escaped. Mike knew why Gavin hadn't come straight back to the compound. The druid settlement lay between Gavin and home. He'd have to go due north and then circle back the long way in order to make it back home. Somehow during that long circle back, something had happened.

He'd never arrived back home.

Mike drew a hand across his face as if to erase his very features. That had been two weeks ago. Somehow, whatever had prevented Gavin from returning home either still prevented him…or had prevented him permanently. He didn't like to think of that but it had to be considered. It wasn't like Gavin to just leave and not come back. The lad was loved and he knew it. He'd also had to know his dear old da would be apoplectic with worry.

No, Gavin hadn't come back because something or someone was preventing him. Mike's stomach muscles clenched painfully at the thought.

"Are we here for the night?" Sarah asked, her eyes still closed.

"Aye. We're protected from the wind yet high up. We should have some warning in case someone comes upon us. Are ye cold, Sarah? I can blast the heater if ye like."

She shivered under the heavy wool rug he'd laid across her knees but shook her head.

"I'm fine."

"It was a good day," he said, trying to force the optimism into his voice for her. Her eyes flickered open and she reached for his hand.

"I didn't really expect to find them our first couple of days out," she said.

"Really?"

She smiled sadly. "Well, all right. Maybe I did. But only a small, desperate part of me."

"We'll find them, love."

"I know."

The daylight was fading rapidly. It probably wasn't much past four o'clock but they would be sitting in total winter darkness in another half hour. They'd bought sandwiches in Dublin for the road but neither of them were hungry.

Truth be told, Sarah wasn't the only one who'd expected more than the day had given up to them.

Were all the days to be like this one? Beginning with hope and optimism until one shaking head after another brought them relentlessly to the night and another day with no word of where the boys were?

"I nearly didn't come last year, you know," Sarah said softly. Mike turned to see her eyes were open now and she was looking out across the Saint George's Channel as if she saw something there. But it was all inky blackness, the water indistinguishable from the dark sky.

"I know. You told me." Mike was well aware of how close the decision had been about Sarah's return to Ireland. With the Americans shutting down all portals—coming and going— and her own parents begging her to stay, it was nothing short of a miracle that she was here with him now.

"But my hardest decision had nothing to do with hot showers or air conditioning," she said. "I don't care about any of that." She reached over and slipped her hand into his. "That was a no-brainer, Mike—giving all that up for a life with you."

He felt his throat close up with emotion and he squeezed her hand.

"That wasn't the hard part."

"I know." And he did, too. He knew it wasn't the convenience and safety of life in America versus the post apocalyptic nightmare that her daily round in Ireland with him often was. It had always come down to one thing: John. And when she was finally able to believe that coming back to Ireland —to the life they could have there with the love of people they knew there—there was always that nagging doubt for her: Had she done the right thing by John?

"He's so smart," she said. "And not just about trapping rabbits or problem-solving the compound's electronic equipment, but really, really smart."

Mike felt a flinch of guilt as she spoke. He was as much to blame as anyone for why Sarah came back. She came back to him. And while there was no doubt that was the best thing for Mike—and maybe Sarah too—nobody in their right mind could believe a brilliant lad with his whole life a head of him was better off in a mud fort in a third world country.

"I was so selfish," she said in a whisper, her eyes closing again. A tear slipped down her cheek. "I wanted to have it all. I wonder if this is God trying to make a point to me."

"I don't think He works like that."

"Maybe He does to the ones who are really thick-headed."

"Sarah…"

27

"Never mind," she said, wiping the tears from her cheek. "There's tomorrow. Maybe we'll hear something tomorrow."

He leaned over and kissed her then eased her seat back into an incline. They were both exhausted, physically and emotionally. All they had left was their hope, their combined strength and their belief in the future. His eyes glanced at her belly again, still protectively covered by their folded hands.

He fell asleep wondering what would have to happen to force them to accept the truth that everyone else in the world probably knew by now—that the lads were gone for good.

The next morning, Mike was driving before Sarah was awake. He knew she'd feel better if they got some miles under their belt before breakfast and he was determined to make that happen. It occurred to him that driving the coastal road might make sense as far as a five-year plan of searching every kilometer of Ireland but it made no sense for two brokenhearted parents attempting to find their children as fast as possible. He pointed the Jeep inland, knowing the roads would be even worse the further south he drove and the further he went from the main highway, but also knowing that searching the coast for the boys was a long shot.

And they weren't at that point just yet.

They drove three hours without stopping, drinking their own water and eating their sandwiches. They didn't come upon another likely looking waystation until long past lunch time. If they were touring the country, this might be a decent day's effort, Mike thought with frustration. But if they were hoping to find word of the lads, it was just about as useless as a day could be.

"Where are all the people?" Sarah asked.

"I don't know," Mike said. "It's not a very populated area." They passed several cottages—all of which were obviously abandoned. "There's a village up ahead."

A sign choked with weeds taller than the pole it hung on announced *Ballycanew*. Sarah sat up straight and craned her neck as they drove down the narrow main road of the village.

"Is it deserted?" she asked. It had started to rain and the holes in the road began to fill and form puddles. More an alleyway than a proper road, it wound tightly through a brief section of attached homes with gabled and peaked roofs. Mullioned windows were set over empty window boxes. This must have been a charming representative of the classic Irish village in its time, Mike thought as he squeezed the Jeep down the road, mindful of the stone wall on one side and the painted doors and shrubbery of the houses on the other.

"The people might just be in out of the rain," Mike said. Ahead was a slight widening in the road which opened onto a small two-story mud and stone thatched house. There were no bicycles out front to alert the uninitiated to the fact that this was the local meeting place, but somehow Mike knew it was.

"Did you find something?" Sarah asked, frowning.

"I think I found the village pub."

"It looks like an abandoned house. From the last century."

"Aye. To your jaundiced American eye, I can see how it might," Mike said with a grin as he put the Jeep into park. "Why not come with me this time? In a village like this, I reckon it's safer inside than out here on the road."

"Maybe they'll have tea," Sarah said, throwing off her rug and reaching for the car door.

"I'll wager they will," Mike said.

*****

How Mike knew that this abandoned shack was the village's popular brewery was a mystery to Sarah. She was just grateful that he did. If she'd been on her own, she'd have passed right on by. That was probably the whole point.

Mike kept his hand on her elbow as he pushed open the door to the house at the end of the village street. The rain had started to come down harder and Sarah was grateful for the shelter of the pub even though her nostrils were met with a dank mildew smell that had her hesitate on the threshold. There were no fewer than half a dozen people in the room, clustered around a polished wooden bar, behind which stood a bartender. The man wore a Nike t-shirt and a baseball cap.

"Feck me," he said loudly. "Trade!"

The five people at the bar turned to see what he was looking at and openly gawked at Mike and Sarah as they came in. Sarah smiled at the faces of the four men and two women. Two lanterns anchored the opposite sides of the bar, throwing shadows around the room. The tension was palpable but Sarah felt Mike move away from her toward the bar as if coming upon this secret bar in post apocalyptic Ireland were an everyday occurrence.

"Do ye have ale?" Mike asked the barman, his big voice booming out friendly and confident. Sarah knew Mike didn't feel quite so hail-fellow as his voice might indicate and she was grateful for his acting abilities.

"Aye, mebbe," said the barman, a sour-faced man in his fifties.

"That's grand," Mike said. "And a cup of scaldy for the missus?"

Sarah watched all eyes shift from Mike to her as if Mike had requested double lines of cocaine for them both. Mike went to a table and pulled out a chair for Sarah, but his eyes never left the occupants and the smile never fell from his face.

She sat heavily on the wooden chair and ran her hands absently over the deeply scarred table. She wondered if this table had been here since the Middle Ages but of course that was ridiculous. Mike went to the bar. The two women were still openly staring at her. She smiled at them and one possibly smiled back. After a moment, Mike returned with a large steaming earthenware mug with a teabag floating in the water.

"No milk or sugar," he said and then patted her hand. He had work to do.

Sarah dunked the teabag absently and forced herself to appreciate that she was dry and that however unsuccessful she and Mike were today, they were at least doing something to find the boys. Although the roof was thatched, she could hear the rain pounding away on it and the windows. There was a good fire blazing in the grate to her left and she felt the warmth on her knees. She shook the rain from her jacket and draped it on the back of her chair.

From where she sat, she could hear Mike in full blarney form chatting up the bar occupants and the barkeep. It always surprised her that fellow Irishmen were just as likely to fall victim to the lavish bullshit that is a true Irishman in full story-telling form. You'd think they'd see you coming for a hundred kilometers but no, human nature being what it was, the Irish were as susceptible as anyone else for buying a lie.

"Is there any news, d'ye ken?" Mike asked from the bar as he tipped back his lager. Real beer was rare these days unless the proprietor had perfected the art of the microbrewery which she'd heard some actually had.

"That's usually what we ask strangers for," one of the men standing beside Mike said, narrowing his eyes at him.

"Aye, to be sure," Mike said goodnaturedly. "All I know is about the plague that's stalled outside our own good shores and naught else."

"And stalled is exactly where it'll stay," one of the women said. "The Brits are shooting any craft found in the water between here and Wales, so they are."

The other woman spoke up, "I thought it was the Irish Garda doing the shooting."

"Sure does it matter *who's* doing the shooting?" one of the men retorted and they all laughed.

"We're looking for our lads," Mike said. "Young fellows, been missing now about two weeks."

"Misplaced your boys, did ye?" the bartender said as he refilled Mike's glass and palmed the gold coin Mike deposited on the smooth bar top.

"One's tall with red hair," Mike said. "His mother would say he looks like me. T'other is young. No more than fourteen."

The bar was quiet. One of the women spoke.

"Nay, sorry. There's nobody new gone through here excepting yourselves."

"Oh, well," Mike said, polishing off his beer and placing the tankard down on the counter with a sharp smack. "We'll be off then."

"Are ye looking in every pub from here to Galway, then?"

The men all laughed.

"Aye," Mike said. "If we have to. I thank ye for your time."

"Good luck to ye, squire," one of the men said to Mike. "These are hard times. Harder still to lose a child."

Sarah felt her eyes smart when he said that. Up until that moment they were just strangers in a bar but suddenly she felt like they were all connected, like they'd all felt pain and loss in the last four years. And she felt his pity and his empathy. She stood up and pulled her jacket back on.

"Thank you, everyone," she said. "You've been very kind." Mike was by her side and slipped a hand around her waist as they turned to the door.

"Oy, hold on," one of the women said as she pulled away from the bar. "One of the lads you're lookin' for wouldn't happen to be a Yank by any chance, would he?"

Susan Kiernan-Lewis

4

Sarah stood on the dock and stared across to where Wales must be. She held her arms tightly to her chest and let the cold wind whip her hair about her face. She didn't care about pain now or discomfort or hunger or anything else.

She knew where he was. A miracle had blossomed into an answered prayer this morning when one woman in one pub they just happened to visit turned out to be the wife of a man who had seen John less than a week ago…and taken him across the sea to the United Kingdom. She watched the seagulls dive-bomb the waves for invisible prey.

Nothing else mattered now. She knew where he was. She didn't yet hold him in her arms but she knew where he was. Mike came up behind her and blocked the worst of the sharp gale from blasting the warm penumbra created by her radiant hope.

"I can't believe we've found him," she said as she stared at the horizon.

Mike didn't answer. She tore her eyes from the water and the promise of Wales on the other side and turned in his arms.

"They won't take us across, will they?" she asked.

He winced and gave a half shake of his head like he was trying to believe it himself.

"The plague," he said.

"But why did they let John cross then?"

"The pilot said it was his last crossing. John just happened to time it right."

"Lucky us."

"Well, it *is* lucky us, love," he reminded her. "We know where he is and now it's just a logistics problem to be solved."

"So how do we solve it?"

He looked out at the water himself.

"Like anything else," he said. "With money."

In the end, Sarah knew, as much as she wanted to jump in the water and start swimming to the other side, she needed to plan. It was hard. Knowing John was in Wales—in Fishguard, more precisely—was immensely helpful because now they only had one small fishing village to take apart brick by brick for what surely must be the only fourteen-year old American boy there. But she also knew that they didn't just need passage over; they needed passage back.

And, of course, there was still Gavin to be found. If it turned out that the reason John was in Wales was because Gavin was there too—well, then they would all just settle in Wales until the travel ban was lifted.

Even Sarah knew the pilot was a poor choice to confide in—as nice and as friendly a fellow as he appeared to be. He knew who they were and he knew what the stakes were. First, he'd be a fool to help them and risk his livelihood by breaking the law, and second, while he might not rat them out, he'd be an even bigger fool to lie to the authorities for them. No, they needed someone who didn't care who they were or what their goals were. Someone who was just interested in the gold coins Mike had to pay for the deed.

"It's not a matter of trust, ye ken," Mike told her as they stood and watched the horizon. "For our purposes, we can't afford to trust anyone."

"I know," Sarah said. "Just pay them what they want. I don't care."

He rubbed her back and leaned down to kiss her on the cheek.

"Will ye not let me go alone?" he said into her ear.

"I'm not letting one more loved one out of my sight."

He laughed. "You might have your hands full laying down that particular law to your boy when ye have him back."

"Hands full or not. He's never leaving me until they haul me out feet first. Nor this one either." She placed a hand on her stomach and Mike covered it with his own larger one.

"Aye. It's a pact then," he said and bent down to speak to Sarah's stomach. "If we let ye come out, it's on the express understanding that ye'll not be going anywhere until we're dead."

Sarah laughed. "You got that right."

*****

The man was shaped like a hunched over shellfish, his back curved over onto himself, his face a gristle of beard framing bad teeth. All the virtues of the man were on display for the world to see, Mike thought grimly as he held up two gold coins in the Rosslare fishgutting shed.

"For passage there," Mike said in a low voice. The floor was still slick with last month's catches. With the Garda patrolling this close to shore, no one was comfortable even taking a dingy out, let alone to where most of the normal fishing sites were.

These days, whatever was caught from the pier was what got sold or traded. Nobody was taking a chance on getting shot for a load of mullet.

Mike glanced at Sarah, huddled in her heavy coat in the corner of the shed. Her eyes glistened in the dim light. He could feel her excitement even from fifteen feet away. They were that close. Tomorrow they'd wake up in the same town where John was. By lunch, they'd have him back again. Bob's your uncle and Nancy yer fecking auntie.

"It's twice the risk for me," the weasel of a man said. Ned, he'd said his name was. "First to get there and then home again. And it's the homeward stretch what's the most dangerous."

Mike watched the man's eyes flick downward to where Mike kept his wallet and his meager cache of gold coins. He'd happily give them all to the little turd if he wasn't completely convinced that they were all that stood between him and Sarah and home. What if John or Gavin were in a situation that required a bribe? You couldn't be too careful or too surprised these days. And while he had nothing to trade save the labor of his body, Mike had a little gold in a world where it still meant something.

Not a whole hell of a lot and not what it used to...but something.

Mike frowned. "If I double it?" he asked. He knew the man wanted to think he'd manipulated Mike and giving in too happily would just prolong the exercise.

"Aye, that would be grand, Squire," Ned said, licking his lips as Mike brought out another gold coin. He snatched it from Mike's fingers.

"Meet me at the boat ramp at midnight," he said and began to move toward the door. Mike put his hand on the man's shoulder. His jacket felt damp as if months of saltwater had become entrenched in his very clothes.

"That's only three hours from now. We'll stay with you."

"Nobody trusts anyone any more," Ned said, shaking his head as if saddened by the fact.

"Aye, that's true enough. And for good reason."

"Sure that's the truth of it."

Mike could feel the man's boney shoulder relax beneath his fingers and he reminded himself that he too had a story and likely a sad one.

"I'd buy you a drink while we wait."

The man's eyes flew open in surprise. He shook his head in disbelief.

"Have ye had many people befriend ye, I wonder?" Ned said to Mike.

Mike considered the question and glanced at Sarah. Her face was clear, her brow unclenched. A smile played loosely on her lips. She knew their trial was culminating in her dearest dreams being realized, thank you God.

"Aye," Mike said. "People have been kind."

"They go one of two ways, have ye noticed?"

Mike laughed. "Aye. I've noticed."

"I'm glad for your luck in finding your lad," Ned said. "And I'm glad for mine in finding you. Do ye think it works that way?"

"I don't know. "How about that drink?"

"Ye'll not needing to be asking me twice. Come. We'll drink to the success of your quest. And then we'll be off."

"Will we need more than we have on us?" Mike and Sarah had parked the Jeep in the woods and stripped it of anything valuable. They hid their food, guns and other belongings in the woods to be retrieved when they came back with John.

"Warm jackets, like ye have," Ned said, squinting at Sarah. "Waterproof boots by any chance?"

Mike shook his head.

"Nay, never mind. The crossing's not that long and ye'll have as long as ye like on t'other side to dry off."

That sounded fine to Mike. They left the shed and walked down the slippery pavers that fronted the docks. It had rained on and off all day but the sky was mostly clear now, although the moon was hidden behind a bank of clouds. As Ned had pointed out earlier, moonlight would not be their friend tonight.

The bar that Ned led them to was more like a lean-to with a couple of tables and chairs set out of the wind. Mike tucked Sarah into the one free table with Ned and brought back two lagers and a hot tea. The tea wasn't real tea but it was hot and the lagers were watered down homemade ales without hops. It wasn't the first time that Mike realized that coming together with people in a pub was not so much about what they were drinking than it was the fact that they were doing it together. The four men standing at the open-air bar looked at them over their shoulders with suspicion at first but soon lost interest.

Mike settled down at the table and Ned lifted his wooden tankard.

"To finding your lads," he said and drank deeply.

"Can I ask you how you survive here, Ned?" Mike said. "Now that the fishing's depressed and there's no ferry across, how do you live?" He leaned across to give Sarah's hands a squeeze as they cupped her hot mug of tea.

"Well, that is an ever-changing proposition," Ned said. "To be sure. What worked yesterday, doesn't work today. What works today, likely won't work tomorrow."

"Do you have family?" Sarah asked.

"I do. A wife I love dearly who lives in Blackwater and a lass. The lass is…" Ned made a face and blew out a long exhalation. "She's simple-minded," he said at last. "A great beauty and a pride to me every day of my life." He spoke with determination as if ready to dispute or fight anyone on the subject.

"I'm sure she is," Sarah said.

"Me wife does washing. I gut fish for a penny a pound or for an outright trade. This crossing?" He indicated the two of them across the table from him. "This'll put my family right for the next six months." Mike couldn't see well in the half light but he thought he saw the man's eyes moisten.

"Sure, it's a hard life these days," Mike said. He looked at Sarah and gave her a small smile. They had so much to be grateful for. The bairn, each other, all the comforts of the compound at Ameriland when so many others were struggling for the basics.

Sarah seemed to read his mind for she reached out and touched his hand on the table.

"Have ye eaten yet tonight?" Mike asked Ned. "We'd be proud to share a meal with you."

"Nay, there's naught but bilge in this place. But once you lot come back—with your lad," he said looking quickly at Sarah. "I'd be proud to have ye come to Blackwater. My Keira is a fine cook."

"We'd like that," Sarah said.

An hour later, it was time to go. Mike felt the chill of leaving the semi-shelter but he stamped his feet to get the blood circulating and rubbed his hands up and down Sarah's back.

"Won't be long now," he whispered into her hair as they followed Ned toward one of the many boat launches.

"Watch your footing, mind," Ned said to them over his shoulder. "It's slick here."

Mike slipped his arm around Sarah's waist and moved down the ramp. He could feel her excitement through her jacket as she hurried beside him. The motorboat that waited them was small. Smaller than Mike had imagined it would be and that worried him. Even from the shore he could see the waves were choppy.

"Have you made this crossing before, Ned? In yon wee boat, I mean?"

"To Wales, ye mean? Only a hundred times. Never mind. It's big enough for the job." Ned held out his hand to Sarah and she stepped into the boat. "Go to the front, lass," he said.

Then he unhooked the rope attached to the rear of boat and tossed it in after her, holding fast to the boat itself.

"Hop in, Squire," Ned said, urgently. "Quietly now. There's patrols on the hour. No sense in straining our luck."

Mike waded into the water, drenching his pant legs to the knees. The boat tilted dangerously as he stepped inside but righted itself soon enough. He moved to the middle seat to leave the tiller space for Ned. He touched Sarah's shoulder.

"Alright then, love?"

She nodded but didn't speak. She was pointed toward Wales. Her focus was all one way now. Mike turned around to see Ned give the boat a mighty push from the shore.

"Hey!" Mike shouted. "What the feck—"

"Good luck, Squire. Keep your head down."

"You bastard! I paid you to take us across!" Mike grabbed the tiller. Sarah turned around, her face white.

"I changed me mind. You've bought the boat. Just point 'er nose straight 'til you hit land."

Sarah grabbed Mike's arm. "Let him go. We don't need him. Let's just go!"

She was right. There was nothing for it. He would have plenty of time later to imagine the pleasure of throttling the little termite when he and Sarah were back in Ireland. But the feeling in his chest—of betrayal and lies—wouldn't go away. This was the most treacherous part of the whole expedition. The sea was full of patrol boats and while the rumors about helicopters in the sky ready to shoot boats out of the water seemed to be only rumors, there was still enough to worry about.

The sound of the outboard motor itself was an announcement of stealth in the still quiet of the night. Should he kill the motor? Would they be able to paddle across? He hadn't thought to ask Ned any of this because he'd done the one stupid thing he'd always taught the boys not to do—trust someone else to handle the details.

Sarah turned around and he managed a smile for her. The fact was, they really didn't need a helmsman. It just felt wrong to Mike for reasons he couldn't put his finger on and hated to admit to. It just felt wrong. Ten minutes into the night he suddenly realized why. It didn't make sense that the night was so dark, the air so silent except for the sound of their own motor.

Suddenly, the night illuminated like a supreme hand had flipped on all the lights. Two large patrol boats shot into stark relief directly in front of them.

Their powerful searchlights swept across the water in threatening bands of brightness drawing ever closer.

Susan Kiernan-Lewis

5

The twin patrol boats loomed out of the darkness. When the powerful search beams crossed and intersected on the small outboard dingy, Mike brought his arm up to shield his eyes from the blinding light.

They knew we were coming.

His gut roiled. There was no hope of escape. The lights illuminated the boat and everything around it in a fifty-yard radius. It was like standing on stage blinded by the footlights— revealed, naked, vulnerable. Sarah never turned around but Mike's gut instinct was to reach forward and clamp a hand on her arm before she launched herself into the water. He knew she was about to do it even though not a twitch betrayed her intention.

He knew because he had the same idea. She put her hand on top of his. He killed the motor and moved to sit behind her and hold her close.

An hour later, they sat shivering in the lighted cabin of the boat of the Garda Siochàna, the Irish government's national police. They were disarmed but not handcuffed. Before being taken aboard, they acknowledged that they were coming from Ireland, not Wales, although that seemed obvious enough with Ireland barely several hundred yards away.

"Were you aware that it is illegal for an Irish National to travel to the United Kingdom?" the young Garda police officer asked.

"Was it on the news channels?" Mike asked. "Because I might have missed it."

"Pretty cheeky, old fellow," the officer said. "We've blanketed the surrounding area with leaflets and made several announcements in the villages."

"We don't live near the coast," Mike said.

"Where are ye from then?" The officer narrowed his eyes.

"I am from Jacksonville, Florida," Sarah said. "And I'm almost positive the US doesn't have a no-fly policy with the UK."

The Garda policeman turned to scrutinize Sarah. She could tell he was surprised by what she said but he made his mind up quickly what to do about it.

"I'm sorry ye weren't made aware of the new law," he said, turning back to Mike. "But that's no excuse for breaking it. We'll be taking you to Dublin for further questioning."

"Are ye daft? Do ye think we're takin' state secrets to Wales for God's sake?"

Sarah could tell that mentioning states secrets had been an error in judgment on Mike's part. That was clear from the way the police officer's face took on an immediately worried look.

"Secure them," he said to his men as he turned and left the cabin.

Sarah moved closer to Mike and took comfort in the strength of his arms around her.

"It's all right, love," he murmured. "We're going to be all right."

But what of John? As Sarah felt the boat turn and set its course northbound, she felt her loss well up inside her until she wanted to scream. Instead, she bolted from Mike to grab a nearby wastepaper basket and vomited noisily into it.

*****

No guns. No Jeep. No money. Just the clothes on their backs and their good word. Their good word made slightly less good by the fact that they were caught attempting to sneak across to Wales in the middle of the night.

Sarah and Mike were marched off the boat in Dublin where they were met by three armed soldiers and a waiting SUV. At four in the morning, all lights of nighttime Dublin were gone as they drove from the harbor to the same government offices where they'd been just two days prior.

This time there was a definitely sinister tone to the visit. The two police officers, dressed more like soldiers, didn't speak, even though Mike repeatedly asked them where they were being taken. Eventually they arrived at the entrance to a maze of darkened government buildings and were taken to the second floor and down a long hall. Their two escorts led them through a door painted seasick green to match the walls then left and closed the door behind them without a word.

Sarah waited several seconds and tried the door handle. They were definitely locked in. The room looked like an old-fashioned motel room with furnishings from the seventies. A queen-sized bed was jammed up against the wall and flanked by Scandinavian style nightstands with matching lamps on them.

Sarah went to the bed and sat down. She turned the side lamp off and then back on.

"They have electricity."

"Well, they would, wouldn't they?" Mike said. He stood by the door as if not convinced they couldn't somehow walk back through it. His pant legs were still wet from when he'd stepped into the sea hours earlier to launch them on their ill-fated mission. She patted the bed next to her.

"Come sit. It's late. We're exhausted. Nothing to be done tonight."

She saw his shoulders heave like he was wrestling with a terrible decision.

"I'm so sorry, Sarah."

"Well, it certainly wasn't anything *you* did, Mike." She went to him and put her hand on his arm.

"I trusted the little weasel who turned us in."

She tugged at his jacket in an attempt to peel it off him. "We don't know what tomorrow will bring or why we're here. Let's be as rested as we can be for whatever we're in store for."

"What did that policeman mean by *interrogating*?"

"I don't know. But I know they'll have to answer to the US and even if that wanker ambassador isn't here any more, they still have to deal straight with me. We'll get all this sorted out in the morning. In fact, I've been thinking, Mike."

He dropped his jacket on the floor behind them and allowed her to pull him to the bed. "Oh, Lord, do I want to hear this?"

"Since we obviously are not going to be able to do the crossing Mission Impossible style, we'll do it through proper channels. I am an American looking for another American. The US will see to it that I'm able to cross to the United Kingdom. I don't know why we didn't think of it in the first place."

"You might have a point," he conceded, kicking off his shoes. "There might be something to this going through proper channels thing."

"You think? Just for a change?" She smiled and pushed him down into a reclining position on the bed before slipping into his arms and placing her head on his chest.

"You might have something, darlin'," he said with a long sigh. Seconds later he was asleep. Sarah stayed still for a moment before standing and taking off her own jacket and shoes. Just before she slipped into bed next to her lightly snoring husband, she said a quiet prayer.

Tomorrow, God. If you please. And we'll all just forget this monstrosity of a night.

The next morning, Mike and Sarah splashed water on their faces from the room sink—a luxury Mike hadn't seen in four years—and readied themselves for whatever the day would bring. Sarah was determined to speak with any US representative besides cooks and secretaries who could help them get to Wales. This nonsense of them sneaking across the Irish Sea to get to Wales would be put in proper perspective as soon as the Irish authorities knew what the stakes were.

Two soldiers knocked on their door at seven in the morning and escorted them back down the same hallway and down three flights of stairs to what appeared to be a subterranean level of offices. The halls had electric lights and the carpet looked new. Sarah decided to take this as a good sign—a sign that the city, or at least its provisional government, was righting itself, and the infrastructure needed to deal with an international incident was in place.

There were no signs on any of the office doors that they passed. Sarah's shoes were still wet from the night before and the dampness of her clothes chilled her, making her wish she could feel warm again. The two soldiers stopped at a double set of doors and rapped loudly against them before opening them and motioning for Mike and Sarah to enter.

Inside was a small bleak lobby devoid of seating or wall decorations. The only furniture in the room was a metal desk, behind which sat a young man in suit and tie, whose long hair hung to his shoulders.

"Right, you're here. I'm Shane Sullivan. Mr. O'Reilly's Junior Minister. I'm sorry I can't offer you a seat but you won't have to wait that long."

Sullivan had a pleasant face but large round eyes, giving him a slightly startled appearance. Sarah wondered if he'd been bullied a lot as a child.

"And who the feck is Mr. O'Reilly?" Mike asked.

To Sullivan's credit, he looked Mike in the eye and answered, "Mr. O'Reilly is the Senior Minister of the provisional government of the Republic of Ireland."

"The *Senior Minister*?" Mike said. "What the feck is that? Do we not have a prime minister, for shite's sake?"

"We do not, sir," Sullivan said. "I'm sure you won't be surprised to realize that we have endured many changes in the last four years. Not all of them bad."

"Shite. What are you? Sein Fein?"

"As it happens, I am not, sir," Sullivan said. "In fact, there are fewer parties than there was before."

"Well, since there were only two before, I'm guessing that means we're down to one?" Mike said. "With no media, it's easy enough to make all kinds of changes I'll wager, but what are you in charge of? A country of people who can't vote, don't have running dunnies, and can't even feed themselves."

"It's still Ireland," Sullivan said. He glanced at his watch. "Mr. O'Reilly will see you now."

"Actually," Sarah said, stepping forward. "I'm an American national and I was hoping to see a representative from my country. I have a problem I need help with."

"We'll do everything we can to help you, Mrs. Woodson."

"It's Donovan," Mike growled.

Sarah was surprised that Sullivan knew of her, regardless of what her name was. Before she could react any further the door behind Sullivan opened and a tall man with flaming red hair stepped through. With the wiry red hair, he looked so much like Gavin that for one mad moment she thought it was him. Mike must have thought so too because he barely stifled a gasp.

"Yes, of course it is," the man said, extending his hand to Mike. "I'm Liam O'Reilly. Please come in."

Sullivan stepped out of the way so that Mike and Sarah could pass him and step into the adjoining office. Shane followed behind them and closed the door.

"Please sit," O'Reilly said as he returned to his desk. Sarah and Mike sat down in two chairs facing him. Sullivan stood against the wall with his arms crossed in front of his chest.

45

"I'm hoping you can help me," Sarah said. "It's extremely important that I get to Wales. I have information that my son—my child—is there."

"I'm very sorry to hear that, Mrs. Donovan," O'Reilly said. "But you'll know that you've broken our laws here in this country, aye?"

"Broken your...I am trying to find *my son*, Mr. O'Reilly," Sarah said, fighting the urge to stand up and somehow make this man understand her.

"I heard you, Missus," O'Reilly said, tapping his fingers on the desk. "I'm not sure what you're asking me to do aside from commute your sentence."

"Jaysus, man!" Mike exploded. "Are ye serious? You're arresting us?"

"What part gave it away?" O'Reilly said impassively. "The escort by the Garda Sìochàna? As I'm reliably informed you have electricity and all the comforts of life-before-the-bomb at your compound." He flipped open a file on his desk and jabbed at it with his index finger. "So I can't imagine you're here to enjoy our hospitality." He looked from Mike's stunned face to Sarah's.

"We're here," Sarah said, trying to keep the tremor out of her voice, "to ask your help in finding our children."

"You and everyone else in Ireland. You do know that your country is experiencing a significant economic crisis, don't you?"

"What?"

"They've pulled their presence from everywhere west of St George's Channel." He picked up a cellphone from his desk and glanced at the screen for a moment. "I'm sure I've the exact verbiage somewhere but suffice to say there is no United States presence in Dublin or Ireland or anywhere in the United Kingdom at the moment."

"I...I don't believe you," Sarah said, an incredulous look on her face.

"As you like."

"My...I have US-secured funds in a bank here in—"

"No."

Sarah looked away from O'Reilly to Mike and then back to O'Reilly.

"There is no US-backed anything any more," O'Reilly said. "All monies have been seized by the republic. We are facing several challenges—although perhaps not on the level of what the US is battling—foreclosures, recession, and the like—but at least they still have running vehicles, electricity and functioning grocery stores. You'll notice that Ireland today has none of those?"

"You took my money?"

"Your *money*, Missus, was in this country at the indulgence of the Irish Republic. Am I right, Mr. Sullivan?"

"You are," Sullivan said.

Sarah turned to Mike. She felt as if she'd been slammed in the stomach. Was it all gone? All the money? Any support from her country? Was that possible?

"It's all right, love," Mike murmured, but his eyes glinted dangerously as if he was ready to erupt at any moment.

"But what do we do now?" she said, ignoring the two politicians in the office.

"What you do, Missus," O'Reilly said, standing up and signaling for Sullivan to open the office door. "Is go back to wherever it is you came from and be glad you weren't shot trying to cross to the United Kingdom. I can see you're not looking too grateful at the moment and I hope that will change for your sakes."

"But our Jeep..." Sarah said, looking wildly about the office as if expecting to find their vehicle there somehow. "How are we to get home?"

"If you've lost your vehicle—when millions have naught but a bicycle and glad for that—then it's your own fault. Go home by putting one foot in front of the other or stay and I'll change me mind about holding you for your attempt to illegally sneak off to a forbidden location."

"Can this be happening?" Sarah said softly to herself. Mike stood up and tugged her into a standing position.

"Let's go, Sarah. Looks like both our countries are done with us."

"Truer words, Mr. Donovan," O'Reilly said, turning away to open a filing cabinet. "Truer words."

Sullivan escorted them to the hallway and gave instructions for the waiting pair of soldiers to accompany them out the main gate. Without a glance at Mike or Sarah, he returned to his office and closed the door. Sarah felt the strength in Mike's hand on her elbow as he walked beside her. She was thinking of O'Reilly's last words as she put one foot in front of the other until they found themselves walking down an outdoor tunnel of barbed wire leading to an exterior gate.

It was still morning but the rain was cold and relentless. Mike led her to the first line of storefronts opposite the government complex where they stood under a narrow overhang to avoid the worst of the downpour. They watched their security detail return and disappear into the complex.

Sarah knew she was shaking but wasn't sure it was the cold and the wet or the fact that she was breaking down.

"Now what?" she whispered. Mike held her in a warm one-armed embrace and kissed her hair.

"We'll be fine, love," he said.

Even she could hear the hopelessness in his voice.

*****

"Should we have them picked up?" Shane asked.

Liam tapped a pen against his bottom lip and stared out the window of his office.

"No real point," he said. "They've got no money, no car." He shrugged. "Why not let nature take its course for a change, eh?"

Shane nodded.

"Did we in fact seize her bank funds?" O'Reilly asked.

"We didn't, no."

"Well, it's a bloody good idea. Do ye see how that happens, Shane? Some of the most fortuitous events in history have come from a totally unexpected source. Take care of it straightaway."

"There are a couple of other matters we need to get sorted," Shane said. "The efforts toward the cure for one."

"I'm assured that that's in process. Or should I say, *permanently* in process?"

Shane knew as well as O'Reilly did that the rampant illness infecting most of Europe and the United Kingdom had been the single best thing to happen to Ireland—before or after the bloody EMP went off. With Ireland shutting its borders and establishing itself as the only country untouched by the plague, it had the singular opportunity to rise above where it had always rested before.

Want a place to hold a high level summit meeting of top world leaders? There's only Ireland left unaffected by death and illness.

Want to invest in a country's natural resources with a workforce that's quadruple the average population of any

*country in Europe? Ireland's workers are second to none in skill
set and ability to work long hours for little to no money.*

*All countries' future economic health would be
dependent on access to Ireland. All industries factories of the
future—garments, plastics, electronics—would need to be sited
in Ireland or perish.*

*And then there was the matter of the obscenely rich. Got
a million or two US and want a spa experience where you don't
have to worry about dying from some disgusting world disease?
We'll even throw in a castle tour and some fishing.*

*And it all depended on one thing—that no cure be found
any time soon.*

O'Reilly wasn't a fool. He knew eventually they'd nail
it. But not this year. And that gave him the time he needed to
build the separatist empire in Ireland that would have the rest of
the world—even that bugger America—coming to him on its
knees for labor, for natural resources—for one spot on Earth that
was safe.

As he had said many times to Shane: *Can you imagine
the power of being the leader of the only country in the world
virtually untouched by the plague? We'll be the next US—only
better because we'll avoid all the mistakes they made.*

O'Reilly knew he didn't have a reach long enough to
control all the world's scientists. After all, until two years ago,
he'd been a middle management politician with an office in the
basement of the government house. But what he did have was a
man in a very high, very trusted position in London government
who was extremely motivated to help O'Reilly delay the cure for
as long as possible.

"There's problems at the mine again," Shane said.

"Jaysus, Shane. Do I need to remind you how important
that fecking mine is?"

The same year of the EMP, Ireland had discovered a
significant lithium depository off their northern shore. While it
would have been a game changer in any economic climate, the
fact of a weakening, sickening Europe and United Kingdom
tipped the promise of wealth and power dramatically in Ireland's
favor.

"The bastards are either revolting or dying on us."

"If they're revolting, then we're feeding them too
much."

"They need the calories to work the necessary long
shifts."

"Bull shite. Who's in charge down there?"

"Kirkpatrick."

"Tell him to cut the rations by a third. If they're still giving him a hard time, by half."

"They won't last at that rate. They're already dying at nearly five a day."

"Then find new ones. Jaysus, Shane! Do I have to do your job too?"

Shane flinched but otherwise showed no reaction to O'Reilly's insult. He stood up and went to the door.

"If the Donovan compound does have a sat phone," Shane said grimly, "we need to get to it before those two get back home."

"Agreed," O'Reilly said, swinging his feet onto the top of his desk and picking up a folder. "And as a bonus, I imagine a compound of hardy souls carving a life out of the countryside will have a few able-bodied men who might be handy, say, with a shovel in an ore mine, wouldn't you say, Shane?"

Shane smiled. "I imagine they will," he said.

6

John awoke from his pallet of blankets on the porch floor. As tired and wet as he'd been last night, there was sickness in the house and it didn't take a genius to figure out it wasn't a safe place for him. He tapped on the front door and opened it to see the old man in the kitchen making tea. John watched him shove a chair leg into the potbellied stove. It was next to the nonfunctioning electric stove.

"I'm Bill Walker," the old man said without looking up. "You'll have a cuppa?"

John remained in the doorway. "Yes sir. Thank you."

"She's gone now," the old man said as he set the kettle on the stove and turned to look at John. "In the night."

John looked in the direction of the bedroom.

"I'm so sorry, sir."

"The doc told us fifty-fifty." The man sat down on a kitchen stool and covered his face with his hands. John didn't hear weeping but he could see the old man's shoulders shaking. He wasn't sure what he should do.

A part of him couldn't believe he'd shot and killed a man last night—without warning. He'd been trained on a lifetime of westerns and American sensibilities. *You don't just kill someone!* Even the worst bad guys got a chance to surrender or rethink their choices before you blasted them.

But not last night. Last night John used the fact that the man thought he was just a stupid kid in order to get the jump on him. Yeah, a part of him couldn't believe he'd done that. But probably worse was the fact that John had fallen right to sleep last night.

The old man stood up as the kettle began to whistle. His face was dry as he poured the steaming water into a teapot.

"I don't have milk. Nobody does."

It made John think of how everyone at the compound had milk and sugar, too for their tea. Plus jam. In fact usually four or five kinds. And always home-baked bread. His mouth watered to think of it. He felt a sickening sensation in his chest. He missed home. He missed his mom and Mike and Gav.

It occurred to John that he probably shouldn't drink the tea, or anything else prepared in this house.

"It's fine black," John said. "What will you do now?"

John had never buried anyone. In fact, he'd only ever watched the compound men do it and he had no idea what the compound women did to the body beforehand. He glanced toward the bedroom again.

"Oh, I imagine I'll just wait and things will go along as they're meant to." The old man poured tea into two mugs. "I'm grateful for your help last night. She was able to go in peace and I'm thankful to ye for that."

"Have they been...coming around before?"

"Oh, aye. They're afraid, ye ken. Of catching it."

"Once they know she's...gone, they should leave you alone."

The old man looked out the kitchen window.

"I'm afraid not," he said. "When I awoke this morning, I felt the first symptoms of the bugger meself."

John's fingers tightened around the doorjamb at his words.

*****

Later that morning, John helped Mr. Walker wrap his wife in a bed sheet and carry her to the curb where she would be taken away for burial—and which would announce to the neighborhood that the sickness had left their house. Then he set out for the clinic in Fishguard. The body of the man with the bat was laying face down in the front drive. Walker didn't seem to think it was a problem. The government health workers who went around scooping up the dead every morning would just add him to the pile.

John was sure he was seeing a preview of life in Ireland if the disease ever jumped the channel. He had to admit it was smart to refuse entrance to anyone from the United Kingdom. As far as Ireland was concerned, the rest of the world was in quarantine. It made sense. John had already made a pact with himself that he wouldn't worry about how he was getting home until he had Gavin. Together, they'd figure something out. It was just unimaginable that they wouldn't.

John knew he was welcome to stay with Mr. Walker as long as he wanted. The only question now was, did he want to? If only a percentage of people got the illness, it was starting to look like the percentage was growing—or people had their data wrong. In any case, staying in a house with one hundred percent sick people in it didn't add up in anybody's balance book. He would have to leave. And after bailing on work at Quig's today, he'd have to find another way to find food, too. But he'd already wasted too much time. If he couldn't find anyone who'd seen Gavin at the clinic, he would have to rethink his strategy. *How could nobody have seen him?*

The walk to Fishguard was hard going because the path wove in and out of a dense tangle of trees and bushes which had grown over the walkway. There was a road but Mr. Walker insisted the footpath was the fastest way. After a while John crested a steep hill and stood on a promontory with his back to the North Atlantic to balance himself against the wind. From the rocky escarpment he looked back at Lower Fishguard. It resembled an artist's interpretation of a medieval fishing village. Fishing boats dotted placid bays and foaming waves crashed on rocks along the coast. While John couldn't see Ireland from here, he could see the flotsam and jetsum of broken boats on the shoreline.

And a body.

Was the world going mad? Further out, he saw diesel-powered patrol boats with the bright colors of the Irish Garda splashed across their sides. So they were serious about not letting anybody in. John's eyes drifted back to the body on the beach. Had that been someone who was trying to get home to Ireland?

He turned his focus to getting to Fishguard. Maybe he'd been wrong and it wasn't Lower Fishguard that Gavin had gone to, although, knowing Gavin, he wasn't likely to make the distinction—at least not in a hastily scribbled note:

John—
Heading to Fishgurd!!!
So go home, ya berk
Gav

After scrambling down a precipitous patch of slippery rocks on the trail, John could see the newer part of Fishguard below him. Steps had been cut into the steep hillside below, and at the bottom stood a long row of shops. Behind them in the distance were several modern tract housing developments. But at the end of the street he could see what must be the clinic. There was a line of at least a hundred people standing in front of a large building. Most were standing, but some were lying down. And some weren't moving at all.

For a moment, John felt a twinge of fear at the thought of going down there into that. He'd thought Lower Fishguard had the disease bad. But it was nothing compared to this.

The wind from the channel clawed at his jacket and his long hair and suddenly the rain began pouring down. Watching his footwork as he descended the steep steps, John reached the street. At the end of it, shoved out on a precipice overlooking the bay, was a four-story mansion that looked like the Haunted House in Disney World. The sign in front announced it as the Fishguard Place Hotel. But it must have been at least four years since anyone stayed there as a paying guest.

John tightened his grip on the straps of his backpack and focused on getting past the long line of sick people to the front door. A few gave him a dirty look as he passed them but most were too sick to care. The illness seemed to have hit everyone equally—young, old, white, dark. John had always been told that the UK was better off than Ireland after the EMP. But what he saw now was worse than anything they had in Ireland.

This was death on two feet.

He was closing the gap to the front door and could see that on the second level there was a screened-in veranda overlooking the parking lot. There were beds on the veranda. As he approached the front of the line, he slowed to try to imagine how he would handle cutting in front of these genuinely sick people in order to get inside. He looked nervously at one of the listless women in line. Her eyes were so glazed and unfocused that she looked like she was already dead.

Did he really want to go in that place? As this thought passed through his mind, he noticed a scrum at the front of the line just outside the front door. Several men were shouting and shoving at each other.

Suddenly, he saw him. In the middle of the crowd, Gavin's shaggy red hair popped up above all others as he pushed a bigger man aside. John stopped, his mouth open as he watched

Gavin present himself to an unseen man in the doorway and then step inside and disappear into the interior.

"Gavin! Gavin!" John shook off his shock and bolted for the front of the line, pushing past the people in line. The front door was closed and a thin man wearing a surgical mask and gloves stood barring the entrance. He put a hand toward John's chest but didn't touch him.

"Whoa, there, laddie. You'll wait yer turn now."

"Buggering sod!" The man next to John snarled. "Get back, ye bastard!"

"My friend just went in there," John said. "I have to go in."

"Well, if he went inside then you really don't," the man in the mask said. "Unless you're sick too?"

The man behind John grabbed his backpack and wrenched it off him in an attempt to get John out of line. "Get out ye bastard!"

The masked man came to John's defense. "I will send you to the back of the line if you don't step back right now."

The man, still holding John's backpack, blinked at the doorkeeper and then meekly nodded. He handed John his backpack.

"Now, I'm just going to have a word here and then the boy will be leaving. Okay?"

The man behind John nodded again.

The gatekeeper turned to John. "Okay?"

"My friend went inside. I just saw him and I've come all the way from Ireland to find him."

"Look, I'm sure the doctors are doing all they can in there, me boyo but if you don't have to be inside…believe me, in there? The healthy get sick and the sick get sicker."

"If they're not getting better why is everyone coming here then?"

"Because they're desperate."

"I'm desperate too."

"Go in that door and you soon will be. I'm sorry. Give me the name of your friend and I'll ask someone."

The doorkeeper adjusted his mask and his eye caught another problem down the line as one woman began vomiting. "Everyone step back!" he shouted. "Do not let it touch you!" He hurried from the door to pull two gawking children away.

The front door was unguarded. John hesitated and reran the image in his mind. It *was* Gavin. He was sure of it. And if

Gav was sick, that was all the more reason why John needed to be with him.

He put his hand on the door, pushed it open and slipped inside.

7

The girl seemed to come out of nowhere although later John would realize she'd been sitting in a hidden alcove in the foyer where was reading a book. There was a mask across her face as she stood looking at John. She had the most expressive blue eyes John had ever seen.

"Only sick people allowed in!" she said.

John hesitated. Within seconds the door bouncer was going to realize that John was inside. John looked over her shoulder at the more than sixty people milling about the lobby. It looked like a scene out of one of the first rings of hell.

The smell alone would qualify it for that.

"How do you know I'm not sick?" he asked.

"I have a gift for the obvious. You're not sick. So you can't come in."

"I'm looking for someone."

"Not in here."

"Yes, in here! I saw him come in." John was desperately scanning the lobby. Gav couldn't have gone far. He'd just come in!

"Give me his name and if he's in here—"

Gavin had his back to the front door. He was being helped onto a gurney of some kind. He had a weird slope to his shoulders and his hair was longer than it should have been.

"That's him!" John said, pointing past her.

"If I turn around to look you're not going to run past me, are you? I've seen American movies. I'm not dumb."

John tore his eyes away from Gavin who, second by second, was morphing into a total stranger. He looked at the girl and the sadness and disappointment welled up in his throat until he thought he'd burst out crying right in front of her. His face must have telegraphed as much because she put a hand out and touched his arm.

"Oy. It's okay. It's going to be okay."

"It's not him," he said, as he watched the tall redhead being wheeled down a long hall. "I was so sure."

The front door opened and the man who'd grabbed John's backpack was ushered in. He didn't bother looking at John but stumbled into the lobby where someone in faded scrubs grabbed his arm and led him away. The masked doorman squinted at John.

"What are you doing here?" he said.

The girl turned and picked up her book.

"Don't mind us, Paul," she said to him. "He's fine. Come on...what's your name?"

"John."

"Now we just need a George and a Ringo," she said cheerfully. "Come on. I have a room down the hall."

John followed the girl down a narrow hall to a half set of stairs. He could see the feet of all the waiting people outside through the windows by his head.

He had been so sure it was Gavin.

They came to a row of doors and the girl used a key to open the first one and ushered him inside. He stepped into a small living room. The effects of his disappointment still filtered through him like a vibrating pain. In the time it took him to see Gavin and realize he'd finally found him, he'd already mentally gone through all the steps of getting him away and onto a boat— all the way to the moment when he presented him to their parents back at the compound with all the resultant joy and unbearable happiness. He'd gone all the way there and now he was left emptyhanded, right where he started.

Hungry. Alone. No way home. No idea where to find Gavin.

"You're a Yank, right?" the girl asked, ripping off her mask and revealing a beautiful smile that matched her eyes. Her hair was brown. Not dark and not blonde. "I'm Gilly."

John felt the exhaustion of his disappointment on his shoulders like a fifty-pound weight. He didn't trust himself to speak without breaking down. He'd been so close. So close.

"I bet you're sick of us Brits offering you tea all the time but I swear you look like you could use it. Sit down. When you leave I'll give you a mask. It might not keep the sickness at bay —nobody really knows how it's transmitted—but it can't hurt. That's what my father says anyway." Gilly went to the kitchenette and plugged a hotplate into a small generator. John's eyes widened.

"Shhh," Gilly grinned. "Don't tell the rabble that we have electricity. Even sick, I imagine they'd riot. Sorry we don't have sugar but there's a little milk."

John sat down and looked around the room. It appeared to have been a servants quarters at one time. The furniture was old—a divan, two armchairs and a small dining table with three chairs around it. There were cigarette burns in the table. Gilly handed him his tea and sat across from him.

"So this is the part where you tell me how an American is here in the middle of all this."

John set his tea down and shook his head as if to clear it. "Who are you?" he asked. "Do you live here?"

She laughed. "I guess it sounds crackers. But my father is the head doc here. We live in Oxford. They sent him down here about two weeks ago when things started to get bad. At first we just came because Dad is trying to figure out a way to stop it, you know?"

"He's a…? John didn't want to appear stupid in front of her but he couldn't find the word he was searching for either.

"Immunologist," Gilly said. "Well, he calls himself a lab rat but same thing."

John waved to the clinic above them. "Is he finding a cure?"

Gilly wrinkled up her nose. "He's trying anyway. It's all pretty desperate." She waved in the direction of the long line of people outside. "Dad says right now seventy percent will die and thirty will live through it."

"But he doesn't know why?"

"That's what he's trying to figure out. Okay, your turn. Pretend like I'm the British TMZ." She held an imaginary microphone to John's face. "Tell us, John. What brings you to post-apocalyptic England in the middle of a plague?"

John laughed in spite of himself. In fact, he laughed so hard and so long, that he thought he might fall off the couch. When she put it that way, the truth sounded ludicrous. He wiped his eyes.

"I'm in Ireland because my mother fell in love with an Irishman and we didn't want to live apart. And I'm in the middle of a plague in the United Kingdom because my stepbrother, Gavin, is missing and I'm trying to find him."

Gilly's eyes were large and she sat back in her chair and watched him.

"What makes you think he's in Fishguard?"

"He left me a note telling me he was heading here."

"But you don't know if he made it. He might have changed his mind."

John nodded. He had to admit that was true.

"You must care for him a lot."

"I lost my dad during the second year after the bomb dropped. So I'm really invested in not losing anybody else I love."

Gilly stared at him, no longer smiling. "I love how Americans talk," she said softly as if speaking to herself. "Not just the accent but the words you use are so strange. I lost my mother last year. To this bloody disease." Her eyes filled with tears and she picked up her tea and sipped it noisily.

"I'm sorry."

"So I know exactly what you mean about not wanting to lose anybody else."

"Is it just you and your dad?"

She nodded. "But you've got a stepbrother and a new stepdad, too? What's he like? Is he evil?"

John laughed. "No, he's awesome. I mean he's the total opposite of my dad but still great in his own way. He makes my mom happy. So that's cool."

"Will you stay for supper?"

"I would kiss the ground you walk on and all your ancestors for giving me supper."

"A simple yes would do," Gilly said, laughing. "How've you been managing up to now?"

"Hand to mouth."

"Not any more," she said firmly. "I'll do what I can to help you, John. How's that?"

"That would be amazing, Gilly. Thank you."

They talked for another hour before Gilly jumped up to make dinner. John knew he'd feel better if he checked in with Mr. Walker but he agreed to hold off until after they'd eaten. Gilly was expecting her father any minute and he could tell she was excited about the two of them meeting.

John evaluated his position. He still didn't know where Gavin was but he'd made a friend and if her father didn't hate him, maybe someone who might help him find Gavin and get back to Ireland. His thoughts flashed back to Mr. Walker and how sad he must be today. John's stomach clenched at the thought of that kind of grief. And now Mr. Walker was sick too. He glanced at Gilly as she brought pans out of the cupboard and began chopping vegetables. She looked to be about his age, maybe a little older. It was hard to tell. Her accent was weird, too. Definitely not Irish.

He stood up and leaned in the doorway of the kitchen.

"So are you English?"

She laughed. "No way! I'm a Scot."

"But you live in England?"

"Because Dad has a lab in Oxford. He's usually a researcher. It was a real coup for the government to have him help out like this. Actually, it was Uncle Dan's doing." Gilly put the vegetables on the stove to boil and wiped her hands. "Uncle Dan is in parliament in London. A really big muckey-muck."

"And is he Scottish, too?"

"Of course."

At that moment, the door behind John opened and a man in a white lab coat walked into the room. He was of average height with a pleasant face. He had a long straight nose and clear blue eyes like Gilly. He shut the door behind him.

"Gilly?"

"In here, Dad!" Gilly greeted her father and then turned to introduce John. "We have a guest for dinner."

"I see we do. Finlay Heaton," he said, extending his hand, his eyes taking in every aspect of John as he stood there.

"John Woodson."

Dr. Heaton's eyebrows shot up. "American?"

"Yes sir."

"How was it today, Dad?" Gilly said, holding her hands out for her father's lab coat. It occurred to John that it should probably be in some kind of sanitation containment but Gilly just took it and hung it up on a peg in the hall.

"No worries, lad," Heaton said. "I left my lab smock to be disinfected. Can I offer you a drink?"

John shook his head. "No sir. Gilly gave me tea."

Heaton moved into the kitchen and Gilly gestured for John to sit down. She picked up the tea tray and left the room as Heaton returned with a glass of whiskey in his hand.

"Where are your parents, lad?"

"My father was killed," John said, keeping his voice impassive. "And my mother is in Ireland. I'm here looking for my stepbrother."

"Bad timing, that. The Garda shot two more local craft just today trying to cross the channel."

Gilly returned with a new cup of tea for John. "So they're serious, then," she said.

"Oh, aye. Where are you staying in Fishguard, John?"

"Well, it sort of changes day to day, honestly."

"Dad, can he stay with us? He's sleeping in *ditches*."

"That's all right, sir. I'm used to it."

Heaton frowned and drank down the rest of his drink. "Let's eat first, shall we?"

It wasn't a feast but it tasted like it to John. His mom used to tease him that, like most teenage boys, he was a bottomless pit when it came to food. He eagerly accepted seconds and thirds when Gilly offered them. The dinner was a revelation in other ways too. Finlay Heaton was attempting to discover the cause of the disease so that he could create possible remedies—something that vastly excited John. He also learned that the Irish Garda not only shot at anyone within a mile of Ireland's coast, but some said you were at risk at any place on the water between Wales and Ireland.

It turned out Dr. Heaton wasn't the head doctor at the clinic. As a researcher, his clinician days were behind him. He helped where he could but that wasn't why he was in Fishguard.

"The World Health Organization thinks it's water-borne," Dr. Heaton said.

"So it's bacterial?" John asked.

"Aren't you a clever lad!"

John blushed. "Not really. We came to Ireland when I was ten and the only real schooling I've had since then is the encyclopedia set my mom and I brought back last year."

"Are the Irish not providing basic infrastructure?"

"I don't really know," John admitted. "We stay pretty isolated from the rest of Ireland in our compound. And there's no one there, really, to teach me."

"Bright lad like you," Heaton said, frowning. "That is a crime against nature. Not even Dublin? Not Trinity?"

"I really don't know." John looked at Gilly. "What are you doing for school? Was that not interrupted over here?"

"Not for long enough," Gilly said, grinning at her father. "Most of the UK got a rudimentary grid built back within eighteen months of the EMP going off so the main cities have electricity and cars again."

"But not here."

"Nay," Heaton said, looking out the window. It was already dark. "Not in Wales nor Scotland either."

"Why is the clinic in a hotel? Wasn't there a hospital in Fishguard?"

"Oh, aye," Heaton said, shrugging. "But it was picked clean within weeks of the bomb. Besides, it's too far out of town. With no cars, nobody could get there. It's the British government that set this clinic up and staffed it. Actually Fishguard is one of our larger sites. Or at least it was."

"What do you mean?"

Heaton sighed. "Well, they're moving most of the operation to a larger hub. Makes sense of course. But tell that to the poor sods around here needing treatment."

"You'll just leave?" John asked.

"Well, Gilly and I were leaving anyway. I've seen what I came to see. The rest needs to happen in a laboratory."

John was relieved when Gilly refused his help to clean up after the meal. He really wanted to check on Mr. Walker. As he gathered up his pack, Dr. Heaton clapped him on the back.

"We'd be glad to have you stay with us, John. We have the room. You're welcome to leave your pack here."

John hesitated. While he was delighted to have a place to stay for the night, he didn't feel good about walking back to Lower Fishguard without his gun. Nor did he particularly want to show Heaton that he had it.

"Is something amiss, lad?"

John heard the sounds of Gilly washing up and humming in the kitchen. Perhaps Heaton would understand. While things hadn't been as bad in England as they had in Ireland, he must have heard the media reports.

"I travel with a handgun. And I hope that doesn't make you think twice about having me stay with you."

Heaton paused and looked at the pack in John's hands.

"When you're out at night, where do you carry it?"

John opened his pack and pulled out the semiautomatic. He checked the cartridge and then tucked it into his back waistband.

"Jolly good. You go and come back safe, eh? I'm only sorry we can't invite the old man too but until I know the parameters of the contagion factor—"

"That's all right, sir. I won't be more than an hour, there and back."

"Cheers. I'll have a word with the door security to keep an eye out for you so you don't get locked out."

"Is he leaving?" Gilly stood in the kitchen wiping her hands on a hand towel. The gesture reminded John of his mother and he felt a sudden longing to see her.

"Just," her father said as he opened the door for John.

"Thank you again for everything. For dinner and just everything."

"Tut!" Heaton said. "It was our pleasure. Wasn't it, darling? Off you go now."

John grinned at Gilly and then trotted down the long hall. The security detail included two men sitting on stools by the front door. From the smell of alcohol wafting in the foyer, they weren't as alert as they could be, but they nodded to him as he passed and slipped out the door.

What unbelievable luck! A place to stay while he sorted out which way Gavin went...*if he went anywhere*. The nagging thought that Gavin had never made it to Fishguard had flitted in and out of his brain ever since the man in the clinic turned out not to be him. John would continue to look and ask around but one way or the other he was going to have to accept the possibility that coming over here might have been a major mistake.

He thought back to how far from the coast it was that he'd found Gavin's note. What if Gav was *planning* on coming to Fishguard but then something happened and he changed his mind? Knowing Gav, he could be half way to Limerick before he remembered he hadn't left any further clues for poor, stupid John who was probably on his way to Fishguard by now.

As soon as John started down this way of thinking, every thought or strategy he came up with began with the default assumption that Gavin was *not* in Fishguard after all and had never been in Fishguard.

There was no moon out when John hurried back over the hill that separated Lower Fishguard from the newer town. It was still early for the stars to reflect much light. He could smell the sea to his right even if it he couldn't see it. It gave him a chill to think of it there, massive, moving, invisible.

He figured if the neighbors saw poor Mrs. Walker's body out this morning, they'd have no reason to bother the old man—unless they wanted vengeance on how their mate, the guy with the cricket bat, ended up in the same body bag. The two who ran away didn't look like the types who'd come back for more but John wasn't willing to trust his intuition.

An image of Gilly popped unbidden into his head and he grinned.

Yeah, she was cute. And while his experience with the opposite sex was extremely limited, *like zero*, even he could tell she liked him, too. Just thinking of her gave him a funny feeling in his stomach. And unlike all the other funny feelings he'd experienced in the past few years, this one didn't make him want to throw up in the bushes.

John waited until the house was in sight and then he stepped into the shadows to wait and watch. The house looked dark, as it had last night and he felt a thin tremor of guilt for the terrible day the old fellow must have spent: dumped his beloved wife out on the curb for body pickup and then returned to a house with the electricity permanently off, there to sit and reflect on his own impending mortality. Bill Walker had surely just endured the worst day of his life.

To be on the safe side, John pulled his gun out and approached the house in a crouch. If someone was lying in wait on the porch or in the thick weeds by the front walk, he'd be ready for them. He slowed his approach and silently crept up the steps to the porch turning so that the door was at his back. He surveyed the front yard. Nothing. Without turning around, he tapped on the door behind him. There was no answer.

Crap shit. With his eyes still on the street in front of the house, John felt for the doorknob. It was unlocked. He pushed the door open and backed into the house, turning around only once he was inside to look out a front window. There was still no movement on the street.

"Mr. Walker?" he called. The house was dark and totally quiet. John stood, undecided. The silence was unnerving and his mind raced to fill in the answers.

The old guy's dead in the back bedroom. Don't go in there.

He's being held at knifepoint by somebody in the back room just waiting for me to wander down the hall to investigate. Don't go there.

John's heart seemed to be pounding in his ears.

Does he need help? Is he back there...needing help?
John's shoulders sagged and for a moment he was tempted to sit on the couch. What difference did any of this make any more? Why had he even bothered coming back? There was nothing he could do for the old guy. Nothing. And he wasn't even going to stay the night. This was all so stupid.

Except John had promised he'd be back.

He straightened his shoulders and took a long steadying breath. He'd promised Mr. Walker that he'd return. Good or bad, that's what that was. Holding his gun out in front of him and promising himself he wouldn't accidentally shoot the old guy, John edged his way down the hall. The first bedroom door was partially open and John edged it all the way with his foot. Just junk and some old broken furniture. Probably the stuff Mr. Walker had been using to fuel the cook stove. John turned to the second and last bedroom down the hall.

Quit freaking yourself out. His hands felt slick on the gun which all of a sudden was very heavy. He shifted it to his left hand and wiped his right hand on his jeans before taking it back up with both hands. This bedroom door was open too. John stepped inside pointing his gun first left then straight and then right, just like he'd seen on a hundred cop shows when he lived in a world with Netflix and a mildly clueless mother.

The room was empty.

The old guy wasn't here. John jammed the gun back into his pants and hurried to the front of the house. He looked out the window and felt a light sheen of sweat erupt across his brow. There was still nothing in sight.

Would he have gone outside? John knew there was a shed in the garden that the old couple were using as a dunny. It was possible he was out there. John wished he'd brought the penlight he had stashed in his knapsack but maybe it was just as well he hadn't. While it would help him see, it would also help others see him.

Quietly, he slipped out the front door and jumped off the porch. There wasn't a sound to be heard anywhere. He walked quickly without running—it would be all too easy to trip over something—to the rear of the house. With his back against the house, he stood and waited for his eyes to adjust. He estimated he should be staring right at the makeshift outhouse. If Mr. Walker was outside, this was John's best chance to find him.

As he waited, he listened but there was nothing to hear. Now that he was standing still, he realized his head was pounding with a dull ache and he wondered for a moment if that was the reason he didn't hear anything. Afraid to test his theory by clearing his throat or snapping his fingers, he passed a shaky hand over his face and brought it back with more perspiration. There was a cutting breeze weaving its way down the residential streets and through where the houses were set. It seemed to slice right into him. For a moment, John wasn't sure how long he'd been standing there and was horrified to realize he'd blanked out for a moment.

Really smart, Woodson, he admonished himself. The setting before him was still dark but he could see well enough now to realize there wasn't a body or anything else visible out of the ordinary. He had no idea where Mr. Walker had gone and tonight was not going to be the night he found out. He was cold and tired. He hadn't slept in a bed in over a week and he ached in places he didn't know were on his body to ache. He said a silent prayer for Mr. Walker, wherever he was, and turned to find the path that led back over the hill to Fishguard.

It took him much longer this time. The wind fought him at the crest of the hill and he stayed as far from the edge of the promontory as he safely could. He heard the water below, pounding angrily against the rocks, and he felt the salt stinging his lips and eyes. Something was wrong. That much he knew but it took all his effort to stay upright on the path and moving forward. Any thoughts that didn't focus on the path or putting one foot in front of the other were dangerous now. When he finally came to the downward slope of the hill that led to the town street, he slipped on a smooth rock and lost his footing. His gun, still wedged into his pants, cut painfully into his back as he tumbled down the hill, crashing into the rocky ground several times, and finally skidding to a stop at the base of a tree a few yards from the street.

He knew he was hurt but he couldn't feel the cuts and bruises. It was like his entire body was insensate to the physical world. Something was ruling him from the inside and nothing that happened to the vessel mattered. He lay against the tree, willing himself to move, to sit up, to keep going. But he couldn't. At one point in his fall, his face must have hit something that didn't give because he tasted blood in his mouth. He smelled the loam and the dirt and the grass where it pressed into his face. His body felt like it didn't belong to him.

He would never know how he got himself back up on his feet and down to the street or how he managed to walk the three city blocks to the clinic and stumble to the front door. When he fell into the arms of the drunken security guard in the foyer, he felt his body shut down entirely, as if it had accomplished what was required and now it was finished.

He felt himself being carried down the hall. He saw flickering lights through his half-open eyelids and heard Dr. Heaton's voice.

"I'm sorry," John mumbled before the darkness claimed him.

8

Where Antonio had found a Catholic priest in Ireland in the middle of the wilderness, Gavin would never know. And he didn't care. All that mattered now was that in one hour, Sophia would be his wife and a few hours after that, his in every sense of the word.

His stomach cramped at the thought and he glanced nervously at his soon-to-be father-in-law as if the man could read his mind. Antonio Borgnino stood beside Gavin, his face solemn as befitting the occasion but with a twinkle in his eye that communicated his good mood. He was a striking man. Even Gavin who normally didn't notice such things, could see that. Jet black hair although he had to be well into his fifties, and dark, nearly pupil-less eyes. Beside Antonio stood Benito, Sophia's teenage brother. Benito wasn't the kind of bloke Gavin would normally choose to hang with—a little too intense for his tastes. *But, hey, you don't get to pick your family, do you?*

Gavin cleared his throat and smiled nervously at the priest who faced him. The man was severe and disgruntled. Not, Gavin, had to admit, unlike most priests of his acquaintance. He felt a twinge of anger when the thought came to him. That bastard Father Ryan had led him with a lie to the woods where the fecking druids had bashed him about. Gavin's cheeks burned at the memory of how Ryan had made him believe that his girl Regan was waiting for him in the woods and that it was God's will that the two be united.

How stupid can one randy fecker be? Gavin thought, shaking his head. He glanced at Antonio who was frowning at him as if worried that Gavin was about to bolt. The very thought made Gavin smile again.

Was the man barking? Would *anybody* in their right mind run in the opposite direction from the vision that was the lovely Sophia? In fact, now that Gavin put the two notions together, if it weren't for that tosser Ryan, Gavin would never have met her and for that reason alone, he could forgive the fecker, lying bastard though he was.

When Gavin had cut through his ties with his hidden boot knife in the druid camp and escaped into the forest, he set out going due north because he knew how widespread the druid's reach was east and west. The plan had been to go north and then east to the coast before coming back around south to the compound. Unfortunately, he'd had to escape with only the pants and boots on his feet, the head wanker druid having stripped him of his favorite shirt. Bastard! Just thinking about that first freezing cold night spent hidden in the leaves and underbrush of the woods with no shirt made Gavin want to go back with a shotgun and find the twitchy bastard.

Instead, he'd been found by Antonio and his family. When they came upon Gavin they hadn't hesitated but swept him instantly into their community. They fed him, clothed him and even promised vengeance for him on the druids—although nothing ever came of that. They were good people and it was nothing short of providence from God Almighty that they'd found him when he needed so badly to be found.

But of all the good fortune that Gavin had to be grateful about nothing could top the one amazing bit of luck that he never in his whole damn life ever thought he'd experience.

Sophia.

Dear God, just thinking of the lass now turned his insides around in seriously gratifying waves of desire. The second he laid eyes on her he knew he loved her. He knew he'd do anything for her. He knew, if God was in his heaven and Sophia was daft enough to have him, that he'd never leave her side not even to save his own life if she'd have him, please God.

Never had he even come close to the way he felt when he was with her. And when he held her in his arms? He swallowed and moved his feet, not bothering to look at Antonio. Holding her in his arms was like a living sacrament and he didn't care how blasphemous that sounded. It was as true as rain in winter.

A flash of color and movement caught his eye and he turned his head with his heart pounding in anticipation of what he knew his eyes would see.

Sophia stood at the end of the path, her mother and two cousins flanking her like attendants. There was a glow from the climbing sun behind her that gave her a radiant outline as she moved toward him. She held a bouquet of winter flowers in her hands. Her long, black hair was down, curled in flowing tendrils. She wore a gown made from several dresses but Gavin didn't notice the seam lines or the different colors on the multiple hems. He saw an angel with dark brown almond-shaped eyes and a smile of promise on her full lips as she walked slowly toward him.

He was getting married today. Married to a goddess he'd never imagined could possibly exist—let alone love him. As he stood there waiting for his bride to come to him, he knew that nothing and nobody mattered except this perfect moment.

71

Susan Kiernan-Lewis

9

For two days, John was only aware of intermittent darkness and wavering light behind his closed eyes. When he dreamed, he felt himself being spooned broth or water. He heard Gilly's voice and her father's like they were calling to him from across a gymnasium, their voices echoing and reverberating. He knew he should tell them not to worry about him but his body was too heavy, his arms and legs unresponsive. He was surprised how philosophical he felt about dying. He didn't have the emotion to deal with it. He was just so tired.

When he finally opened his eyes, it was because the dream he was having was so physical that he wanted to see for himself what was happening. His whole body vibrated and hummed in a very pleasant fashion so he was pretty convinced he'd made it to heaven, which was good. Mom would be sad but only because she didn't know yet how awesome heaven was.

"You're awake. Dad! He's awake."

At first John couldn't understand where he was or what was happening. It had been so long since he'd ridden in a vehicle that for a moment, he flashed back to being a child again in his car seat, cartoons on the car video, Mom and Dad in the front seat. He licked his lips.

"Are you thirsty, John?" He saw that Gilly poised a water bottle in front of his face.

"I…where…?"

"We're going back to Oxford," Gilly said, pushing the bottle into his mouth. He drank deeply, deciding to process her words in a moment. They sat in the back seat of a large SUV. Dr. Heaton was in the driver's seat. John was wrapped in a blanket with a large pillow behind his head.

"I'm sick," he said. God. It was all coming back to him. He had the sickness. He left poor Mr. Walker's house and…that's all he remembered.

"You're a lot better now," Gilly said.

"How are you feeling, laddie?" Dr. Heaton called to him. "I told you he was coming around."

"Dad thinks maybe flu. What with sleeping in cold ditches and eating bad."

"I…it wasn't the plague?"

"Blimey, no," Gilly said. "But it was still bad, mind you. I was sure you were going to wake up with brain damage. I'm not completely sure you haven't."

John closed his eyes. He had just enough energy to smile. He felt so weak, and so very comfortable. He wasn't ready to address the fact that they were taking him to Oxford. There was no way Gavin was in Oxford. Neither was it a direct route back to Ireland. All in all, being on his way to Oxford wasn't great.

"We had to leave," Gilly said. "And we couldn't leave you there."

"I…'preciate all you've done for me," he said with his eyes still closed.

"Go back to sleep, John."

He could feel her tucking his blanket around him.

"When you wake up we'll have roast beef."

Since that seemed the perfect ending of his fairly perfect dream, John nodded and fell back to sleep.

*****

By the time they reached the outskirts of Oxford, it was nearly dark. Normally a two-hour drive from Wales, because of the number of abandoned cars on the roadways and the necessary detours due to permanently closed roads, it had taken them six hours to make the trip.

True to Gilly's word, they stopped at a pub in the village of Compton Abdale for dinner before continuing on to Oxford. John was surprised to see the small pub had electricity and a full menu. Even in just two days of being sick, he could tell he'd lost weight when he walked from the car to the pub. Gilly led him to a booth by a roaring floor to ceiling fireplace and his legs nearly gave out before he got there. The fire smelled like cherry wood. He was still dopey from his deep sleep and stared into the dancing flames. Gilly chattered away but didn't seem to need encouragement or participation.

When Dr. Heaton came to the table, he brought three glasses of beer with him.

"There's the stuff, lad," he said, pushing John's glass to him. "Liquid bread. It'll help fix the wobbles."

"Or cause them," Gilly said, giggling.

John drank his beer down. Warm, thick and foamy. It was delicious and made his head spin.

"Whoa, slow down, laddie. A little goes a long way in the beginning."

The proprietor brought a tray with their food and for a moment it was all John could do but stare at the steaming plate of roast beef, mashed potatoes and roasted carrots on the plate. It had been so long since he'd eaten good food that his hand trembled as he picked up his fork.

"You'll be wondering why we kidnapped you, I imagine," Dr. Heaton said, winking at Gilly. "We couldn't leave you, lad. Gilly and I had to make an executive decision."

"I'm grateful to you for everything you've done," John said, trying not to talk with his mouth full. The dinner definitely took precedence over conversation tonight.

"It's rather urgent that I get back to my lab. We couldn't wait. You're not but three hours from the coast."

"If that's what you want, John," Gilly said, meaningfully. "I mean you can't cross back over anyway. Why not stay with us for awhile? At least until Ireland eases up on travel?"

John really didn't know what to think at this point. He knew he was taking a detour in his plan to find Gavin but until he got strong again, staying with Gilly and her dad sounded like an intelligent move.

"I'm grateful to you," John said, finally slowing down on his meal. The warmth from the crackling fire and his now full stomach combined with the lager to make him long to lay his head down again.

"Well, that's settled then," Heaton said with a smile. He looked at his daughter. "Are you ready to be home, darlin'?"

Gilly looked over her father's shoulder to the proprietor. When she did John noticed for the first time that they were the only ones in the pub.

"Did you talk to Mr. Smails?" she asked.

"Aye. There's nothing to worry about."

"But the sickness? Is it still bad?"

"No change. Eat your supper and let's get home. Young John there looks like he's ready to park his cot in front of Mr. Smails' hearth."

John smiled, his eyes drooping sleepily. He put his fork down and propped his head up on one hand. And promptly fell back to sleep.

Life in Oxford was not something John was prepared for on any level.

He woke up the next morning feeling much stronger and ready to begin to sort out his new plan for returning to Ireland and finding Gavin. The Heatons lived in an Edwardian semidetached house walking distance to the college. John figured it must have been pretty old even before the EMP sent everyone back to the eighteen hundreds but it was cozy and it was warm against the cold December temperatures. He was grateful to have found the Heatons and that they seemed to like him well enough to help him. But he couldn't stay any longer than another day at the most.

He found his clothes and realized that they'd been laundered at some point in the last few days. His bedroom was upstairs with a window facing the back garden. He hoped the doc wasn't sleeping on the couch downstairs. He'd hate to think he took his bedroom. When he stood in the hallway, he was surprised to see Gilly coming up the stairs with a steaming cup of tea.

"Oh! You surprised me," she said. "I was just bringing you a cup of tea. You look good this morning. How do you feel?"

"Good."

"Well enough to come downstairs for your tea?"

"Sure." He wondered how long she'd been up but the light in the hall window seemed to suggest he hadn't slept the whole day away. He followed her down the steep stairs leading to the salon. A fire was blazing in the grate and a teapot with cups and toast on a plate were sitting on the kitchen table.

"Dad's already gone to the lab. But he said we could meet him for lunch if you were up for it."

"That sounds great." John sat down at the table in the small kitchen. The window over the sink looked out onto the brick side of another house not six feet away. Gilly set his tea down and shoved the toast toward him.

"I can make you an egg if you like?"

"No, thanks. Toast is great."

"I know you want to get back to Ireland as soon as you can." Gilly said. When he looked at her, he could see panic in her eyes. He was surprised because up until this moment, she'd always been so happy and so sure of herself.

"Well, my family is there. Great toast by the way."

She looked at him as if trying to decide something and then stood up.

"It's nearly lunchtime, so I'll just change, shall I? Won't be a tick." She turned and walked back up the stairs. John sat and drank his tea and felt a little more relaxed, as if Gilly had taken some of the tension out of the air when she left.

He stood to look out the kitchen window and was surprised to see a boy about his age pulling up on a bicycle. John watched as the boy set two bottles of milk and a package of what looked like bread loaves on the back porch. As if feeling someone's eyes on him, the boy looked up and saw John in the window, grinned and waved.

Thirty minutes later, Gilly locked the townhouse. A thick hedge of bushes lined both sides of the front walk. John could see thorns and imagined in the summer the hedge was full of roses. He'd left his gun in his bedroom. He was anxious to get some exercise and to try to strength his legs. Gilly assured him the walk to the college wasn't long. They walked through the largely residential neighborhood and met nobody. Not mothers pushing prams or bikers or students.

"Where is everyone?" he asked.

"Oh, they're here," Gilly said, looking up at one of the houses as they passed. It looked vacant but then John caught a glimpse of a moving curtain in the window. "When the sickness came, people started staying inside. Like that would save them."

"Is the sickness bad here?"

"Not as bad as Fishguard," Gilly said. "I don't know how it's been in the last couple of weeks, obviously, but it's not the Oxford I grew up in, let's just say that."

They walked silently until they came to a cobblestone alley that led to a stone archway into Trinity College. The sounds of their shoes on the cobblestones echoed loudly in the walkway. John saw bicycles everywhere, parked in bike holders, propped up against walls and trees, fallen over in a tangle of rubber and chain.

"Don't they have cars in this part of the UK?" he asked.

"They do. Mind you, not like they used to."

"It's like the whole place is depressed," John said.

"You're not wrong there."

The college setting reminded him of what Disney World would feel like if they closed it for a day but you got to roam around. Here was this world famous university that felt like a ghost town. It began to snow in big fluffy flakes drifting lazily to the ground. John couldn't help but feel it gave a decidedly magical air to the scene.

"Here we are," Gilly said as she walked up to a large wooden door and yanked on the handle. They went up two flights of stairs worn slick with generations of use, and then down a narrow hall. Dr. Heaton's lab was visible behind a long wall of glass enabling anyone to watch the work in progress. Standing in the hall were two men and a woman in white lab coats seeming to do just that. Gilly nodded at the group and hurried past them but John was startled by the animosity that seemed to roll off the glowering threesome.

Gilly tapped on the glass and John saw movement inside as her father turned his head to see them and wave to them.

The contrast between Heaton's lab and the rest of the college was dramatic. Outside was cobblestones and ornate archways. Inside, the lab was all bright lights and streamlined countertops packed with chemistry paraphernalia and microscopes. Dr. Heaton wore a white lab coat and latex gloves.

"Is it safe to come in?" John asked Gilly.

"Must be," she said, opening the door. "Hey, Dad."

"Hello, you, two," Dr. Heaton said, turning to face them. "Well, you're looking better, laddie."

"Thank you, sir," John said, gazing around the lab. He felt his heart start to race.

"Like science, do you?"

"I think so."

"I've an idea," Dr. Heaton said. "Before we head to lunch, I'll give you a tour. Gilly darling, you'll be bored to tears. Why don't you go down to the salon and fetch your old Dad a hot cuppa?"

Gilly hesitated for a moment and glanced at John. Something was going on. That was clear. There was no point in having a cup of tea now if they were going to lunch. But Gilly just shrugged.

"Sure," she said. "Back in a tick."

As soon as the door closed behind her, John turned to Dr. Heaton expecting him to lead him around the long tables. He was surprised to see the man staring at him.

"Sir?" John said, unsure of what was going on.

"She's gotten attached to you, my Gilly."

"She's a great girl," John said, feeling uncomfortable. Had he said something inappropriate?

"Aye, she is that. I have a problem, young John, and I need your help with it."

"Sure. If I can." John felt his shoulders tense up under his jacket. Now that he was inside, he was feeling too warm with it on.

"Gilly has had a terrible time with the loss of her mother last year. She'll have talked to you about that?"

"Yes sir. She said her mom died of the sickness."

"Aye. She's had...problems adjusting to the loss."

"I'm sorry, sir."

"I'm going to ask you to stay with us a little longer, son." He held up his hand as John started to speak. "I know. You're in a hurry. You have a mission. I know. But I think I might be able to help you with your problem if you think you can help me with my problem."

Did he know a way back to Ireland?

"I am in a position to arrange medical transport to Ireland because of my position. If you were to agree to stay with us—just until the lass can handle it, mind—I'd be happy to see you back to Ireland where you won't be dodging bullets as you go."

John turned to see the figure of Gilly as she walked toward them down the hall balancing a mug of tea in her hands.

"How long would you need me to stay?"

"Not long. Three months, maybe?"

Three months. Mom will have a nervous breakdown in three months.

"Will you think on it, lad? For Gilly's sake?"

"Yes sir. I will."

*****

The routine of life in Oxford took on a comforting monotony for John, punctuated with predictable episodes of pure joy. Once he accepted that he would be staying—at least for a while—he found he could turn his attention to the world around him and table his plans. *Wherever* Gavin was, John would find him one day. He knew exactly where his mom and Mike were and would return to them when he could.

Meanwhile, he'd discovered a brand new world peopled by scientists who understood him better than he'd ever imagined possible. As soon as Dr. Heaton saw that John had a keen interest in the lab, he began bringing him to work most days. Their conversations were complex, educational and engaging.

Sometimes Gilly came too. But often she didn't, seeming as if the comfort and security of knowing that both her father and John would return each afternoon for tea, board games, dinner and long walks was enough.

John never really saw the depression in Gilly that Dr. Heaton had hinted at. But even he saw the difference in her affect after only a week of the three of them living together as a family. She was more independent, happier to be left to her own projects—usually knitting or crocheting—and willing to spend whole afternoons with her girlfriends who lived on the same street. Dr. Heaton had arranged for John and Gilly—along with other classmates—to attend tutoring sessions in the college classrooms with various professors. While John attended these classes with pleasure, his greatest passion was visiting Dr. Heaton's lab, which he anticipated every morning with enthusiasm.

As the weeks went by, John realized that Finlay Heaton was the first person since John's dad who spoke John's same language. It wasn't just their mutual love of science but a love of learning. There was a symbiotic connection between the two of them that was palpable.

It was clear that Heaton's objective—to find a cure for the water-borne disease that was ravaging the UK and the continent—was also a considerable feather in his cap. Even in the few weeks that John had been in Oxford he had picked up on the thinly veiled disrespect in which Dr. Heaton was viewed by the other scientists in the lab. That he would be formally tasked by the government to find a cure for the plague was generally greeted in the department with unabashed and open astonishment.

As Dr. Heaton had explained it to John, the disease involved both a bacterial and a viral infection. The bacteria acted as transports for the virus. What worked to kill the bacteria still left the virus intact. And the usual methods of killing the virus— high temperatures and chlorine washes—left the water toxic for consumption.

One Oxford scientist in particular, Dr. Sandra Lynch, seemed to make it her goal to come by the lab daily to goad Dr. Heaton. In John's opinion she was too tall for a woman, easily over six feet. Her hair was pulled back in an unattractive ponytail that made her ears stick out while her thick-lensed eyeglasses made her eyes look froglike.

Dr. Heaton gave John basic lab chores, like cleaning test tubes and dusting the microscopes. But often he just talked to John about life, about the disease, about the way things were and the way they'd become.

"Did you know that smallpox killed fifteen million people a year until 1967?" Dr. Heaton said as he squinted through his microscope.

"I thought smallpox was eliminated."

"It was. Ten years later it didn't exist because of the vaccine."

"So is our plague like smallpox?"

Dr. Heaton looked at John and frowned. "It is and it isn't. More like a super cholera, which is also transmitted through water."

"Wouldn't it be easier to figure a way to prevent it than cure it?" John asked.

Heaton walked over to his desk and picked up a thick sheaf of documents that had arrived from London that morning by courier. "Very possibly. But that's not the job, lad."

"I mean, isn't coming up with new antibiotic therapies or vaccines going to take forever?"

"Welcome to the world of science."

"It seems you're spending a whole lot of time trying to figure out what it is that's making people sick instead of how to stop the disease from spreading."

"Ah, the impatience of youth. Finding the cause of the disease will help us fight it."

"Maybe the cause doesn't matter."

"How can it not matter? It's knowledge, John. And knowledge always matters."

"But when you're trying to fix a problem, isn't some knowledge more important than others? Why not just do the easy thing first and move on from there? That's what I'd do."

"You call creating a prophylaxis the easy thing, do ye, lad?"

"Well, comparatively, yeah."

They sat in silence for a bit.

"Ye should be in school, John," Dr. Heaton said. "And then college. Not planting turnips in Ireland."

"My family's there."

"I know, lad.

One night, after he'd been in Oxford for three weeks John was surprised to see that Gilly had invited Dr. Lynch to join them for dinner. If he read Dr. Heaton's face correctly, it was a surprise to him, too.

Gilly's English professor, a brittle and timid older woman named Bertie Mangham, was also waiting for Dr. Heaton and John when they arrived home. The fragrance of chicken stew reached out to John from the moment he entered the foyer. Just being in a house again felt so…normal. Not that the cottages of the compound didn't have a homey feel to them, but there were times living with the Heatons in Oxford that John actually forgot that the bomb had ever dropped.

Tonight was one of those nights. John could see Gilly had gone to no little effort to create a special dinner for all of them. They ate off her mother's china and drank wine from crystal goblets. Dr. Lynch and Bertie knew each other and because they weren't in the same field, were friendly with each other. Dr. Heaton was a gracious host, giving each woman equal attention. The conversation was often academic but also very lively. Bertie, when she had a glass of wine in her, relaxed and was surprisingly witty. Even Dr. Lynch, usually so proper and stiff, seemed to loosen up as the evening went on.

Later, when they all retired to the salon and the fireplace to play Scrabble, Dr. Lynch shared the small settee with Dr. Heaton. John was sure he saw her smile at one point during the game. The laughter, the conversation and the warmth washed over him like a caressing wave. He envied Gilly's easy and constant access to these sharp minds—from birth, really. He tried to imagine what it would feel like to live in a town like Oxford, totally committed to the life of the mind and intellectual pursuits.

At one point in the evening, he glanced at Gilly and she was giving him an eyebrow-arching, smug look like: *See? These are your people.*

The hell of it was she was totally right.

Susan Kiernan-Lewis

10

Mike guessed it would take them three days of steady walking to get back to the Jeep. It was the middle of December, cold and wet. Sarah wasn't complaining, but he knew she was physically miserable. Hell, they both were.

Mentally was a whole other animal entirely.

No matter how many times he told her this wasn't the end, he could see she wasn't buying it. In her mind, John was a mere hundred kilometers to the east and a little thing like a country's militia and ice-cold north Atlantic waters weren't gong to keep her from her lad.

Except they were.

Thank God, those pikers O'Reilly and Sullivan hadn't taken Mike's few gold coins. They had enough to stock up on food—a cooked guinea fowl and two loaves of bread—to get them as far as Arklow. Mike had sprung for a bottle of brandy too. It was dear but it'd help keep them warm and maybe buy them a moment or two of forgetfulness. That was well worth the price.

At first, they kept near the coastline. It was colder to be sure but Mike knew Sarah took comfort seeing it, knowing her boy was just across the way. They walked beside the coastal road the first day, confident they wouldn't run into anyone. And they didn't. Toward the end of the first day, they grew tired, and the dregs of their mutual despair began to bubble up to the surface.

They found an abandoned house overlooking the water whose front steps opened onto a walkway leading up to the road. It was a dreary structure, with only one small window among three sides of bleak grey stone. Mike found it difficult to believe anyone had chosen to live here. But the Crisis had changed things for everyone and it might easily be inhabited—as forlorn and unwelcoming as it appeared to them.

He positioned Sarah on the road overlooking the house.

"Stay here until I get back, aye?" he said. He noticed she'd spent much of the day with her own thoughts and he wasn't sure that was a good thing.

She nodded but didn't answer. Nor did she look at the house with any curiosity. She just stood, waiting. He hated leaving her up here, exposed and without a weapon, but he hated worse the idea of ushering her into a house without checking it out first. He slid the fifty feet down the steep walkway to a gap in the broken stonewall encircling the house. The trees and bushes within the wall were overgrown and hedged the house in tightly.

When he got closer he could see it wasn't falling down. In fact the house looked as if its exterior had been recently repaired in spots. But there was a chimney and no trail of smoke coming from it. On a cold day like today—with the rain spitting every few minutes—there should have been a fire. He peeked over the wall to see if there was anything alive within—a goat or a dog—but there was no sign of life. When he got to the front steps, he glanced up at the road to see that Sarah was watching him. She might well be on the verge of total despondency but she wasn't totally oblivious—at least not where Mike was concerned. He waved to her and then turned to the house and rapped on the front door.

The sound of movement inside made him jump to the side of the door in case it swung open followed by a shotgun blast.

"Who is it?" a woman's voice called out. "Phelan? Is that you?"

"Sorry, Missus," Mike said. "It's just a traveler with his exhausted and pregnant wife hoping to find shelter for the night."

He wasn't out of the woods yet. A woman—especially a panicked, frightened one—was just as able to shoot a hole in him as a man was. Mike felt very vulnerable with only his boot knife sheath—and that empty.

The door creaked open and the long barrel of a rifle emerged.

"Show yourself," the woman said, her voice hard but shaky.

Mike put his hands up but before he revealed himself to the woman and her gun, he heard Sarah coming around the house.

"Mike? Did you find someone?"

Mike's feelings were at war with one another. On the one hand, Sarah's presence was likely to put the gun woman at her ease. On the other hand, he'd have felt better if she'd stayed on the road and out of range. The woman stepped out of the house and pointed the rifle at Mike's chest but her head turned to watch Sarah as she appeared in front of the house.

"Oh!" Sarah said, affecting to be out of breath from the jaunt down from the road, her eyes on the woman's gun. "We come in peace, I swear."

The woman immediately dropped the nose of the gun.

"You're American?" she asked, frowning.

"Canadian," Sarah said.

"I'm Kate Donovan."

"Sarah Donovan. And this is my husband, Mike."

"Donovan, you say? Are ye from Roscommon by any chance?"

Mike shook his head. "Closer to Tipperary."

"Well, then. There's a few of us then, aren't there? Come in. Me husband will be back soon. There's a fireplace in this dump but no firewood. D'ye have food by chance?"

"A roast chicken and some bread," Sarah said. She stepped into the dark house, whose small window provided little light through its dirty panes. "We're happy to share for a place to stay."

An hour later, Phelan Donovan showed up with an armful of wood and he and Mike soon had a fire going in the hearth. Sarah feared they would all be spending the night in the forecourt of the place when the chimney started smoking but it was just age and a few old birds nests and it soon righted itself. Mike and Sarah shared their food and the brandy. There was no furniture in the place but Sarah didn't care. She snuggled up next to Mike, feeling stronger after eating. The fire warmed her face as she fought to stay awake against the exertions of the long day.

"I was an IT specialist with Accenture," Phelan said, hugging his knees as he stared into the fire. He was middle-aged but in good shape, lean and hard. "Sometimes I can't believe the life we used to have." He looked at his wife, Katie who nodded in agreement.

"We lived in Dublin," she said. "I was taking some classes but basically we were just enjoying being childless in Dublin. We went clubbing every weekend. Life was so good. No offense, Sarah. Kids are great. Just not for me and Phelan. Especially now." She looked at her husband. "Can you imagine?"

Sarah felt her heart tighten. *Yeah, trust me, do not have kids so you can be worried sick about them twenty-four seven.*

"You're smart," she said to Katie.

"Sarah, darlin," Mike admonished. "You don't mean that."

Sarah turned to the couple. "We've both lost our sons and are on the road looking for them."

"Lost them? Blimey," Phelan said. "How?"

"How indeed," Sarah said miserably. "It doesn't matter."

"And now you're pregnant again?" Katie asked timidly, glancing at Sarah's stomach.

"It was an accident," Sarah said, almost bitterly. She didn't look at Mike. She knew her words were hurtful but she couldn't seem to help herself. *Another child to worry myself sick over. And look at these two! Happy as larks with just themselves to fret over.* Tears burned her eyes.

"It's been a long day," Mike said.

Sarah turned to lean into him, her sadness a living breathing thing that sat on her chest and sucked all the breath and the life out of her.

Just like the day that's coming, she thought. *And the one after that and the one after that.*

*****

As they prepared to part ways with Phelan and Katie the next morning Mike split the rest of their bread with them. It seemed that after four years of living in Dublin in their old apartment, a band of toughs had pushed them out and they'd fled the city. That was barely a month ago and the pair had lived hand to mouth ever since.

"You're welcome to travel with us," Mike said. "We have a Jeep hidden in the woods near Rosslare. We can drive you as far as Kilkenny. From there we need to split up but you can walk the rest of the way to Ameriland. There'll be a place there if you want." He grinned at Katie. "There's no nightclubbing but we do have electricity."

"Saints be praised," Katie said. "Electricity? Christmas came early."

They walked together the rest of that day. Mike was able to trap a rabbit which they cooked over a small fire on the beach at midday. They stopped early for the day when they found another vacant shelter to spent the night.

"Do people have jobs in your Ameriland?" Phelan asked after they'd had dinner in the small stone house. "Because I'm handy."

"We used to have electronics and video surveillance," Mike said. "But we had a bit of insanity recently and most of it got rubbished."

"Electronics?" Phelan looked at his wife and then back at Mike. "I bet I can fix it."

"Well, it would be worth a lot to us if you could. That's grand."

"What about me?" Katie said. "I was an executive secretary in my life before the Crisis."

"Not much paperwork at the compound," Sarah said with a sad smile. She wanted to involve herself in the conversation but the pain in her chest was like a hard knot that got in the way of eating and drinking and thinking and talking.

"But if you're good at organizing," Mike said, "there's lots of ways you can contribute."

"Failing that," Katie said, I have my two hands. "I can knit, I can milk goats, I can garden." She turned to Sarah. "And I can help with the babies."

"We weren't entirely honest with you earlier," Phelan said in a low voice as he took the brandy bottle from Mike and stared into the flames in the fireplace.

"Oh, aye?" Mike said in a tense voice.

"About being childless," Katie said hurriedly.

"So you do have children?" Sarah asked.

"No, we were dishonest about us being happy and childless," Katie said. "We were undergoing infertility treatments when the bomb went off. The truth is we were trying like mad to get pregnant." Her eyes went to the soft swelling under Sarah's jacket.

"Oh."

"No big deal," Katie said, tossing a small stick into the fire. "Just...I think I'd like to mind the kiddies if people need that."

"They do," Sarah said, with a sigh. "Kiddies always need minding."

The weather turned nasty in the night and Sarah heard the pounding of the rain against the hard slate roof—and the sounds of Katie getting sick over and over again. The smell of the vomit and Phelan's concerned murmuring combined with the terrible storm to ensure that nobody slept. Mike held Sarah as if by doing so he could somehow change whatever was happening to the couple on the far side of the abandoned cottage.

Once, he put his hand on her stomach and she patted his hand reassuringly.

"I'm fine. *We're* fine. Do you think she has the illness?"

He shook his head. "I don't know. I thought it hadn't come to Ireland. What's the whole point of shooting boats out of the water if it's here?"

"But she looked fine yesterday." She shivered and Mike rubbed his hands up and down her arms to warm them.

"I can start another fire," he said.

"Is it light enough to leave? I'd rather just get going."

Mike took an intake of breath as if he would speak but didn't.

"She's not going to be able to go, is she?" Sarah asked quietly.

"I doubt it."

"Make the fire."

Mike disentangled himself from Sarah and began to build up the wood in the cold hearth. At one point, he stopped and handed Phelan a water bottle for Katie and then went back and lighted the kindling. Sarah watched the fire catch and bring the room to life with a warm glow. An hour later, Mike spoke to Phelan and came back to Sarah. She saw he had the rifle in his hands.

"Where are you going?" She dreaded him telling her they wouldn't be leaving today. Even though it was hopeless and there was no way to go where John had gone, it still felt less monstrously awful to be moving. If there was an answer out there to finding John or Gavin, one thing Sarah knew was that it wasn't going to be found on the inside of an abandoned cottage twenty miles from Rosslare.

"I'm going out to bag a rabbit or two," he said. "We'll roast them and then leave them here. He says she's done this before and she'll be right as rain by nightfall. Or tomorrow latest."

"So we can go ahead and leave?" The relief was paramount. She knew it didn't matter and they should probably just stay put and wait but right now the only thing that was keeping her sane was movement. She was pretty sure Mike felt the same way too.

"As soon as I get back and dress the meat. They'll follow when they can. I've given him directions to Ameriland."

"Is she contagious?" Sarah said, sitting up and brushing off her hands.

"Phelan says no. And she's asleep for now so just sit tight 'til I get back." He gave her a quick kiss, then stood and said a few words to Phelan before slipping out the door. Sarah could see when he opened the door that it was still dark out. Phelan stepped outside too, probably to relieve himself.

She moved to the fire and held her hands out to feel the warmth. She tried to imagine that John was just a few miles from where she was sitting right his minute. In her mind, she imagined a kind woman was feeding him soup and being charmed by his cheerful affect and his southern manners. He really was the best of both her and David. Her heart pinched painfully at the thought of David and the memory of how quickly life could turn to terror.

The door suddenly flew open with a loud bang. Sarah gasped and turned on her knees to face it. Three men filed in. They looked to the fireplace where Sarah knelt and then to the pallet in the corner of the room where Katie lay. The man in front held a gun in front of him and pointed it at Sarah. Her heart pounded loudly in her ears, obliterating all sound in the room.

The two men behind the gunman turned as if startled by something and Sarah saw Phelan's white shocked face appear in the doorway. The sound of the gunshot reverberated wildly off the stone walls of the cottage. Phelan sank to his knees.

Susan Kiernan-Lewis

11

Katie's scream filled the house. Sarah lurched to her feet. She needed to get to Katie to make her stop. But out of the corner of her eye she saw the man's arm raise up. She tried to make her voice form words to tell Katie to be quiet. And then the explosion resounded off the rough stone walls.

Katie, finally quiet, lay on her back, the hole in her chest pumping the life out of her in a steady fountain. Sarah dragged her eyes away from the dying woman to look at the gunman. He was in his forties, balding, with a big paunch. He pointed his gun at Sarah. Her first thought was a prayer that they hadn't hurt Mike on their way here.

"Oy, don't shoot 'er, Pete. I'll be takin' a piece of that first."

The shooter lowered his arm. A much taller man pushed past him. His face was pocked and one eye looked as if it had been stitched closed. He shoved a handgun into his jacket pocket.

"Let's go," he growled as he grabbed Sarah by the arm and yanked her toward him. "I ain't pretty but you won't be looking at my face." He glanced around the room as if in search of a bed or a table.

"They got shite here," Pete said, walking over to Katie's body and toeing it with his boot in disgust.

"What did you expect?" Sarah's assailant said. "Check the berk in the doorway. He might at least have fags on 'im."

The world seemed to slow down. Everyone was moving in halftime. Sarah felt the man's hands on her arm gripping her flesh like steel pinchers but she didn't feel the pain of it like she should. It was almost like the video part of her brain was off track and the physical sensations weren't matching up with what was happening.

She didn't look at Katie or try to wonder if Phelan might still be alive. She only knew the moment she was in was being played out for her one frame at a time. The man ripped her jacket open and began to twist her shoulder around to push her onto the floor face first. She tucked her head at this movement and rammed it full force into his nose, feeling the cartilage crunch. A split second later she brought her knee up hard and slammed it into his testicles.

He whimpered and sagged against her. Over his shoulder she saw Pete watching them, his eyes wide.

"Feck me, ye fecking bitch!" Pete bellowed. "What have ye done to Jeff? I swear I'll make it hurt before I shoot ya!"

When Sarah heard the gunshot, for a moment she thought he'd made good his threat until she saw the third man—the outside watchman—fall backwards into the house. He was holding his stomach and blood gushed out of it. Pete turned and fired his gun blindly at the open door. Sarah heard another shot and saw Pete's head snap violently backwards. He dropped his gun and slowly crumpled to the floor.

"Mike!" she screamed. "There was only three!"

Please God, let it be Mike.

Mike stepped into the room, filling the door for a moment and blocking out all light. He looked at her ripped open jacket and then at Katie's body. He walked to Sarah and shoved two more cartridges into his rifle.

"I'm fine," Sarah said. But he took her arm in his free hand and led her past Jeff, moaning and writhing on the floor.

"You bitch, you bitch," Jeff said, rocking in agony.

"Wait for me outside," Mike said, giving her a gentle push toward the door.

"Mike—"

"Just do it, Sarah. Go on now."

Sarah hesitated and then ran from the house, stepping over the two bodies and Phelan who was face down just outside. Dawn was breaking and there was a soft glow over the sea. The early morning chill pierced through her jacket.

She heard one gunshot ring out from inside the stone house.

*****

Daniel Heaton sat at his desk in the Palace of Westminster. Sometimes it was all he could do to believe that he came to work here everyday. *Imagine, a Scotsman, an indifferent student and son of a butcher—sitting as a Member of Parliament.* Everyday he passed through the Peers Lobby and walked down the Central Hall to enter the House of Commons where the country's Members of Parliament met. Even as a lad, he'd never aspired to this.

His office, although not lavish, was decorated with taste and style. At times like these, sitting in his office and looking through the window at the city stretched out below, he felt glad he'd never married. The fact was, the opposite sex had never interested him but, truth be told, neither had the same sex. Daniel Heaton had been happy to accept early on that his was a singular nature. He was sure he was well enough liked on both sides of the aisle and he never had trouble finding someone to go for the odd pint now and again.

But still, the only person Daniel Heaton MSP had ever really been remotely close to was his brother Finlay. He was fond of Finlay's girl Gillian, of course. But he saw them rarely and was sure they didn't pine to come to London any more than he longed to visit the sticks. Still, it was pleasant having a relation you had positive feelings for— probably even love. Made you seem more human in conversations with others. Yes. All in all very useful.

The phone rang and Heaton frowned. The plague had eliminated all tourist and school children tours of parliament but it had unfortunately also decimated support staff in the House of Commons. While there was a central operator ensuring that the more rambunctious nutters didn't get through to an MP or in his case an MSP, it was still bloody tiring dealing with constituent contact when he'd been so comfortable with virtually none before.

"Hello?" he said cautiously into the receiver.

"How's the cure coming?" A strong Irish accent purred in Daniel's ear and he felt a flutter of nausea trickle through his gut. Liam O'Reilly. On paper, such a good idea. In the skin-crawling flesh, less so.

"These things take time," Daniel said knowing it wouldn't be enough to pacify the man.

"Indefinitely would be good."

"I do understand your position, Liam. You've been quite clear on the matter. I'm confident a cure is not immediately forthcoming. At least not from the UK. Which is the whole reason I assigned it to my brother."

"And if Europe finds one first?"

"The signs aren't pointing that way but if they do, I have people in position who might be able to intercept it before it gets to the World Health Organization."

"Jaysus, Heaton! Do you have to say this shite over the phone?"

Daniel sighed at the man's quick temper.

There was a reason nobody liked the sodding Irish.

"We're lucky to have mobile service at all," Daniel said. "Trust me, our national security is not in a position to monitor every phone call. Besides, aren't you using a burner phone?"

"I have a lot riding on this, Heaton. There must be no cure any time soon."

"Not to worry, Liam. My brother is a lovely man but he couldn't find a wildly-flatulent ox in a china shop. His reputation for incompetency is renowned in scientific circles. Even the berks here in London had heard enough of his lunatic theories to be astonished when I named him as lead on the project."

"Do you know how close he is to finding something?"

"My eyes and ears in Oxford tell me he's working on a new and improved bucket purification system." Daniel snorted. "Unbelievable. Even for Finlay."

"So he's not reporting to you himself?"

"A very secretive man, my brother. Even when his secrets are total rubbish."

"Yeah, well, make sure he doesn't accidentally stumble onto the cure."

"Trust me, my dear Liam, there's no fear of that."

*****

The days that followed the morning Mike and Sarah buried their new friends were filled with relentless, long marches. Mike hunted rabbits which they cooked and ate by day, leaving the evenings to hunger and hiding in the cold, wet woods. While they had a gun now what they had lost that terrible morning was one they found hard to forget. And they were still eighty miles from where they'd left the Jeep—if it was even still there.

Eighty miles was three days of walking in the cold and the rain with little to no food, with discouragement and heartbreak instead of hope that they might be reunited with the boys, and with fear and trepidation at just how quickly warmth and laughter can turn to horror.

Sarah couldn't stop thinking of poor Katie, how desperately she'd wanted a baby of her own and how much hope she seemed to hold out that she could have that some day—at the compound with Mike and Sarah. To watch both of them come alive with hope for the future reminded Sarah of how she used to feel when the future was something to hope for.

And then to watch it die like so much else had died. So many others.

But worse than the realization that death and evil were right around every corner and under every rock was the stark slap-in-the-face realization that the idea of finding their boys alive in this wicked new world would truly be a miracle. And one thing Sarah knew like she knew every callous on her hand and every blister on her feet—miracles weren't being granted any more.

The final day before reaching Rosslare they walked the last thirty miles straight down the highway, abandoning the protection of the woods. Sarah's legs ached badly but she pushed past the pain. Her world was broken down into little bites now. *Just make it to the next rise and then you can have a sip of water. Just make it to the Jeep and then you rest.* The idea of the Jeep had grown to enormous proportions for Sarah. She knew John wouldn't be waiting for her there but she couldn't help but think all would be well, the pain would subside...and she'd feel the baby inside her again.

Ever since they'd left Dublin the first time, she'd felt the little tickling bubbles inside her that she knew was the baby moving around. She'd hesitated to tell Mike because even if he'd put a hand on her belly, he wouldn't have been able to feel it. It was something only between Sarah and the baby. And as she remembered with her first pregnancy with John, it was a special time that would only last a very brief time.

But she'd felt nothing since the moment her would-be rapist had laid his hands on her. And while she knew she'd experienced more physical pain from attacks in the past, for some reason when that creature touched her she felt the blood in her veins freeze. Had he been so evil that he had the power to extinguish the life in her belly just by his touch? Or had she been so horrified by what she'd seen—the senseless murders of the young couple—that something had seized up inside her, taking the baby with it?

"Won't be long now, love," Mike said as he walked beside her. His long stride made it impossible to keep up with him but he slowed his pace for her. If he felt even a tenth of the anxiety and impatience that she did, she could only imagine what that must have cost him. He'd said very little since the horror in the little house above the beach. They'd worked silently to bury the Donovans then simply turned without a word and made their way south.

Now they were nearly there.

"Do you remember exactly where?" Sarah asked. She didn't think she could bear another night of sleeping in the woods.

"Never fear."

She didn't want to tell him she could feel the warmth between her legs that told her she was bleeding.

If only they could get to the Jeep, everything would be all right...

They walked another hour, unmindful of the concern that they hadn't stopped to find and cook a rabbit. There was food in the Jeep. They walked as the light began to fade from the sky as the late winter afternoon descended upon them. It didn't matter. They were nearly there and that was all that mattered.

Mike saw it first. He sped up as he turned into the woods and slid down a small incline. She could see past him and glimpsed the metal of the vehicle glittering out from under the bough of tree branches he'd covered it with. Before she got thirty feet from it she knew there should have been more branches, more leaves...

She approached the Jeep after Mike and touched the back fender. All four tires had been slashed. The cloth roof looked like someone had taken an axe to it. The seats were gone entirely and so was everything they'd left in the back.

"I hid our guns in the woods," Mike said grimly, looking at the ruined vehicle.

Sarah looked at him in shock.

"Why? Why would someone do this? What possible reason would someone want to do this?"

It made no sense. Steal the seats, fine. But slash the tires and destroy the roof?

"People," Mike said with disgust.

Sarah's legs gave out beneath her and she sagged to the ground, not caring that the sharp stubby stumps of damaged trees cut into her thighs.

"Sarah?" Mike was by her side, a steadying hand on her arm as if to pull her upright again.

"I needed it to be here," she said, sobbing. "I needed to drive away from this nightmare! This fucking, monstrous excuse for a life!"

Mike knelt beside her and wrapped his arms around her. At first she struggled, so angry with the world and God and Mike that she wanted to hit him or scream until her vocal cords were raw.

Her sobs came pouring out of her. Mike tightened his hold on her and she let the tears and the sobs wrack her, not caring, never caring again. When she was finally quiet, she simply lay limp in his arms until the cold from the oncoming evening slipped between her and the ground and gently, insistently urged her to move.

"I'm okay," she whispered unconvincingly to Mike. "I'm sorry."

"Don't be sorry, darlin'," he said softly. "Never be sorry to me. I love ye so much, Sarah. It breaks my heart. But we can do this. You know we can."

Don't tell me to be strong for the baby. Don't make me tell you that the baby is gone. I can't bear any more today.

There was no sense camping near the Jeep. It offered no protection against the elements and it served to remind both of them of the evil that dogged their steps. Mike left Sarah leaning against the front fender to see if the hidden guns had been found. Sarah watched him go and listened as the woods became quiet once he'd left. It was as if the woods had swallowed him up and now she was alone. All alone with no food, no water, no hope. She stared into the dark gloom where Mike had gone and allowed herself to think for a moment of what she might do if he never came back.

The minutes stretched into an hour. Something was wrong. He hadn't hidden the guns that far away. She looked around the Jeep. He'd left the rifle with her and she went to it now and picked it up, and checked that there was a cartridge in it.

She moved away from the Jeep into the woods in the direction Mike had gone.

Susan Kiernan-Lewis

12

Gavin leaned over the back of the wagon and pulled out the frying pan. The Italians had five wagons and ten horses. As a wedding gift to the happy couple, Antonio had given Gavin and Sophia their own wagon and one horse. That was a big deal. The wagons and horses were the only thing that allowed the big family to move about at will. Antonio said they represented their freedom and Gavin could see that. What he didn't understand was why Antonio was so keen on keeping on the move.

Whenever Gavin suggested he'd like to bring Sophia to the compound to meet his family, Antonio was all in favor of it. But there never seemed to be a good time.

"Did you find it, Gav?" Sophia called to him.

Five days married and she still hadn't realized what a terrible mistake she'd made, Gavin thought to himself, grinning.

"I'm coming," he said as he moved toward their campfire in front of their tent. He had to admit he liked camping out. Always had as a kid or with John. A shadow of melancholy passed across his brow as he thought of John—which in turn led to him to think about this da. He hated that he hadn't gotten word to them yet. Worse, he'd actually left John a note when he'd gotten to Cashel and had a wild hair about going across to Fishguard to see his grandda. He'd run into Antonio not an hour later and then once he'd clapped eyes on his future bride, well, the idea of running back to fetch a note that John probably would never find anyway seemed a little crazy.

But he did need to get back to the compound to let everyone know he was all right—and to tell them what a bleeding lying wanker Father Ryan was. Hopefully, the bastard hadn't pulled anything else in the meantime.

He tried to imagine how furious his family would be when he came back to the compound. *On the other hand, da will have to pull his punches when I waltz back there with my beautiful Sophia.*

He handed the pan to her as she stood by the campfire, her hands on her hips. She wore jeans instead of dresses as some of the other women in the camp did and he loved that about her. As gorgeous as she was—especially on their wedding day—she seemed more comfortable in pants. And as Gavin was particularly fond of how she looked in pants, it all worked out. He leaned over and kissed her neck which made her squirm away from him.

"I was just trying to imagine what my da will say when I bring this home." He patted her bottom and she turned and raised up the frying pan over her head, laughing as she did.

"He'll think what everyone else thinks round here," she said, letting him draw her into his arms for a kiss. "That you've lost your damn mind."

"Then let me be crazy," he murmured as he kissed her. "Let me die crazy in that case." She deepened the kiss. The sound of a harsh throat clearing made him lift his head and he felt Sophia stiffen in his arms.

"Not to interrupt anything," Benito said as he came from the bushes. Gavin wondered how long he'd been standing there. "Papa says to pack up. We're moving."

"Again?" Gavin said in astonishment. "We just got here day before yesterday."

While he wasn't familiar with these woods, and they hadn't gone near a town since he'd travelled with the Borgnino's —nearly a month now—he couldn't shake the feeling that he wasn't far from the compound—maybe a day's walk. The idea of moving again, possibly *away* from the compound, made Gavin realize fully for the first time that he was ready to go home.

"I guess marriage suits you," Benito said to his sister. Sophia scowled at him. Gavin knew the two didn't get along. He considered that a character reference in Sophia's favor. Benito was hard to like. He was fat and unctuous and he was forever sneaking up on the two of them as if trying to catch them in the act. "Guess he's better'n me?"

"Screw you, Benito," Sophia said, her voice low.

Gavin didn't know what made him do what he did next. He'd certainly heard lads say worse in his life and all of it in fun. But the words were barely out of Sophia's mouth before he took two steps and buried his fist in Benito's stomach. Maybe it was the way she said it, in a tone of deep-seated loathing but a feeling overtook Gavin as powerful as any he'd ever felt.

Revulsion. Fury. Protection.

As Benito hunched over on the ground, vomiting and holding his stomach, Gavin stood over him, his fists still clenched.

"If you ever talk to my wife like that again," Gavin said, panting, his face flushed with fury, "I'll make you eat your foot."

"Papa will kill you for this," Benito wheezed, looking up at Gavin.

Sophia spat at her brother. "Papa prefers my husband to you and you know it."

Gavin pulled Sophia back from Benito as her brother fought to get to his feet and scramble away. After Benito staggered away, Gavin pulled her into his arms and felt her tremble.

Was there truth to what Benito said? Had he known Sophia in that way? Gavin's stomach turned and he rubbed Sophia's back as if to erase the image. She pulled back and held him with both hands to force him to look her in the face.

"He lies, *amore mio*. He is just a rodent trying to poison our happiness."

He nodded and drew her in close.

"It's time for us to find our own home," he whispered into her hair. "It's time to go."

That evening, the whole tribe gathered around the center cookfire. There were twenty-five people in all—uncles, aunts, cousins, and siblings. Antonio was the eldest and the unmistakable patriarch. As Gavin and Sophia settled into their places by the fire, Gavin noticed Benito sat with some cousins the furthest distance from the group. Sophia was right. Although Antonio's only son, Benito was a clear disappointment to his father. At first Gavin hadn't noticed it because he'd been too focused on Sophia. But now that he held his beloved every night in the privacy of their own snug bed in their own tent, he began to relax and look around him at his new world. The things that he'd been so grateful before—a hot meal, a coat—he now expected as his right as a part of the family.

In fact, now that Gavin thought of it, almost since he'd arrived he'd been treated as nothing less than the heir apparent. Whatever role Antonio had been attempting to groom Benito for had been passed to Gavin. Antonio stood in the center of the camp and lifted his hands to his family.

"Everybody have enough to eat?" he asked, as he always did before starting a family meeting.

"Si, Papa! Si, Antonio!" the gathering chorused back to him good-naturedly.

Antonio was a good leader. He always made sure they camped someplace near natural water or in a forest where they were protected and could trap or hunt something to eat. Nobody ever went to bed hungry and nobody ever found a reason to question Antonio on any of his decisions. He worked for the good of all. Gavin saw many similarities between Antonio and his own father. Both Antonio Borgnino and Mike Donovan were natural born leaders. Both bristled when their word was questioned or when their orders weren't followed immediately and without question.

The difference between the two that Gavin could immediately see was Antonio's natural sense of pleasure in life that he didn't see in his father. *Da was always busy putting fires out or ripping someone's head off for fecking up.* When he drank, he glowered and went to bed early. Whereas Antonio was gregarious and talkative. When Antonio drank he sang and he danced. If there were grumblings in the family about Antonio's style of leadership Gavin didn't see it.

Gavin grinned while remembering how many times the compound considered voting out his father out of power.

Practically on a weekly basis.

"Happy?" Sophia said to him. She sat so close her hip was nearly in his lap. Her hands were entwined over his knees. As cold as it was, she wore her blouses low to show as much cleavage as possible. Even shivering wouldn't deter her. Gavin ran a hand down her back and cupped her bottom.

"So happy," he said.

"Tomorrow we go toward the coast again," Antonio said. "The game is scarce and we go where the fish never let us down."

"Which coast, Antonio?"

"I'll tell you tomorrow!" he said, laughing. The crowd laughed with him.

"Are we really not going with them?" Sophia asked in a soft voice.

"Would you mind?"

"Well, they are my family," she said, biting her lip.

"How about just for a visit then? We'll go to the compound and you can meet my lot...they have hot baths there, you know. And electricity."

"I know. You told me. It sounds wonderful."

"They are going to love you, Sophia."

"I hope so."

The two of them stayed just long enough to joke around with some of Sophia's cousins. Sophia's mother Bianca must have been beautiful once. She was taller than Sophia and more feminine but also much quieter. Gavin thought she and the vivacious Antonio were an odd pairing but maybe they balanced each other out. He rarely saw them connect in any way although they shared the same tent. He vowed to himself that he and Sophia would never act like they didn't belong to each other.

"Ready for bed?" he asked her.

"For hours now," she said teasingly as she slipped an arm around Gavin's waist. They walked away from the heat of the main fire and back to their tent. They'd let their own fire go out.

"Don't bother with it," Sophia said when he stopped to kick at the embers. "I'll keep you warm, *amore mio*."

He turned and scooped her up in his arms. She squealed with delight as he carried her into the tent. The smell hit them both immediately. For a moment, Gavin stood, holding Sophia, stunned and unsure what to do. When she started gagging, he swiveled around and stepped back out into the cold evening.

If he'd thought for a moment that that little turd Benito had taken his licking like a man, he was way wrong. The pile of animal feces heaped on their marriage bed told a very different story.

*****

Gavin waited for the next morning only because Sophia begged him to. To confront Benito now, in the middle of the family gathering, would only make it worse, she said.

"And not just for him, *amore mio*. It would be giving the little *verme* exactly what he wants, to have disrupted our love."

So they cleaned up the mess, tossed the bedclothes in the bushes to be dealt with later, and snuggled down into each other's arms in a pile of all the coats and clean blankets they owned. After an exquisitely exhausting night spent in Sophia's arms, Gavin had to admit that leaving the unsavory business of dealing with Benito until morning had been the right thing to do.

But the next morning, he took the soiled bedclothes and found Benito eating his breakfast in front of the cookfire. He was sitting by his father who was talking seriously to an older cousin. Gavin knew the cousin, a tall man with a lazy eye named Paco who had two teenaged daughters who caused him no end of pain and trouble. Clearly, Paco was going for guidance to the head of the clan.

Gavin stomped over to Benito and dumped the sleeping bags and duvets on the man's head. Benito fought his way out of them and, in the process, dropped his piece of rabbit pie in the dirt.

"Hey! *Bastardo!*" Benito yelped.

Antonio whirled around to watch the two, his face a growing thundercloud.

"What is the meaning of this?" he said, between clenched teeth. It occurred to Gavin that he'd just been in the process of telling his poor unfortunate cousin how to handle his family when his own family imploded on his doorstep.

"Benito left Sophia and me a pile of raccoon shit on our bed last night," Gavin said heatedly.

"He lies!"

"If not you, then who? After I punched you in the stomach yesterday—"

"*Che cosa?*" Antonio said, looking from Gavin to Benito. "He hit you? Why?"

"A misunderstanding!" Benito said.

Antonio backhanded his son so hard the boy fell down. He sat in the dirt holding his cheek and glaring up at his father.

"You will clean Gavin and Sophia's bed clothing and I will inspect it to ensure it is done properly. You will apologize to both of them tonight at the campfire. *Capito?*"

"Yeah, sure," Benito muttered, not looking at either of them

"Now!" Antonio roared. Benito grabbed the soiled bedding and fled the campfire.

Gavin really wished Antonio hadn't done that. Not that he was ever going to be friends with Benito but now it was looking pretty much impossible. The cousin Paco had stayed just long enough to see the show and then disappeared into the woods. Everyone was dismantling and breaking down camp for the trek to the coast. Gavin figured this was as good a time as any to tell Antonio that they wouldn't be coming with them.

"I am sorry for that," Antonio said, waving in the direction that Benito had gone. "He is a serious...*delusione*... disappointment to me. His mother's child."

"Look, Antonio. I can't tell you how much it means to me that you took me in. I mean, if it wasn't for you, I'd probably still be wandering shirtless through the fecking woods."

Antonio slapped Gavin on the shoulder and laughed. "Not to mention enjoying the warmth between my *bellezza* daughter's thighs, eh? Have you thanked me for that yet?"

Gavin was momentarily speechless. He didn't know if Antonio was joking or if what he said was a cultural thing that didn't translate in Ireland.

"In any case," Gavin said, "we've decided not to go with the rest of you to the coast. Mind you, we may catch up with you later."

The smile on Antonio's face looked frozen, as if someone had taken a still shot of him. His eyes lost all merriment.

"Oh, you've decided, have you?"

"Aye. I've a mind to see me own family so they can meet me bride."

"Are we not family to you?"

"You are, sure, Antonio. But I have a father and I guess I haven't been acting like he means much to me but you know, he's me da and...and I miss him."

"I see. You a-miss him," Antonio said, mocking Gavin's words. "Before, you are not acting anything like this. It is like you have no family."

"Well, I'm sorry if I gave you that impression but I do and I hope you understand. Sophia and I will be going to the compound today."

"No problemo, Gavin," Antonia said, his eyes glinting like malevolent slits from a suit of armor. "You will of course send my daughter to me to say goodbye, yes?"

"Sure. And again, thank you for all you've done for me."

"Not at all, Gavin. Not at all."

Gavin headed back to the tent with a plate of breakfast for Sophia but she was nowhere to be seen. That wasn't unusual. She often hung out with her cousins, gossiping and braiding each other's hair. It *was* strange though today of all days, Gavin thought. A travel day was a whole lot of packing and work. Perhaps Sophia wanted to spend time with her family before they split up. Satisfied that this was the reason for her absence, Gavin collapsed the tent and rolled their bedding and clothing to fit in the back of the wagon.

The excitement he felt at the prospect of seeing his father and everyone again at the compound was mixed with the anxiety caused by the fact that it was midday and he still hadn't seen Sophia. The other wagons had begun to line up. He noticed they were pointing west. It looked like Antonio had decided which coast to set out for. Gavin frowned. He wouldn't have recommended going west this late in the year but something about his conversation with Antonio this morning made him think his opinion might not be welcome.

He waved to several people riding by in wagons until he finally saw Sophia running up to where their own wagon was parked.

"Hey, where've you been all day?" he called to her. "Saying goodbye to folks?"

Her face was as serious as he'd ever seen her. Even the usual olive glow of her skin had a white pallor as if she'd walked across a grave.

"Sophia? Are you all right, luv?"

She climbed into the wagon and sat with her hands on her lap in the front seat. She looked at him. "I've decided I don't want to be a part from my family," she said.

"Are you serious?" Gavin climbed up on the wagon. From this height he could see the line of wagons moving out of the woods. Their wagon was last in line. Leaving this late meant they'd be traveling at night.

Sophia did not look at him. "I'm young and not used to being away from my mama," she said. Those words didn't sound like the Sophia he knew. They sounded like words in a script she'd memorized and was spouting back. Badly. Words her father had written.

"Did you see your father?"

"I did." She held her chin up looking like she was ready to defend her decision and her father too if it came to that.

"And he talked you out of leaving with me?"

"No," she said, pulling her shawl around her. "I just don't want to leave my family." She turned to him and said fiercely, "*You* go if you're so determined!"

Gavin picked up the reins. He urged the horse forward with a flick across its hind quarters.

"We're married now," he said. "We're not going separate ways. We'll stay with your family if that's what you want."

She sighed and placed her hand on his thigh. But she still stared straight ahead. They rode silently for several hours, with just the sounds of Antonio up ahead calling encouragement or shouting orders. When it got dark, Sophia unpacked a small package of cold chicken and they ate without stopping, their horse following the one in front who followed the one in front of it.

What madness was it to travel in the dark? To what purpose? Were they in a hurry? Was someone following them?

After they'd eaten, Sophia dug out one of the heavy blankets from the back of the wagon and they huddled under it to stay warm. By the time Antonio finally led the caravan off the road, Sophia had fallen asleep on Gavin's shoulder. She awoke as the wagon pitched and rolled over the uneven ground.

Gavin didn't recognize the area but it was so dark he likely wouldn't have even if they'd been right outside the compound. It was a cold night but dry. Antonio sent word back to them that they were to sleep in their wagon tonight and not to build a fire. Gavin unharnessed the horse and hobbled him, letting him graze nearby while Sophia prepared a soft spot for the two of them to life down in the back of the wagon. Gavin wasn't finished questioning Sophia about why she changed her mind about leaving with him but they were both too tired to face it tonight.

*****

An hour after they stopped, Gavin and Sophia held each other under the blankets in the back of their wagon. Gavin was sure he was so tired that he'd fall straight to sleep without the worry of needless thoughts and questions dragging him back to consciousness. His da used to always say there was nothing like an honest day's work to have a man sleep soundly each night no matter what else might be worrying him. He missed his father, missed even his bitching and moaning.

He held Sophia to his chest and was surprised but not shocked when she reached for him under the covers. They coupled noisily in a burst of energetic youth and need. They both knew there was something she wasn't telling him. A fool could see that. But the honesty of her body, and her love for him was the gift she gave in the midst of the lie. In a way it felt like her way of asking him to trust her. At least for now. He kissed her face as she succumbed to slumber and he wondered how he'd so quickly learned to read her so well.

He must have dropped off himself because the next thing he knew, the spot beside him where Sophia should have been was cold and vacate. He sat up and saw her looking over the side of the wagon.

"Sophia?" he whispered. She turned to look at him, her face ravaged with sadness. In the quiet space where her reply to him should have been, he heard crying. He stood up to see where the sound was coming from.

"Gavin, no!" Sophia cried hoarsely, pulling him back to a seated position.

The sobbing was coming from the wagon in front of them. Gavin knew it belonged to Sophia's Aunt Bella.

He turned to Sophia in bewilderment. "What is—"

"Please, Gavin, don't. It's over. He'll leave her alone now."

He looked at the dark hulk of the wagon in front of them.

Bianca?

"I'm begging you. If you love me, leave it alone. You will only make it worse."

Gavin turned and listened, his heart pounding in double time, to the quietly fading sobs of Sophia's mother.

13

Walking in the woods holding a loaded rifle at night wasn't the smartest thing Sarah had ever done. But it was either that or go back to the Jeep and wait and she was *done* waiting. Why the hell hadn't Mike come back? It occurred to her that he might have spotted a hare and decided to bag dinner. But in the dark? Was that likely? It was possible he'd think a roast rabbit tonight would make up for whatever worry his not returning right away might cause her. She shouldered the rifle grimly. He was a man after all.

She walked a quarter of a mile in the general direction that Mike had gone when she saw a firelight flickering through the branches and bushes in the distance. A campfire or at least some kind of settlement. When she stopped walking she heard voices. Sarah frowned. There was no way Mike hadn't heard or seen this.

Did that mean he was there? Was he being held captive? She checked her rifle again. He'd been unarmed before he could reach the cache of hidden guns. If he was intercepted before he could get to it…

Suddenly the branches parted in front of her and someone jumped in front of her and screamed. Startled, Sarah screamed too and swung the rifle down but he was too close to get a bead on…and too short. She stumbled backwards, clutching the gun to her chest, her mouth open in astonishment.

"I found 'er! I found 'er!" the child screeched, jumping up and down. "Da! She's right here! Da! Hurry!" The child reached up and tugged at Sarah's jacket.

It was a little girl with golden curls that bounced maniacally as the child jumped. In the dark, she looked like an angel from a fairy story—or even one of the little people come to life.

"Sarah? Is that you?"

Mike!

"I'm bringin' 'er, Da! Don't worry!" the child said, turning and leading Sarah toward the flickering light that now blossomed into a full campsite. As Sarah approached, she tried to shake loose of the child's grip. As she stepped into a clearing she could see people centered with a small cookfire.

"Sarah, over here!" Mike called. He sat in one of the salvaged Jeep seats, his bare foot in the lap of a young woman who was carefully wrapping it in a bandage. A tall man with wispy reddish blond hair hurried over to where Sarah and the child had stopped.

"Mrs. Donovan!" the man said, "I was just sending someone out for you. Come sit by the fire. Himself has had a tumble as you'll see."

"He stepped into one of Da's traps!" the little girl said, still holding Sarah's hand.

"Elise, petal," said the woman bandaging Mike's foot. "Let Mrs. Donovan sit, if you please."

Sarah looked at the man and then back at Mike who had a remarkably sultan like pose going on and didn't seem inclined in the least to be moving his foot away from the woman or her lap.

"You did what?" Sarah asked as she approached Mike. "I was worried sick about you!"

"Ah, that's our fault," the man said. "We should've sent the little uns for you sooner."

"I told you, Da!" Elise said indignantly.

"I stepped into a rabbit trap," Mike said, patting the vacant Jeep seat next to him. "Just about took me foot off at the ankle."

"Seriously?" Sarah hurried to him and dropped to her knees to look at his foot but it was bandaged tightly. Without antibiotics even a small cut was dangerous these days. "Did you wash it first?"

"Aye," the young woman said, patting the bandage and then leaning across Mike's foot to shake Sarah's hand. "I'm Molly Connor."

Sarah sank into the chair next to Mike and shook her hand. "Sarah Donovan," she said with a sigh. The exhaustion of the day and the anxiety of her ten-minute walk in the woods was culminating in a ferocious headache.

"Sure, we've heard nothing but Mrs. Sarah Donovan for weeks now, haven't we?" Molly said.

"It's Darby Connor," Mike said, reaching out to take Sarah's hand. "Cor, darlin', your hand's like ice."

The man who initially greeted her came and draped a blanket across Sarah's knees. She could see at least a dozen people in the background in tents and there were two other smaller cookfires scattered among them. Ponies stood quietly next to their carts and munched oats in bags hung from hooks on trees.

"You don't remember me, Missus?" Darby said. "I came to your compound last month looking for medicine for me family."

She did remember. There was so much going on at the time that it was all just a blur. He'd come saying there was sickness in his village and that two girls had gone missing on Midsummer's Eve there last summer.

"Of course, Mr. Connor," she said wearily. "Imagine bumping into you here."

"Well, we're traveling these days," he said easily, placing a hand on the young woman's knee. "Living off the land well enough. Staying healthy, too."

"Have you run into more sickness?" Sarah asked. She eyed Mike's foot wondering how bad it was and if it would prevent them from traveling. He didn't look like he would be hoofing it down the road any time soon.

"Pockets," Darby said. "Here and there."

"The government says it's not come to Ireland yet," Sarah said.

"They're wrong," Molly said.

"Or they're lying," Darby said. "Enough of that. Now that we're all together, you'll stay with us, I hope for as long as you need to or want to."

"That is very kind of you, Mr. Connor."

"Call me Darby, please. And giving me raisins, chocolates, energy bars and enough antibiotics to last me family a full winter, *that* was kindness beyond any I'd any hope to expect."

The little girl crept back to Sarah and slipped her hand into Sarah's.

"What do you say, Elise?" her mother said.

113

"Thank you," Elise said smiling at Sarah. "Da said you was our angel."

Sarah leaned down to the girl and whispered in her ear, holding back tears as she spoke. "And now you're mine."

The pony cart was piled high with duvets and blankets by the time Mike and Sarah climbed into it for the night. They were fed, warmed and cared for by the Connors and their tribe— a merry group of friends and family who had once been officemates and neighbors and were now a small traveling village unto themselves.

"I'm so sorry I didn't crawl right back to you, darlin'" Mike said, slurring his words a tad from the copious wine and brandy they'd all drunk after dinner in front of the fire.

"How bad is it, do you think?" Sarah whispered.

"It'll be a day or two before I can walk decent."

Sarah wasn't disappointed to hear they wouldn't be immediately on their way again. Sometime during the evening as she held Elise in her lap and listened to Molly talking about how to braise the rabbit so that all the parts cook without overcooking any one part, Sarah realized she missed the fellowship and warmth of a community. She missed Fiona. She missed Siobhan, too, and her heart squeezed painfully to think of her.

But the care and affection so willingly given to both her and Mike by the Connors—all on account of a spontaneous act of generosity on Sarah's part—had filled up the cistern in her heart and helped her to feel human again. And while it didn't eliminate the memories of poor Phelan and Katie and the suddenness with which they were taken, it did help to soothe and ameliorate the pain by supplanting it with love and care.

As Sarah looked at her husband's face as he slept, she realized that if part of her despondency had its roots in her urge to give up, then the Connors' kindness had strengthened and galvanized her spirit. As she'd looked around the campfire earlier and watched their faces, she realized it wasn't a picture of people untouched by horror or evil she was seeing, it was a picture of people banded together in spite of it, and bonded by their conviction that evil would not win.

The gentle snores coming from Mike made Sarah smile. She was glad his foot wasn't bothering him. She also knew that Gavin had been missing longer than John and unlike with John, they'd had no clue as to what had become of Gavin. And yet

Mike had been resolute and strong, unfailing in his good humor to go forward and support Sarah when she flagged.

No, we won't give up and we will find them. Sarah leaned back into the cushions of the pony cart and saw the stars overhead in the winter sky, bright as diamonds. *And we won't go home or stop until we do. Desperate and foolish it may be,* she thought as she closed her eyes. *It still beats the alternative.* And as she drifted off to sleep she felt the gentle flutter of a thousand butterflies tickling her on the inside.

*****

The morning after Gavin listened to his mother-in-law sob herself to sleep, he fed the horse and tacked him back up in harness. Sophia spoke little. Bianca didn't appear the next morning and by the time they were ready to leave, only Sophia's Aunt Bella sat in the driver's seat of the wagon in front of them.

Gavin turned to Sophia as she sat mute and still by his side.

"You want to explain what happened last night?" He felt Sophia flinch at his words and he stared at her with bewilderment. Did she think he was capable of hitting her?

"Sophia. Look at me."

She turned to him, her eyes fearful.

"It could've been any reason," she said quietly. "But most likely it was because of what Benito did. To us."

Gavin reined the horse to a stop and put a hand on Sophia's shoulder. She shrank from him.

"I'm not asking what possible reason your father could've had for whatever he did to your mother last night, Sophia. Ye ken there is *no* good reason, don't you?"

She looked at him in confusion. "I'm pretty sure it was on account of Benito."

There was obviously no getting through to her. Gavin turned his attention back to the horse and urged him forward. "So he's done this before."

"Papa gets angry sometimes."

"We're leaving, Sophia," he said firmly, his eyes on the road ahead of him. "We can't stay here."

She put a hand on his arm. Her eyes pleaded with him.

"Please, *amore mio*," she said. "For my sake, please no."

"It's mostly for your sake that we have to," he blurted in frustration. "Or Jaysus, any kiddies we have. The man's a lunatic. You know that, right?"

"He's my father, Gavin." She dropped her hand from his arm. Gavin couldn't help but wonder when the light had gone from her eyes. Was this the real Sophia?

"Is this how you want to live? Listening to your mother get wailed on anytime his lordship is mispleased? Did he beat you, too?"

Sophia didn't answer.

"Sophia?"

"Did not your own father whip you when you misbehaved as a child?"

Gavin rubbed his hand across his face. "He walloped me, sure. From time to time. Is that what we're talking about?"

She looked away. "He wouldn't do it now that I'm married."

The thought came to him like an adder's strike—was that the reason she married him?

"We need to leave, Sophia. I don't want to kill your father—or your fat little slob of a brother either for that matter. Even without formal laws in Ireland, it wouldn't set well with me."

But could he leave knowing Antonio was beating Bianca? Could he escape over the horizon with Sophia knowing that poor woman was taking the blows whenever her bastard husband had a mind to do it? Antonio was likely to beat the woman to death if they left. Sophia put her hand back on his arm as if reading his mind.

"Even if he never caught us—and he would because he's heard you talk of your compound enough—he would punish my mother for our crime. I couldn't bear that."

"She'll just have to come with us. There's plenty of room for her at the compound."

"She would never agree to leave him."

Jaysus! Was there no answer to this monstrous riddle? Was the bastard going to keep everyone in line because he knew love was their weakest link and could always be used again them? Gavin gritted his teeth and drove the horse in silence. Finally, he dropped a hand to Sophia's knee.

"I don't know the answer, luv," he said. "Not yet. But I do know that staying isn't an option for us."

"Even if our leaving gets my mother killed?"

"It won't be our leaving that does it," he said, narrowing his eyes at her. "Ye ken that, right? If your father hurts Bianca for whatever reason, the blame is his own."

"I don't think I'll feel like the blame is his own when it was my leaving that made him do it."

They travelled the morning in silence. It was crowding in on late December and they were already seeing patches of snow that didn't burn off by noon. If he had to guess, Gavin figured they were just east of County Clare. It was easily another two or three days travel before they reached the coast. The caravan of wagons stopped on the road at midday and Gavin stood up to see if he could see why. A child riding a pony cantered down the side of parked wagons until he reached Gavin and Sophia. The boy was about eleven and although John was three years older than that now, the boy reminded Gavin of John when he was younger.

"Lunch!" the boy yelled. He tossed a package to Gavin. "Zio Antonio says we'll make camp tonight." Then he turned and trotted to the wagon in front of them and repeated the process. Gavin handed the package to Sophia. Inside was cold cooked sausages and roasted peppers wrapped in congealed fat. Sophia dug out a dishtowel from the back and spread it across her knees. She lay the opened package on it and they ate in silence. When they were finished, she put away the wrappings, turned to Gavin, and put her hand on his arm.

"I married you because I love you, *amore mio*. From the moment I see you, I know this."

Gavin relaxed. It didn't fix everything. But it fixed a lot.

"And whatever you decide to do…for us…" She nodded resolutely. "I say, *si*. It is what we will do."

"Even leaving."

"*Si*." Her eyes were on his face and they glistened with tears, but also with determination. "Even leaving."

That night, Antonio had the wagons park in a semicircle like wagons in the old west, Gavin couldn't help but think. The wind blew stronger the closer they got to the sea and the wagons served as an effective windbreak. No one bothered putting up tents, though. It was still an interim camp, even with a couple of campfires to warm everyone up. Like everyone else, Gavin and Sophia would be sleeping in the back of their wagon again.

Normally, Antonio took Gavin with him when they went looking for small game for the evening meal. But tonight, there were three rabbits roasting on the spit and Antonio never approached Gavin. That was just as well. Gavin wasn't sure how he would face the man after what happened the night before. He and Sophia took their places by the fire waiting for plates of meat to be passed down to them. Gavin took his boots off and perched them near the fire to dry. They'd been wet so long now that he feared foot rot. His feet were cold and his sox damp, so he straightened his legs to toast the bottoms.

From where they sat, Gavin could see Bianca as she carved meat and spoke to some of the children, but her face was turned away. Suddenly, Antonio clapped his hands and demanded silence. For the first time since Gavin had been traveling with the family, Antonio did not ask if everyone had enough to eat. When he didn't, Gavin felt the tension in the air as everyone else must have noticed the omission too.

"I know we are all tired from our travels today," Antonio said to the group. "But there is family business to attend to and it must be done."

Gavin glanced at Sophia but her face was unreadable.

"My son, Benito, has shamed me to my new son-in-law and my daughter. Where are you, Benito?"

Gavin saw Bianca approach Antonio. When she did, he could clearly see her face was battered. Both eyes were black. Her lip was split and her nose broken. Gavin felt a wave of nausea. Antonio kept his hand raised, oblivious to the stark evidence of his handiwork behind him. The light had died at four in the afternoon and with it any natural warmth. A cold breeze sliced through the little camp.

"Stand, *por favor*," Antonio said loudly to Benito. Gavin could see the young man's face was set in a snarl of defiance but he obeyed.

"Apologize," Antonio said. Gavin watched Bianca's face flinch as if the word itself were a physical slap.

Benito stood with his fists clenched. "I regret my actions."

"Louder! And speak to your sister not to the back of Zia Bella's head."

A weak titter of laughter moved through the group. Gavin's face burned for Benito's humiliation and for the glances both he and Sophia were enduring from the rest of the family. Why was Antonio doing this? To ensure Gavin never had a decent relationship with Benito?

"I regret my actions," Benito said loudly to Gavin and Sophia. "And beg your forgiveness."

Before Gavin could respond in any way, Antonio said, "A real apology is underscored with pain. To show you mean it."

Gavin saw Bianca come forward. Her hand hovered over Antonio's arm as though she was afraid to touch him. Her eyes were on Benito.

"You will strip naked before everyone," Antonio said loudly. "All your clothes in the lap of your sister for as long as she deems necessary but not—" he said, turning to Sophia, "before one hour has passed."

Was the man totally mad? Both Sophia and Gavin got to their feet.

"That will not be necessary, Squire," Gavin said. "I accept your apology, Benito. We're good."

"But *I* do not accept it!" screamed Antonio.

"Antonio, please," Bianca moaned, her hand finally touching her husband's shoulder. Antonio's reaction was fast and brutal. He turned and backhanded the woman, snapping her head at an unnatural angle. Sophia screamed as her mother staggered backwards. Bianca lost her footing and fell backward into the fire, knocking a roasted spit of rabbit into the dirt. Gavin dashed for her, reaching her before anyone else moved. He dragged her out of the fire, slapping the flames out of the sleeve of her shirt. She was limp in his arms.

He turned in time to see Sophia launch herself at Antonio, her fingernails out like talons to rake her father's face. Antonio grabbed Sophia's arms but the look on his face was one of bizarre joy. Gavin jumped to his feet. But before he took two steps, strong hands grabbed him and pressed him to his knees.

"Get off me, ye berk!" he shouted as he watched Sophia grapple with her crazy father.

"Take her! Take her!" Antonio shouted. Three men emerged from the seated family to pull Sophia away.

"You bastard!" Sophia screamed, spittle flying as she lunged again for her father, her face a mask of rage.

"Let me go!" Gavin yelled as Antonio turned to face him, his face flushed but his eyes alive with pleasure.

"If a husband cannot control his wife, it is the duty of the father to it for him." Antonio spoke loudly to all present but his eyes were on Gavin and the message was clear: *Cross me and pay the price*.

Antonio strode to a nearby stack of firewood and grabbed a squat log which he carried back with both hands and slammed down in front of Gavin. The two men holding Sophia dragged her to the stump and forced her to her knees.

119

"What are ye doing, ye crazy fecker?" Gavin screamed as he thrashed against the men who held him. One man snaked an arm around Gavin's neck.

"Benito!" Antonio shouted.

Within seconds, Benito—still shirtless—appeared and sank to his knees in front of his sister. Gavin watched as Benito pried Sophia's hand from her breast and pressed it flat on the stump.

"Noooooooo!" Sophia screamed, her head flung back as she fought the men who held her.

Antonio held Gavin's eyes as he pulled the small hatchet from his belt.

14

It happened so quickly, Gavin didn't believe it wasn't a stunt. Yet his eyes had seen it. Seen the hatchet come up and slam down sharply onto the stump. Seen the finger fly off into the dirt. Sophia remained kneeling, her eyes large, staring at her hand, the blood running down her arm. The little finger was gone at the second joint.

"Sophia!" Breaking free of the men holding him, Gavin knocked the log out of the way and caught Sophia by the shoulders as she began to fall. Her face white with shock, she fainted in his arms. He grabbed her maimed hand and held it up while looking helplessly around. Bianca lay motionless by the fire—whether dead or alive, Gavin had no idea. He stared at Antonio.

"I did it from love!" Antonio shouted. "And trust me it's been coming a long time." He turned to the family members who were staring in horror at the blood on the log. "*He* should have been the one to correct her! I was wrong about him. He is not good for my Sophia."

Gavin ripped the tail of his shirt in a long strip and bound it tightly around Sophia's hand. She moaned and stirred in his arms. Benito stood in place, bare-chested and shivering, staring at the small finger on the ground as if transfixed. Gavin stood with Sophia in his arms. He watched the men who'd held him, the brother who'd held Sophia's hand down, and the monster who stood raving before him.

The atmosphere around the campfire was one of terror and apprehension. Gavin's need to protect Sophia—to get her away—warred with his need to attack the man who'd hurt her. His arms trembled as he held her.

Paco held a hand up in front of Gavin. "Let us have the girl. We will see to her wound."

"Are ye daft? You're the fecking bastard who held her while the mad bastard did it!"

"You do not know our ways," Paco said.

"You'll leave us tonight," Antonio said.

Gavin knew immediately that there was no way Antonio was going to let him stay or leave alive. Sophia cried out, triggering Gavin to the decision that until then he had no idea he'd made. He turned to Paco and shoved Sophia into his arms.

"Hold this," he said as he snatched the handgun from Paco's front pocket and pointed it in Antonio's face. Antonio stared at Gavin impassively as if he knew for a fact that the gun was not loaded. Or perhaps just that Gavin could never use it.

"Have you thought past this point, *amico*?" Antonio said, wagging a finger at Gavin. "You are thinking, perhaps, you will walk backwards out of the camp all the way to your compound?" His lip curled in satisfaction.

"Nay," Gavin said in defeat. "You're right. That won't work."

He shot him in the chest.

15

John loved the walk from Gilly's townhouse to the university. There was bus service to the campus from the residential areas as well as the city center where the Heaton's lived. The trains continued to run too although mostly just to London and back.

"When I first came here," John said to Gilly as they walked, "I thought the place was deserted."

"Hardly. You do know that Oxford is the oldest university in the English-speaking world?"

"I didn't know that."

As they approached the intersection of St Giles, Magdalen Street and Beaumont Street, John looked toward the Martyrs' Memorial as he always tended to do. He'd already read the plaque several times and knew all the ghoulish details of the events of 1517 burnings but he was drawn to the plaque every time they passed.

To the Glory of God and in grateful commemoration of His servants, Thomas Cranmer, Nicholas Ridley, Hugh Latimer, Prelates of the Church of England who near this spot yielded their bodies to be burned, bearing witness to the sacred truths which they had affirmed and maintained against the errors of the Church of Rome and rejoicing that to them it was given not only to believe in Christ, but also to suffer for his sake; this monument was erected by public subscription in the year of our Lord God, MDCCCXLI.

Today Dr. White was seated on the steps of the memorial smoking furiously, his eyes darting everywhere. When he saw John looking at him, his lip curled and he tossed his cigarette down in disgust before reaching for a new one from the pack in his jacket pocket.

"Jeez," John said to Gilly as they hurried down the side street toward their classroom. "What is his problem?"

"I know, right? But most people would excuse him for how he behaves because of his wife and son."

John gave her a sickened look. "What happened to them?"

"They both died of the disease last year. Worse than that, they were out of the country visiting relatives at the time in Germany so Dr. White didn't even get to see them in time."

"That's terrible," John murmured. "Explains why he's always in a bad mood."

"He and Dad used to be great mates."

"Really?"

"Oh, yes. They had a falling out. I have no idea why. Here we are."

They hurried through the massive stone archway into Balliol College. Because of her father, Gilly and several other children her age were allowed to finish their secondary education in classrooms situated at the college. Later, when the infrastructure was fully back, she would go on to sixth form at Oxford College to earn her A-levels. The class was far beyond the elementary school level John had been at before he left Jacksonville in 2011, but he surprised himself, and the teacher, by managing to keep up with everyone in the class.

He was in fact was amazed to realize he understood as much as he did. When he was in the class grappling to catch up or to understand, he found he didn't feel frustrated at all but like a fire was being lit under him. Listening to the lectures made him feel like he wanted to take off like a Saturn V rocket straight up into the stratosphere.

After school, Gilly usually went to the homes of a few girlfriends in the class and John went to Dr. Heaton's lab. The routine worked well on every level for everyone. Today, John shouldered his bookbag and was about to make the sharp turn that led him through an internal courtyard and the wing of the college that housed Heaton's laboratory when he spotted someone he thought he knew.

Instantly he recognized the reason he knew the boy sitting at the base of the Martyrs statue feeding stale chips to a scrappy terrier was because he was the delivery boy at the Heaton's house. John had seen the boy on and off for five weeks now deliver milk, collect empties and peddle away to the next house in the street. Seeing him sitting there playing with his dog, his bike and basket full of empties to signal the end of his work day, John felt a twinge of longing for Gavin. In the compound, his world was largely taken up with hanging out with Gavin. Seeing the boy now made John realize how much he missed company of his own kind.

Impulsively, he hurried over to him.

"Hello," John said, holding out his hand. "My name's John. Cute dog."

The boy dropped the chips he'd been feeding to the dog and jumped to his feet, startled.

"Cor, you about gave me a heart attack!" he said, but he laughed when he said it. "I'm Geordie. This here's Ginger. You American or is that a fake accent?"

John laughed. "It's not fake. You live around here? I've seen you make deliveries on Canal Street."

Geordie wrinkled his pug nose and bent to pick up the chips he'd dropped on the stone steps. Ginger had already cleaned up most of them.

"Everybody knows me. I live at Rosemont. About two kilometers south of here."

"Rosemont? Sounds like a retirement village."

"Ha! You're not wrong. But brace yourself, it's a commune. Not the one where we're all naked," he said hurriedly.

"Oh? Where is that one?"

They both laughed.

"I like you, John. What the hell are you doing here? I thought the American tourists were the first ones to take a hike."

"Only the smart ones. It's a long story."

"I've got time. But can you tell it and walk? My granny will hand my head to me if I'm late. D'ye want to see Rosemont?"

John hesitated. He knew Dr. Heaton was expecting him at the lab. That is, if he looked up from his work and noticed. But it was a rare sunny day in December and after a day of school, John longed to be outdoor.

"That'd be cool," he said.

*****

That evening after his visit to Geordie's commune, John walked home in the dark. It had started to rain halfway back and he was drenched by the time he got back to the townhouse.

Gilly had not been happy about it.

"I was worried sick about you," she said when he came into the foyer shaking the rain off his bookbag and jacket. "And so was Dad. He had no idea where you were when you didn't show up at the lab."

"Really? He noticed I didn't come?"

"Of course, he noticed!"

Dr. Heaton entered the room, patting the pockets of his cardigan as if looking for something. "Hello, there, John," he said amiably. "Good day at school, was it?"

John gave Gilly a smug smile which he instantly regretted. It was true Dr. Heaton hadn't been worried, but Gilly clearly was. She turned on her heel and stomped into the kitchen.

"Hello?" Dr. Heaton said, looking after her as she left. "Everything all right, petal?" But he settled himself in his chair by the fireplace and began humming as he opened the book he'd been reading.

John went into the kitchen to find Gilly noisily adjusting the different pans on the stove.

"I'm sorry, Gilly. I lost track of time."

"Well, that's all you had to say," she said, deliberately not looking at him. John knew how she felt. Sometimes it felt good to hold a grudge and when the person you're holding it against is apologetic, it makes it hard to stay mad. He intended to make it impossible.

"No, it's no excuse. You take such good care of me. If all I did every day was just make sure you were happy it wouldn't be enough for all you've done for me."

"Oh, go on," she said, but she was smiling now. "I just know what an idiot you are and how easily you can fall into a ditch and drown."

"Yes, that is certainly one of things I'm constantly trying not to do," John said, attempting to sound simple minded.

She hit him on the arm and sat down on a kitchen chair. "So where were you that was so enthralling you lost track of time?"

"You know the delivery kid who brings the milk?"

Gilly frowned as if trying to place him.

"Well, never mind. Anyway, I ran into him outside class. His family lives in a commune near town so he took me there. Gilly, it was so interesting."

"Really? A commune? Like a religious commune?"

Now it was John's turn to frown. "I didn't see anything like that. But they grow all their own food and they don't go to doctors or anything. Geordie's grandmother is an herbalist. It was really cool to see how they live."

"Cooler than electric lights and refrigeration?"

John laughed. "No, you're right. It's primitive. But they've had very few people get sick with the illness."

"And you think that's because of natural living?"

"Geordie's granny says she thinks the plague is what happens when science gets too far away from the natural ways."

"You don't believe that nonsense?"

"I believe in science," John said firmly. "But I also know my Aunt Fiona was into homeopathic remedies and they always seemed to work. Geordie said I could bring you out sometime if you wanted to come."

"I think I'll pass. But I'm glad you had fun."

*****

For the next couple of days John went to Heaton's lab right after classes. He kept an eye out for Geordie but wasn't surprised when he didn't see him. Geordie had mentioned that he didn't usually have loads of free time. As John walked down the stone walkway leading to the science labs from class one afternoon, he recognized Dr. Davis and Dr. White standing at the archway that led into the building, both in white lab coats and both smoking. They watched John approach but continued to talk.

"You know it was his brother that got him the job. How could it not be?" White said with disgust.

"Man's an idiot. He couldn't find the cure for ripped paper. It's absurd." Davis said, between puffs on his cigarette.

"The worst of it is watching him prance about the lab. As if." Dr. White eyed John with unconcealed disgust as John passed and entered the building. John knew there were professional rivalries in any professional arena but he was astounded at how personally vicious Heaton's colleagues were.

John hurried up the stairs to the lab. As he walked down the hall, he saw Dr. Heaton and Dr. Lynch through the window separating the lab from the hall. He tried to slip inside unobtrusively.

"Hello, there, John," Dr. Heaton said. "How was class?"

"Good."

"We're going to have to convince you to stay longer. Classes will be back full tilt everywhere fairly soon, don't you think, Dr. Lynch?"

She shrugged. "The full impact of the disease seems to have skipped Oxford for all intents and purposes. Have you heard anything from London? Is it diminishing elsewhere?"

Dr. Heaton shook his head. "Daniel says it might not be getting any worse but certainly no better."

John knew Dr. Heaton's brother Daniel had a high political position in British Parliament. He also knew that it was pretty much accepted throughout Oxford that *Daniel* was the reason Dr. Heaton had gotten the research funding in the first place. If that was true and making or keeping friends in the scientific community in Oxford mattered, then Daniel definitely hadn't done Dr. Heaton any favors.

"What is that?" Dr. Lynch came to Dr. Heaton's bench to peer at the flask he was holding up. "Have you found a vaccine?"

"No," Dr. Heaton said. "This is something else."

"What stage is it?"

"Well, as I said, it's not a vaccine," Dr. Heaton said patiently.

"Then what is it?"

John wanted to interject that Dr. Heaton knew what he was doing but he knew the doc wouldn't thank him. It was just galling to see how little everyone thought of him.

"It's a failure, if you must know." Dr. Heaton set the flask into a holder and picked up a white bucket and set it on the bench next to him. "Which is why I finally got smart. Ye see, Sandra," he said with excitement, "it occurred to me that using two buckets like they do in some third world countries to purify water is ideal for the areas in the country without electricity. This way, it's gravity driven."

"I understand the mechanics behind a water purification bucket system," Lynch said with exaggerated patience. "The problem isn't the bacteria in the water, it's the *virus,* as you well know. Why are you wasting your time with buckets?"

Dr. Heaton removed his glasses and cleaned them with a soft cloth he had tucked in his top jacket pocket.

"There are people far smarter than I who are working on the cure for this terrible disease." He nodded at the bucket. "Until those smarter minds come up with a cure, I'm working on a way to contain it."

"You're working on coming up with a better bucket."

John could hear the sarcasm in every syllable of her voice.

"Exactly," Dr. Heaton said, clearly oblivious to the insult.

Dr. Lynch sighed, patted Dr. Heaton on the shoulder and left the lab. Just the way she did it—like it was no good even talking to Dr. Heaton—made John flush with embarrassment for the man. After the door closed behind her, Dr. Heaton turned and stared out the window, his fingers tapping the bucket idly. Every time John looked at the stupid bucket he was filled with an agitation that made him want to pick it up and throw it out the window.

If the two bastards badmouthing Dr. Heaton on the front steps had seen Dr. Heaton with his bucket, it was no wonder they were having a field day at his benefit. Had the doc totally given up? Did he really think a revision of the bucket system was the answer?

Even John knew that was lame and he was just a kid.

Susan Kiernan-Lewis

16

The drive to the commune was brief, not even twenty minutes in Heaton's SUV. If it hadn't been so cold, John would have suggested they walk or even take the bikes he'd found in the garage. But he was probably pushing it to get the doc out of the lab for even a morning. He'd put a note in one of the milk bottles the day before telling Geordie he was maybe coming out the next day with the doc and hoped to meet his grandma.

Since there was no road leading into the commune, John and Dr. Heaton parked outside on the road. The last time John had been here was early afternoon and the sun had taken the bite out of the wind. Today, the snow and the brisk breeze made every step into the little community a wretched one. Geordie must have been watching for them because they no sooner stepped under a large bower of bare branches at the entrance of the commune when he emerged from the door of the first cottage.

"Oy, John!" he called. "You made it, mate!"

"I did," John said. "Glad you got my message. Is it okay to visit?"

"Too right," Geordie said motioning him and Dr. Heaton up onto the porch. They hadn't gotten two steps toward the porch when John realized that Dr. Heaton had stopped. When John turned to see why, he saw the doc had picked up a bucket that had been lying on its side on the pathway.

Dr. Heaton had his reading glasses out and was examining it, frowning intensely. It was a water filtration bucket. John felt a wave of discouragement to see him so focused on it. In the six weeks since John had been accompanying him to the lab and overhearing the other scientists and Sandra Lynch—as well as long talks with Dr. Heaton

131

himself—even John knew that the bacterial part of the infected water wasn't the problem. *So why did the guy keep obsessing about the damn bucket?*

"Dr. Heaton, sir? I wanted you to meet Geordie's grandmother. The herbalist?"

"Yes, yes," Dr. Heaton said, putting the bucket down and tucking his reading glasses back into his top jacket pocket.

John knew that their visit today was probably the second most ridiculous thing anyone could do to solve a problem of this size but one thing was sure, the *first* most ridiculous thing had to do with a bucket that everybody had already used and found useless. Besides, John didn't really think Geordie's grandma had any magic cures up her sleeve. He really just wanted to unstick the doc from the rut he seemed determined to stay in.

When he'd suggested the two of them get out of town for a field trip, Dr. Heaton had been happy to oblige. John chose to believe that was because, deep down, the doc didn't really have confidence in the direction he was going with his research. Sometimes an outing helped clear the brain and restart your engines. John felt that was true when he had something he was trying to figure out. If he left the playing field and went some place totally different, often an answer would present itself. He didn't dare hope that kind of lightning bolt would strike today. But it couldn't hurt to try.

They mounted the steps and John quickly Dr. Heaton to Geordie.

"So you're our delivery boy, eh?" Dr. Heaton said. "And here I thought it was the fairies and the little people making the cream and eggs appear every morning."

Geordie laughed politely and John blushed at the awkwardness among them.

"I told Dr. Heaton all about your grandma," John said. "He's really keen to meet her."

"Oh, well Granny's always up for company, so you're welcome, Doc," Geordie said, as he led them into the cottage.

Once inside, John shivered in relief from the cold. The cozy little home was just one big room anchored by a large stone fireplace where a blazing fire was burning. He could see the fireplace was also used for cooking, like they did at the compound back in Ireland. Seated by the fire was a dumpling of a little old lady bundled up in blankets and crocheted shawls. Her bright eyes and rosy cheeks made her look like Mrs. Santa Claus.

Geordie made the introductions and pulled up chairs for everyone in front of the fire. John could see immediately that Dr. Heaton had no real idea of why he was here. He turned and smiled blandly at Geordie's grandmother.

"Staying warm, I hope, Granny?" he said.

John turned to her. "Geordie says you're a whiz with herbs, Mrs. Bancroft. I'll bet that's fascinating."

The little old woman's deep-set eyes crinkled when she smiled.

"Oh, Geordie said you was a Yank. Sound just like telly, you do. When we had telly, that is. Word is it won't be long we'll have it back. But probably not here in the commune. You know we say *herbs* and pronounce the H but when you say it, it's silent?"

"I know," John said, grinning. "When Geordie first told me you were working with herbs, I thought he was talking about a couple guys named Herbert."

Mrs. Bancroft laughed. "So you're interested in herbs, are you? It only takes the world coming to an end to reinvigorate an interest in the natural botanic arts."

"Were you involved in herbal therapies, Mrs. Bancroft?" Dr. Heaton asked politely.

"Alternative medicine, they called it, don't you know," she said affably. "We've a little more respect these days but back then—before the bomb—they thought we were all witchdoctors."

Geordie stepped away and John leaned in just in case she was hard of hearing. He couldn't easily judge her age but she looked more like Geordie's great-grandmother. She might be and he just called her his grandmother.

"Geordie told me there's not many people in your group who got the sickness," John said. He saw Dr. Heaton's head snap around and he felt the doc's posture go rigid. Even without looking, John knew he'd overstepped his bounds. Now the doc knew what the visit was about—that John thought he was nuts too with his buckets. His stomach flopped painfully and he wished to hell he'd never suggested the visit.

"There were one or two," Mrs. Bancroft said. "I'm not a miracle worker. But I'll wager we're faring better than most." She looked at Dr. Heaton. "Is it still bad out there? The plague?"

Dr. Heaton cleared his throat. "I'm afraid so."

"Tch!" She shook her head and stared into the fire. "There are some saying it's the natural way. We've always had plague, you know."

Before John could respond, Geordie returned and set a tray down on the small footstool in front of the fire. On it was a chipped teapot and four cups and saucers.

"Is it the Dandy tea, Geordie?" his grandmother asked, leaning forward to sniff the fumes coming from the pot.

"Of course, Granny. Wouldn't risk getting me ears boxed by bringing the wrong tea. Were you hoping for Earl Grey?"

"Young scamp," she said, smiling at him.

"I don't believe I've ever heard of Dandy Tea," Dr. Heaton said.

"It's dandelions," Geordie said as he poured each cup and handed them around. "We all drink gallons of it." He handed John his cup and said under his breath, "Mind you, it tastes like donkey piss."

"What's that, Geordie?" Mrs. Bancroft said as she scanned the tray. "No honey?"

Geordie jumped up to fetch the honey.

In for a penny, John thought and took a long breath. "I was just wondering if you had any ideas why so few people here were affected by the sickness when it's all over everywhere outside of here."

"Well, we're very careful to boil our water, of course. *And* we filter it."

"And that's it?" John asked, ignoring the movement next to him that indicated the doc was about to make their excuses to leave.

"Pretty much," she said, shrugging.

Geordie returned with the honey and spooned a dollop into her cup. "Anyone else?" he asked.

John and Dr. Heaton both shook their heads.

"That's not all, Granny," Geordie said. He turned to John and Dr. Heaton. "We boil and filter *all* the water in the commune. Even the stuff we use to wash our clothes with. Can you imagine?"

"You're just a lazy little sod," his grandmother said good-naturedly.

John and Dr. Heaton laughed but John knew he was in for it once they were alone. He cursed himself for insisting the doc come with him to the commune.

Oh, well, at least the old lady had a pleasant diversion, he thought.

*****

With the fifteen head of slowly ambling cows blocking the road back to Oxford, it occurred to John that it would've been faster to walk back home. He and Dr. Heaton sat in the SUV waiting for a slow-moving herd of Holsteins to get out of the way. The tension in the car seemed to be building minute by minute as John agonized over the audacity Dr. Heaton must think he showed to assume the commune could tell them anything about the disease.

He glanced at Heaton's profile. The man was concentrating on the road when there was nothing to see or do but hold the steering wheel and sit.

What was I thinking? A stupid kid? Was I really trying to tell a scientist at Oxford University that there might be a connection between the commune and their lack of sickness? That's just dumb and one thing is sure, it is not thinking like a scientist.

Dr. Heaton's eyes blinked as he stared at the road.

Was the doc even thinking about John's crime of arrogance? Maybe he was redesigning the bucket in his head or something and not even thinking about this embarrassing waste of time...

"It's bloody odd how they've had so few people sicken," Heaton said, frowning.

John felt his pulse quicken. "I guess," John said.

Heaton turned to look at him. "The question is, is it something to do with country living? Or what they're doing at the commune specifically?"

John felt a flutter of hope that the doc wasn't mad at him after all.

"Good question," he said, hoping not to derail the direction the doc's thoughts seemed to be heading.

"May I apologize to you, John?"

Is he serious?

"I was unbearably rude. To Mrs. Bancroft and to you."

"No you weren't. I didn't think you were."

"It's just that I get caught up in my own little world, aye? So many scholars do and to get out like this and gain a fresh perspective, well it's immeasurably helpful. So forgive me and thank you, lad."

John wanted to let out a loud whoop or at least do a fist pump. He settled for a big grin.

"Do you think it could be like a family trait?" John asked. "The reason they had fewer people sick? Like maybe they have a genetic resistance?"

"Good question, lad! Very good question."

John felt the flush of pride that he usually felt when he was with Dr. Heaton. It was more than just the fact that they seemed to speak the same language although there was certainly that. As long as John had been speaking, he'd had adults become ruffled and unhappy to hear what he had to say—as if a kid shouldn't talk sense or at least not demonstrate openly that he can.

And Dr. Heaton was the only person besides John's father, David, who'd ever listened to him as an equal. He gave weight to John's opinions and listened with his whole head and heart. And for that, if for nothing else, John knew he loved Finlay Heaton. That probably explained why when he thought about leaving to go find Gavin or to make his way back to the compound—as happy as that thought always made him—it also made him sad. Because now that he'd found Dr. Heaton and Gilly, he wanted them in his life going forward.

"I'm looking forward to you meeting my brother Daniel," Dr. Heaton said. "He's very sharp. In many ways sharper than I am. He's more of the world, if you know what I mean."

John did. He often caught himself being amazed at how the doc could spend time with Dr. Lynch and not feel her disrespect or especially Dr. White who was out and out hostile to him.

"I guess most academics are like that," John said.

"Well, that's the stereotype anyway. Ethan White isn't that way," Heaton said as if reading John's mind. The cows had finally moved all the way off the road and Heaton inched the car forward. "We used to be close friends once," he said quietly, as if instead of cows he was seeing happier days with his old friend Ethan White.

John didn't answer. From what he'd seen it wasn't just a matter of Dr. White not wanting to be pals any more. When it came to Finlay Heaton, the guy really acted like he hated him.

*****

The E-shaped Ionic colonnade and portico of the old house of Parliament in Dublin sat just south of the Liffey River on College Green by the West Front of Trinity College. Featuring a majestic curving façade, the impressive structure hid a hodgepodge of sheds, and separate bigger buildings within its walls.

The parks surrounding Trinity College were home to thousands of people with most of them living in tents. Liam O'Reilly sat in the passenger seat of the town car he and Shane Sullivan had driven from the government compound. He stared up at the historic building.

"Do you know much about it?" he said pointing to the building. Two men in rags walked by, eyeing O'Reilly and Sullivan in their car. O'Reilly wasn't worried. There was an armed escort parked behind them. The men kept moving.

"About what every Irish school child knows," Sullivan said. "That it was the seat of Irish government for years. And that the English sold it to the Bank of Ireland and demolished our House of Commons."

"You know your history."

"I know what the English have done to our history."

Ahhh, there it was. Sullivan's particular chink in his armor was the fact that he didn't realize how reactive he was to certain things. O'Reilly could literally make the man froth at the mouth any time he liked by the mere mention of the English and what they might or might not have done to Ireland.

O'Reilly glanced appraisingly at his aide. The problem with that was that Sullivan loathed the English so intensely that O'Reilly was more than occasionally concerned he'd have trouble working with them. In today's post-EMP pre-plague Ireland, one didn't always have the luxury to pick and choose one's allies.

O'Reilly had always been careful about who his friends were. He'd come up the hard way, without the benefit of easy connections. But then the bomb dropped four years ago and everything fell higgelty-pigglety...right into its proper place.

First, the president left—on the heels of the fleeing US Ambassador—for his home in the south of France after a full two weeks of attempting to reinvigorate the power grid in Dublin failed. The prime minister packed up the dominant parliamentary party soon afterward saying he would govern Ireland from Wales. Or was it Dubrovnik? Before they ran out of beer, there were more than a few laughs in the pubs after *that* announcement. In fairness to the PM, the man did eventually manage to get some of the cell towers rebuilt. And a barge of working government vehicles came over soon after he left.

When the dust cleared, only the Senate of Ireland remained, of which O'Reilly had been a low ranking member. Most people knew the Senate to be the weaker of the two parliamentary groups but with no prime minister, no president and no dominant party, well, it was a new era in Irish politics. With some of the underdogs finally on top, whoever was left to bully through the bad years of intermittent electricity, nonexistent infrastructure and spotty communications—not to mention sudden swamping of two million people who'd swarmed the capital in the days and months after the EMP dropped—well, there was a prize to be had.

It was clear to O'Reilly that someone needed to step forward. Someone unbothered by the occasional piles of shite to be slogged through. Someone willing to do what was necessary to bring Ireland back. He'd made sure that someone was himself.

"What would you say," he said, turning to Sullivan, "if we moved government back here?"

Sullivan's eyes blinked rapidly as if trying to process his words. "Make it our parliament building again, you mean?"

"Aye."

Sullivan looked at the building with renewed wonder and interest. "The English forbade us to ever use it as a government building again," he said in a hushed tone.

"Sod the English. It's a new world, Sullivan. Especially for Ireland."

Sullivan smiled. And when he did, it occurred to O'Reilly that he'd never seen him smile before.

"Mind you," O'Reilly said frowning as a family of four homeless people approached them. The woman held a large hat out, her face pleading, and he shooed her away with his hand. "We'll have to clean up the streets a good bit first."

Sullivan's mobile phone rang and he answered it, still smiling. O'Reilly watched the smile dissolve from his face.

"Bloody hell. Are ye sure?" Sullivan said into the receiver.

"What is it?" O'Reilly said. "What's happened?"

Sullivan disconnected the phone and stared at it. "I was afraid of this. I'd heard some rumors…I needed to make sure."

"What is it, man?" O'Reilly clenched his jaw and felt the frustration pour out of him.

"It's confirmation," Sullivan said grimly. "The sickness has found its way to Ireland."

Susan Kiernan-Lewis

17

Mike and Sarah spent a full week with the Connors, moving with them, living with them. In that week, Sarah felt her resolve grow strong and that gave her comfort.

You only hurt when you give up. If you never give up, you can keep the pain at bay. She decided this would be her motto in the coming weeks and months.

However long it took.

The day they parted, the Connors loaded them down with food, oats for the pony they were loaning them, a cart and more hugs and good wishes than they could ever use in a lifetime.

"Promise you'll come to Ameriland," Sarah said to Molly as she hugged her goodbye. "If you want to stay, you'll always have a home there. All of you."

"Expect us," Molly said. "I've been sick of traveling for weeks now."

"But no interest in going back to your village?"

"Nay. The Wiccans have taken over there. Or are at least too close for comfort."

"Not human sacrifice?" Sarah asked.

"No, thank God. But not our type, all the same."

"Come to the compound," Sarah said, hugging her again.

"Good luck finding your lads," Molly said. "I know you'll find them. And I'll include them in me prayers every night."

"Thanks, Molly." Sarah knelt and gave Elise a kiss. "Bottomless bowls of raisins for you, darling, when you come."

"Promise?"

"Absolutely, I do." Sarah couldn't stop the memory forming of John at this age, so willing to believe, so ready to be enthused about everything.

"Are you sure you won't stay for Christmas?" Molly said. "The lads are determined to bag a boar. We'll feast for days."

"It sounds great," Sarah said. "But we've already stayed longer than we should. We need to get going."

"Well, I know how you feel. I'd be the same, I'm sure," Molly said as her hand dropped to the head of her child.

Sarah walked over to the pony cart and gave Darby a quick hug.

"I can't thank you enough for all you've done," she said. "Don't forget us in Ameriland. We'd love for you to join us."

"Pretty sure you'll see our lot there before long. Good luck to ye, Sarah." He gave her a quick kiss on the cheek and handed her up to Mike who was in the driver's seat of the cart.

They waved goodbye and pointed the pony south. Their best guess was that, eventually, Gavin would head for home if he could. Meanwhile, Mike and Sarah needed more supplies before they went back out searching. And then there was always the hope that when they rode up to the gates of the compound, one or both boys would be waiting for them. Sarah tried not to focus on that particular fantasy too much but she felt her body leaning forward as if eager to propel the cart faster toward home…and John.

Mike drove the pony with one arm around Sarah. It was cold and though the Connors had given them their extra blankets, they weren't enough. Sarah's feet already felt like blocks of ice. She stamped them against the buckboard from time to time to try to bring feeling back to her toes.

"Darby said there's a hotel or hostel of some kind in the next town," Mike said. "We can get more information."

Sarah nodded. What information could they possibly get that made any difference? She instantly felt guilty for the thought. While it was true there was nothing she could learn on this side of the channel about John's whereabouts, there was still Gavin. She had to admit, finding him would help staunch the terrible feeling of her loss.

The sign for the next town read Carrick-on-Suir. It was a good mile before the actual village showed up and then it was just a string of ten buildings of varying heights, sizes and colors built on one side of the road. The other side was a long line of what was once parallel parking abutting a heavily lichened stonewall. This must once have been a pretty tourist village, Sarah thought as they rode down the main street.

"Which one is it, do you think?" she asked. As usual, all the buildings looked deserted but Mike rode straight to the one building that—to Sarah—looked no different from the others.

He handed her the reins and reached down to pick up the Glock semi-automatic from the floor of the trap. He'd found all their guns and ammunition untouched in the woods once he was able to hobble about on his injured foot. He placed the gun on her knees.

"Shoot first. Ask questions never."

"I hate that," she said, as she took the reins. "Didn't running into Darby and Molly teach us anything?"

"Aye," Mike said as he climbed down from the cart. "That there are good people in the world and we're lucky to know them. Mind the front door. I won't be long."

He wasn't either. Before Sarah had time to fully become nervous about sitting out in the pony trap, exposed and vulnerable, he was back, swinging up into his seat and taking both the gun and the reins from her. She felt her pulse accelerate. His excitement was contagious.

"News?" she asked as he hurriedly prompted the pony into a trot. "Did someone see him?"

"Not as such. But they said there's a large group camped not far from here."

Sarah bit her lip. "Is that good? Don't we want to stay away from big groups living in the woods?"

Mike reached an arm around her shoulders and gave her a quick squeeze.

"Normally, aye, maybe," he said. "But this group is a family. Where there's wives and kiddies there's less likely to be blackguards to deal with."

"If you say so." Sarah thought of the Connor family and friends and she relaxed a bit. It was true that it was difficult to set up a permanent camp the way she and Mike had done. It wasn't unheard of but it wasn't easy. The problem was, unless you did it, you couldn't plant or have much in the way of livestock. Even four years after the bomb, most people were living off their wits —hunting, stealing from others or starving—as though they were waiting for the lights to flick back on any minute.

"Are they gypsies?" she asked.

"The lads in the pub weren't exactly sure," Mike said, his eyes on the road ahead of them. "But foreign to be sure. Italian, they thought."

*****

The Italian camp was only about a mile away from the village. The pony was tired and wanted its dinner. The last thing Mike wanted to do was misuse the poor old thing—especially since he'd promised to return the beast to Darby one of these days. But they were so close. Maybe the Italians hadn't seen anything but at least he'd lay his head down tonight knowing he'd done everything he could for one day to find his lad.

They kept to the road and trotted slowly, keeping a sharp eye out. It wouldn't be totally unusual for a large family moving about like this to have look-outs—or even snipers if they felt threatened. That was the last thing they wanted to encounter.

"Mike, there!" Sarah said, pointing into the woods. They could see the flickering of firelight and when Mike stopped the cart in the road, they smelled the scent of meat cooking and heard the faint sounds of people's voices.

"That's got to be them, don't you think?"

"Aye." He handed her the reins. "Stay here."

"You must be out of your mind if you think I'm going to let you leave me here. No way."

"Sarah, love, why must ye argue with every little thing I ask of ye?"

"Are you serious?" Sarah said, her voice rising. "I am not splitting up again. *Ever.* I would think you of all people would understand why."

He sighed heavily. "Of course I do, Sarah. But the baby —"

"Don't worry about the baby. It's fine. I'm fine. We're both fine."

"You're not."

"As fine as any normal person can be under the circumstances."

He sighed and jammed the gun into his belt before holding a hand out to help her down.

"We'll need to be quiet."

"When it comes to noise, *I* am not the problem," she said pointedly.

He held her hand and they walked across the road to a stonewall beside the road. Mike hopped over it easily and then helped her over. Even at five months, she could feel her center of gravity had shifted just enough that she couldn't always predict how to stay balanced. It was very cold and a few snowflakes dropped in lazy, fluffy spirals around them. They entered the woods and walked toward the sounds of people.

Sarah knew that taking people by surprise could be just as bad as giving them too much notice that you were coming but there was nothing for it. There were only two options and most people would opt for the element of surprise if given a choice. As it happened, she needn't have worried. The Italians—looking to be at least thirty in all—were too busy having their dinner to worry about someone sneaking up on them.

Sarah and Mike stood on the outskirts of the clearing and watched as the family stoked their fire, piled roasted meat on plates and settled themselves around the cookfire. They could see a half dozen or so wagons formed in a half circle but there was no sign of tents. A shrill whinny from behind the wagons answered the question about where the horses were tethered.

"Ready?" Mike asked her, his voice tense with anticipation.

A part of him thinks Gavin will be here. Would she be thinking that too if she didn't know for sure how impossible it was to hope for John? Probably. She gave Mike's arm a reassuring squeeze and they walked out of the woods.

A little girl saw them first and promptly screamed and ran to her mother.

"We are friendly! We are friendly! *Amiegos!*" Mike called out, holding up his hands to show he was unarmed. Unfortunately, his arms outstretched served to call attention to the fact that he had two handguns jammed into his waistband. But all in all that might not be a bad thing.

Everyone around the fire stood up and all conversation ceased. A tall man with a lazy eye met them and held up a hand to signal that they should stop where they were.

"We don't welcome strangers," he said in a heavy Italian accent.

"We're not looking for a meal or a place to stay," Mike said easily. "Just a little information."

"Not a good place for that either," the man said, his eyes scanning Sarah from top to bottom.

145

"I'm looking for a lad. My son. Tall with ginger hair. Name of Gavin."

The man looked like he'd been slapped. Even Sarah could see that the name meant something to him. Was it possible? Was Gavin here? There was a rustle of activity from the group of family and then a thick-set boy stepped out of the crowd and stood next to the man with the lazy eye.

"We haven't seen anyone by that description. Now, go," the boy said, his face contorted with malice.

Sarah's heart sank. She could only imagine how Mike must feel. One disappointment after another. She touched Mike's elbow. The boy was right. They weren't wanted here. It was time to go. Mike stiffened at her touch and dropped his hands. Sarah watched in astonishment as he pulled both handguns out of his belt and aimed them at the two men in front of him.

Oh no no no. This is not good, Sarah thought in bewilderment. *What is Mike thinking?*

"We told you, *signore*," the fat teen said. "We have seen nobodies by this description."

"Oh, really?" Mike said. "Then why is it I'm seeing my son's boots on your feckin' feet?"

18

Mike pointed the gun at the teenage boy's head.

"I'm in no mood for your lies or bullshite. Answer me or I'll shoot me way through your entire camp one by one."

"He left," the man with the lazy eye said.

"Without his shoes?"

"He left in a hurry."

Mike cocked the gun.

"Tell 'im, Paco!" the fat boy said in a high, panicked voice. "They think we killed 'im!"

Paco held up his hands. A crowd had begun to gather behind him. The thought came to Mike that if the rest of them didn't mind losing these two, the crowd could probably overpower Mike in the next few seconds.

"Why is this tub o' lard wearing me son's shoes?" he said through gritted teeth.

A woman pushed through the crowd and put a hand on the boy's arm. Her face was badly bruised yet she stood tall and raised her chin proudly.

"My name is Bianca Borgnino. We did not hurt your son but he had every reason to think we would. We have today buried my husband who your son murdered."

"I don't believe it," Mike said.

"It is the truth. He killed my husband, the leader of our family and Benito's father, and then he ran. So fast that he did not take the time to put on his shoes that sat drying by the fire."

"When?"

"Last night."

"I don't believe her," Sarah said at Mike's elbow. "Gavin wouldn't kill anyone. And he wouldn't leave without his shoes."

Bianca turned to look at Sarah. "You are his mother?"

"Close enough," Sarah said.

"Perhaps we none of us truly know what our children are capable of."

"Prove to me he left here alive," Mike said.

"You can search the camp," Paco said.

"There's only one grave," Benito said with a leer. "Maybe we put two bodies in one hole?"

Mike dropped his gun arm and jammed the heel of his palm into Benito's throat, dropping him to his knees. Bianca screamed and ran to her son.

"The Irish boy is not dead!" she shrieked, cradling her son's head in her lap. "He left here alive, shoes or no shoes. He and Sophia."

"Who is Sophia?" Sarah asked and pulled Mike away from Benito.

"His bride," Bianca said, not taking her eyes off her son's face.

Only a punch to the gut could've stopped Mike as abruptly. "What did you say?"

Paco went to where Bianca crouched with Benito on the ground.

"His *wife*," Paco ground out. "Bianca's only daughter. And the daughter of the man your son killed. You have your information. Leave us in peace. I hope you do not live to find your son but if you do, I hope he is dead."

The venom and hatred in the group was palpable. No faces stared back at Mike from the crowd that didn't wish him ill.

Had Gavin lived with this lot? Had he really married one of them?

"I wish you endless tears that only a mother can shed," Bianca said, then spat in the dirt at Sarah's feet.

Sarah tugged once more on Mike's jacket. He turned away in bewilderment and disgust.

*****

All they knew...all they needed to know...was that Gavin was alive and he was near. If he'd bolted from the Italian's camp last night, he would head south toward the compound. Was he really barefoot? And with a wife?

Mike didn't say a word as they walked to where they'd left the horse and wagon. Up until then, they'd planned on returning to the village for the night. It was getting dark and it was already too late to make any distance today. But Sarah couldn't blame Mike for not pointing the horse's head back to the village.

If it had been her who'd just heard news of John—and the direction he'd likely taken—she'd travel all night if necessary. She could do no less for him.

"He'll have gone to Ameriland," Sarah said as they rode down the darkening road.

"You'd think so anyway," Mike growled.

"What do you mean?"

"Well, how is it he's way the hell out here? We're practically to the western coast—nowhere near the compound. Does the lad not *want* to come home?"

"We'll hear the whole story once we find him," Sarah said, slipping her hand onto Mike's knee. "I'm sure there was a good reason."

"I hope so. After all this, I'd hate to have to kill him right after I find him."

Good intentions and enthusiasm only went so far and they were soon helplessly in the dark. Hobbling the horse on the road was safe enough—most bandits or marauders tended to stay away from dark roads at night. And they'd be well away before light. Mike let the horse graze on the side of the road while Sarah attempted to make a bed for them in the back of the cart. They ate some of the food Darby and Molly had given them, and then held each other close for warmth and comfort as they fell asleep.

In the middle of the night it began to rain. Sarah had prayed it would hold off and had to assume the good Lord had His hands full elsewhere. All things considered, a sleepless night and wet clothes weren't the worst thing that could happen to them.

Unless the worst was still in the offing.

Mike dragged the bedding out and placed it under the cart. It was at least protection from the rain which began to come down in sheets, splashing rivulets and rivers on both sides of the cart but thankfully not under it. Sarah surprised herself by falling back asleep.

When she awoke, the rain had slowed but not ceased. It was still dark but Sarah could tell that dawn was near. When she crawled out from under the wagon, her knees and back screamed in protest. For a moment she tried to imagine the baby inside her —comfortable, safe, and oblivious to the elements that were torturing her and Mike.

She looked around. He was nowhere to be found. It was possible he'd gone to relieve himself. She stood next to the wagon, using it as a support until her knees were working properly again. The only sound in the early morning was the patter of the rain against the leaves and pebbles of the dirt road. She realized she'd heard that same background noise in her dreams all night long.

He should have been back by now.

Damn! What did I say about not splitting up? How tricky is that to remember?

She moved to sit in the driver's seat of the wagon which afforded her a better view down the road. That was when she realized—the horse was gone. They'd left him grazing along the side of the road, hobbled. She looked all around but could not see him anywhere. She held her breath and tried to listen for any sounds under the rain, anything she hadn't been aware of before. It was faint, but she did hear something. Footsteps, steady and coming toward her. She reached down and grabbed the semi-automatic on the floor of the buckboard. Her fingers tightened around the handle.

"Sarah?" Mike called out in a low voice. She felt her whole body sag with relief.

He morphed out of the darkness and swung up onto the wagon with her and ran a large hand down her back.

"We lost the horse," he said. "Damn thing's probably half way back to Darby and Molly's by now."

"How far from the compound do you think we are?"

He let out a heavy sigh. "Two days? On foot any way."

"It's Christmas tomorrow," Sarah said, her throat closing up as she fought to keep the sob from erupting.

"Oh, darlin,'" Mike said, drawing her into his arms and kissing her face. "I'm so sorry, lass. I'd give anything to have your John back by Christmas."

"I know," Sarah sniffled. "But we still have a chance to find Gavin."

"We'll find them, both, Sarah. I problem we will. We'll not stop until we've got him back."

She patted his hand and forcibly collected herself.

"Let's go. The sooner we start walking…"

"Aye. I'll shoot something later. We'll have a hot lunch."

"Are you sure you want to stop long enough for that? Gavin can't be that far ahead. Let's just keeping going. Plenty of time for hot lunches after we're all together."

She could tell he was relieved to hear her say it. They left the wet bedding and the frying pan that Molly had given them, carrying only what they absolutely needed—guns and ammunition. Two days wasn't the end of the world. Sarah knew she could handle two days. Walking, blisters, and a hunger that started in her stomach and spread through her whole body. But there was an end in sight. In two days she'd be warm and the walking would be done.

Except there would be no John at the end of it.

They walked down the road until it was full light. Blessedly, the rain stopped, but dry or wet it didn't matter at this point. One foot in front of the other. Going home now and home was where they'd find Gavin. They had to believe that. To even imagine that they'd arrive back at the compound and he wasn't there…it was a scenario so unimaginable that it wouldn't fully form. Sometimes she and Mike held hands and sometimes they just walked side by side, allowing the other to set their own pace. They'd left the compound nearly a month earlier with a working Jeep full of people, provisions and hope.

They were coming back with nothing but their lives and the clothes on their backs.

They walked without stopping until the late afternoon sun began to set, leaving them chilled and squinting into the dim light of the dying day. Sarah had two biscuits left—both were stale and hard—but she and Mike could suck on them as soon as it was too dark to walk. While there was still light enough, Mike found a small clearing off the road and into the woods with a flattened patch that looked like it had been used often for a campsite. He began gathering kindling to start a small fire to warm them. Sarah put the paltry biscuits on a flat rock beside the fire and went into the woods to relieve herself.

They'd spoken little on the walk. It was exhausting trying to be excited about arriving back at Ameriland for any reason other than food and refueling and to briefly give Gavin a hug—and maybe an ear boxing. John wasn't back at the compound. That was one thing they knew for sure. John wasn't in Ireland and the attempt to be cheerful or optimistic was more than Sarah could manage.

Her thoughts had taken her mind off where she was going and she realized that she no longer heard Mike snapping branches and humming to himself as he typically did when he worked. It was darker in the woods, but a half-moon peeked through the branches above. Quickly, she lowered her jeans, relieved herself, and pulled them back up. Then suddenly, for no apparent reason, she felt vulnerable and afraid. She'd gone too far. She turned around quickly to head back in the direction she'd come and her foot caught a raised root.

She pitched forward to her knees and grabbed at a nearby branch for support. The branch came off in her hand and the ground beneath her fell away as she clawed desperately at the air. Her scream robbed her of her last strength as she fell through the earth itself.

19

It was dark and wet and crawled with life. Sarah slapped at the tendrils of roots and worms clinging to her hair, her clothes. She tilted her head up to see the moon through the tree branches above. She screamed, flinging the creatures and the dirt from her hair, the terror and revulsion grabbing her like a living thing. She didn't dare touch the dirt walls of the pit—dark and invisible in the evening light. Her foot touched something soft. An animal. And her scream retched out of her in one agonizing wail.

"Sarah! Lass! What happened? Where are you?"

"Mike! I'm in a hole! Don't fall in! Don't—"

The light from the moon blinked out as Mike's form filled the opening of the pit, his cursing trailing him as he fell with a heavy thud beside her. She reached out to touch him. It was too dark to see more than shadows.

"Mike, there's something in here..."

The sound of the gunshot thudded into the thick walls of the pit and Sarah screamed. Mike reached for her and pulled her into his arms. She was shaking violently.

"What...what was it?" she stuttered.

"We'll find out in the morning," he said gruffly.

"Oh, my God, do we have to stay here all night? I hate things that belong in the earth crawling on my skin! You've got to get us out of here!"

"Steady on, love," Mike said soothingly. "We'll get out. Just let me think for a moment."

"I'm flipping out, Mike." Sarah saw the rim of the pit was at least five feet above her. "I can't do this. I can't do this. I've got to get out of here." She felt his hands sure and strong holding her firmly around the shoulders as if he could somehow help her keep it together, keep from flying apart.

"Whoever built this pit is likely to have heard my gunshot," Mike said reassuringly. "We won't have to wait long. I'm sure."

"You're just saying that so I won't freak out! Where's your gun? Shoot some more in the air. Help! Help!"

"Sarah…"

"No! Give me your gun!"

"Sarah, stop it, lass." Mike shook her gently. "Take a breath."

She sucked in a noisy breath and squeezed her eyes shut.

"Let it out, darlin," he said softly, rubbing her back. "It's going to be all right."

"I just really don't think it is," she said, fighting back a sob as she covered her face with her hands.

"Nothing is ever going to be all right again, Mike. If I can't find him, if I can't hold him, I just don't think I…" She broke down in agonizing howls of pain and loss, finally letting go of the reserve and the strength she'd needed to go on. There was no going on now. Now she was done.

"Sarah, please, love…" He held her tightly, rubbing her shoulders and back, his hands warm and firm.

"Oy! Whoever's down there," said a voice from above. "If you don't throw your weapon up here right now I'll shoot ye like fish in a barrel!"

Mike squinted up at the opening of the pit.

"Gavin? Is that you?"

*****

Shane walked down the long corridor to O'Reilly's office. It had rained on and off all day and night. Not that it mattered. He lived like a fecking mole these days, spending more time underground than out and about. And what was out and about anyway? Watching the riff raff burn rubbish in the streets? Was this the Ireland he and O'Reilly had inherited? O'Reilly didn't seem to see any difference between the country they'd lost —the country before the EMP went off over the Irish Sea—and the one they had on their hands right now.

And yet. The idea of starting over in the old parliament building had its merits. Problem was, O'Reilly knew it would be just the carrot for Shane that it was. O'Reilly didn't give two shites about where the seat of power was located. He didn't care about history, or how Ireland looked on the world stage or where it was poised to be in a year's time.

Jaysus. How could the man be so obtuse?

He passed a cadre of Garda Síochána guards and noticed their shirts were hanging out of their trousers and their dress shoes were replaced with trainers.

How close to losing the support of the Garda were they? *Or am I just being paranoid?* He forced himself not to look at the men's faces as he passed. The last thing he wanted to do was convey any nervousness or hint of insecurity to them. *Like effing pit bulls. Everything is fine until they smell your fear.*

His phone vibrated in his slacks pocket and he pulled it out and studied the screen. He took a long breath and deleted the received text. *No guts no glory. But no sense in being foolhardy.*

He went into his office. The door to O'Reilly's office was open.

"That you, Shane?" O'Reilly called.

Shane walked to the door that separated the two offices. O'Reilly was smoking a cigar and squinting at his computer screen.

"Why is our Internet bollocks?" O'Reilly said.

Maybe because our infrastructure got fried about four years ago? But Shane didn't answer.

"Sometimes it works great," O'Reilly said. "Other times it's rubbish." He looked up at Shane. "Did you hear any more about those wankers over in Cows Lane off Lord Edward Street?"

It seems the Garda had broken up a rally late yesterday afternoon that was annoyingly well attended. The rally—mostly people who would normally be in college and not causing trouble—was the first grassroots effort to promote the idea of storming the government compound and bringing rule back to Ireland.

Two dozen people had been rounded up by the Garda.

"Apparently they don't want whatever government they currently think they have. They're frustrated with the rate of rebuilding in Dublin."

"Shite. They're not the only ones," O'Reilly said, tossing his keyboard down with disgust.

"What's your intentions with them?" Shane asked.

"Jaysus, you're a formal berk, Shane," O'Reilly said, shaking his head. "Take 'em to the camps. We need the manpower and I need this pain in my arse here in Dublin gone."

"It's probably just the beginning," Shane said. "The people are unhappy. There'll be more."

"That's grand. We've plenty of work in the mines. More is good. Now. The bigger problem at hand."

Shane nodded.

"The plague is definitely in Ireland. Do you have any idea how far from a cure they are in the UK?"

"Well, since I've been paying good money to ensure the finding of a vaccine was indefinitely stalled, I'd say we're not close, wouldn't you imagine?" O'Reilly said sarcastically. "Which village is it affected?"

"On the western coast."

"How many people?"

"Five hundred maybe."

"I'm thinking I'll send a Garda contingency down there. Fast. Effective. Make this problem go away. As if it never happened."

Shane pressed his lips together. *Did the bastard really think there was no more accountability? Is that what he was counting on?*

"But if they've got it," Shane said patiently, trying not to telegraph his frustration, "it got in and if it got in then it's only a matter of time before it comes at us from another direction, so... what you're suggesting, it's not a solution."

"Few things absolutely are, Shane, but it'll buy us some time."

"Look, why don't we quarantine them? Throw up fences and keep it top secret."

O'Reilly's mouth fell open in exaggerated astonishment and Shane felt his own anger building deep in his gut.

"I'm not being squeamish, Liam," Shane said. "You know I'm not. But sooner or later, if we do something like this... someone's going to talk."

"Someone like *you* maybe?" O'Reilly's face was impassive as he said the words. His eyes dead, his mouth pressed in a straight line.

"Are you serious?"

"No, no," O'Reilly said, rubbing a hand through his hair and turning back to the computer on his desk. "I'm just knackered. I trust ye with me life, Shane. You're right, sooner or later some wanker will start a newspaper and then we'll be in the shite. No, we'll create a walled compound. Anybody gets sick, we put them there. Top secret. It'll be our very own Area 51. No one will ever know."

"Except eventually they will. Or are you counting on Ireland never getting cell phone towers again?"

"Not any time soon. Besides, by the time word spreads, we'll have the cure."

"Change of tactics?"

"You do give me points for flexibility, don't ye, Shane?" O'Reilly said with a dry smile. "Things have changed and so must we. If there's a cure, we need to have it. And we need nobody else to have it."

Shane sighed. At least that made a little more sense than paying *not* to find a cure.

"Lotta people dying out there, Liam," Shane said as he walked back to his own desk.

"I'm not a monster," O'Reilly called after him. "If they have enough money, the cure will be available to them. That's only free market enterprise. America was bloody built on it."

*****

Sarah was sure it must have taken everything Mike had to allow her to climb up the rudimentary ladder of branches first. But maybe not. Perhaps just knowing his boy was there, alive and laughing was enough. It would have been for her. She hugged Gavin briefly before Mike made it up the ladder. She saw the intense delight on his face as he gazed on his son, lost for so long. Father and son held each other in a brief but forceful bear hug until Mike pounded Gavin's back several times and stepped back with an enormous grin of pure joy flooding his face.

"We found ye, lad. By God we did. Where's the gun ye nearly took me head off with?"

Gavin laughed. "Would I be trying to trap food if I had a gun?"

"I can't believe we found you," Mike said, shaking his head in wonder.

"I'm so sorry, Da. One thing led to another. I never meant to be gone so long."

"It doesn't matter," Mike said, and Sarah could see that it really didn't.

Mike held his hand out to Sarah.

"Young John's missing," Mike said. "Gone looking for you."

"Aw, shite, no," Gavin said, shaking his head. "I was afraid of that."

As they walked to Gavin's campsite, he told them his story. From Father Ryan's lie to Gavin marrying his beloved in the woods to...everything that had happened after. When he and Sophia fled the Italian campsite, they'd run until Sophia collapsed. Gavin had found a dry crofter's cabin to stay the night. They'd walked all the next day too—heading due south and keeping in the woods and off the roads. They'd been at their present campsite two nights because Sophia wasn't ready to go on. Yesterday, when he was out looking for something to eat, he found the pit and covered it up, in the hopes of snaring food.

"I think you bagged a fox," Mike said. "He was none too pleased to be sharing his place with us."

Even Sarah could tell Gavin had changed in the six weeks he'd been gone. A boy had left and a man now strode into the rough campsite where a young girl sat waiting. And not just a man because he'd married—that in itself was enough to shock anyone—but in the manner that he'd been forced to rescue her.

That had changed him.

When they arrived at the campsite where Sophia was waiting, Sarah couldn't help but notice how much the girl looked like her mother—right down to the hunted look of fear and sadness in her eyes.

"Sophia," Gavin said, "this is me da and stepmum."

"Hello, lass," Mike said. He didn't reach out to shake her hand. She sat with her mangled hand roughly bandaged and held to her breast.

"You look like him," she said in a strong Italian accent. "Like Gavin."

She's still in shock, Sarah realized as she sat down in front of the campfire. There was a rabbit on a spit over the flames. Sophia turned away to stare into the fire.

"Are you in pain?" Sarah asked. She had no pain relievers with her but they were well equipped back in Ameriland.

Sophia shook her head and smiled sadly, still only looking into the fire. "I am good," she said.

"I didn't want to rush her," Gavin said, sitting down on the other side of Sophia, his feet wrapped in rabbit furs.

"I like what you've done with your footwear," Mike said grinning.

"Aye? Just like the American Indians, so it is," Gavin said.

"I can't believe we've found you," Sarah said. She reached out and gently touched Sophia's uninjured hand. Sophia continued to stare at the flames but slipped her hand into Sarah's. Sarah was struck by how childlike the girl was. She couldn't be nineteen years old and she'd already suffered so much.

"You'll be okay now," Sarah said softly.

Sophia nodded. "I know. I know this from the moment I first see *mio cara*."

The next morning, Sarah was awakened by the sounds of Mike and Gavin breaking camp. She felt guilty about not being able to fully revel in Mike's elation. She felt like a bad wife and a mean-spirited soulmate to allow her own desperate sadness to seep into these moments of rare joy. But she couldn't help it. They were all going to bundle up their pathetic belongings and limp the last fifty miles of cold, wet road to the compound—where there would be warmth and hot toddies and going to bed every night with full stomachs.

And John would be nowhere near any of it.

The thought of the journey was almost more than Sarah could bear. She watched Sophia as she slept by the fire. *How nice to be oblivious*, Sarah thought. *How perfect it would be to just close your eyes and wake up when this nightmare had played itself out instead of having to endure every miserable, agonizing moment of it.*

Mike left Gavin and came to sit down next to her in front of the fire.

"Thank God," Sarah said. "One down."

Mike took her hand. "Aye. One to go."

"I can't go with you," she said, surprising herself that the words were on her tongue, let alone in her head. She hadn't known before she spoke that that's how she felt.

"I can't go back without him. Not even to restock or get the other truck. I'm sorry, Mike. I can't."

Mike squeezed her hand and they watched Sophia wake up and look around the campsite in a growing panic until she saw Gavin, a backpack on his shoulders, come out of the nearby bushes. Then her face relaxed.

"Ye know he's nowhere in Ireland," Mike said gently.

"I know."

"All right then."

Gavin sat down next to Sophia and gently lifted her wounded hand.

"Are ye about ready?" Gavin said to Mike and Sarah. "We should make it by nightfall tomorrow if we put our minds to it."

"We'll not be going with ye, lad," Mike said. "You two go on. Your Auntie Fi will see to your bride. You'll both be well. And we'll be along anon."

Gavin gaped at them. Sarah turned to Mike in stunned surprise.

"Where the hell are ye going?" Gavin asked.

I would love to know that too, Sarah thought, as Mike's big calloused hand squeezed hers.

"We're going to Rosslare," Mike said.

The minute he said the name, Sarah's shoulders relaxed and the tension she'd been holding dissipated.

Yes. That is exactly where we're going.

"Rosslare?" Gavin said, frowning. "Blimey, why? Didn't you say he's in Wales?"

"Aye, but we can't get to Wales," Mike said, smiling sadly at Sarah. "So Rosslare is as close as we can get."

"That makes no sense," Gavin said.

"It will when you're a parent."

"You'd go to Rosslare when you know he's not there? Instead of coming to the compound where there's comfort and family and safety?"

"It's a different kind of comfort," Mike said. "Did I ever tell you the story of the Irishman, many years ago, who worked as a day laborer and had five bairns?"

Gavin slowly shook his head.

"He was a good father and loved his children dearly but the one lad—the youngest—was his favorite, as much as you're not supposed to have those." He smiled.

"This lad was smart and cheerful—a grand little fellow and everyone loved him. One day, the lad took sick and died as bairns do. The father was devastated, so he was. After the child was laid to rest in the parish kirkyard, the man found it hard to carry on with his life as it was before. He ate little and began to disappear for hours several times a week. His wife became worried and decided to see for herself what he was getting up to.

"One day she followed him to the church graveyard when he was too focused on his own grief to know she was there. She watched hidden from the bushes as her husband lay down on the grave where their lad lay buried, his head by the gravestone, and he stayed that way for half an hour or more."

Mike paused as if bolstering himself for the telling of the rest of the story and Sarah's eyes filled with tears as she pictured the heartbroken father.

"After her husband left, the wife went to the grave of their little lad. She walked around it and saw a rock that shouldn't have been there next to the headstone. She picked it up and saw there was a hole underneath."

"A hole?" Gavin said. Even Sophia had turned toward Mike to listen.

"Aye. A hole just big enough to fit a man's arm into. And just deep enough that when the grieving father lay on his stomach and pushed his arm into it his fingers could touch the wooden coffin that held the child he loved so much."

They were all silent for a moment. Finally Gavin took in a long ragged breath and spoke to Sarah. "You need to be near where he last was."

Sarah nodded, not trusting herself to speak.

"We'll go too," Gavin said, reaching for Sophia's hand.

"Nay, Gavin. Take your lass home. Take her to the compound."

"It's my fault he's in Wales. If I hadn't left that fecking note…"

"It's doesn't matter, lad. Your coming can't change the past."

"How about the future?" Sophia said softly. Three heads turned to look at her, her eyes clear for the first time since the attack. "We are a family now. We should stay together."

Gavin looked at both Mike and Sarah. "Sophia's right. Families stay together. We'll all go to Rosslare and wait for John there. Together."

Tears gathered in Sarah's lashes as she realized that in the space of fifteen minutes she'd begun to hope again for a miracle. And that miracle began with a walk to Rosslare with these three people on a cold, wet Christmas Day.

Susan Kiernan-Lewis

20

The snow in Oxford piled up in great banks of white, making the inside of the little brownstone all the cozier. It was impossible for John to believe that tomorrow was Christmas Day. He hated not being home for it and knew his mother and Mike were having a sad day—especially if Gavin hadn't found his way home yet. He imagined it was snowing in Ireland too. He wondered who was helping Mike with the horses now that he and Gav were gone. It was Christmas Eve. And while that holiday in the compound didn't look anything like it had in Jacksonville when he was a kid, John had to admit it was still pretty wonderful.

The whole place would be busy with baking pies and roasting pigs and chickens. They even had a big Christmas tree in the middle of the camp decorated with ornaments people brought from their own homes or found in abandoned cottages. The gifts were modest—certainly not on the scale of the Xboxes or iPads he'd once known. But somehow it was still magical.

The longing he felt today for his mother and for Gavin and Mike was as physical as if someone had slammed his hand in a door.

"Penny for them, then John?" Gilly said from behind him.

He tossed the book he was trying to read on the couch next to him and moved the magazines off the cocktail table to make room for the tea tray she was carrying. She placed the tray down and sat opposite him.

"Nothing, really. Just wondering what my mom is doing today is all."

Gilly poured tea into three mugs. Obviously her father would be joining them soon.

"I hate you not being with your family for Christmas. Blame the weather," Gilly said handing John his mug. "If it weren't for about six inches of snow, you'd be on your way home by now."

John spilled hot tea on his hand and quickly placed the mug on the coffee table.

"What are you talking about? I'm not supposed to leave for another two months."

"Oh. You mean the deal you made with my father?" Gilly blew on her tea as if she were totally relaxed but John could see her fingers trembling.

"I told him that was nonsense. I told him there's no reason why you shouldn't go home."

"In fact, it's already done," Dr. Heaton said as he descended the stairs from the bedroom and walked into the salon. It was a rare day off for him and he clearly didn't know what to do with himself. He and John had visited the commune twice in two weeks in order that the doc could carefully examine their buckets and filters. John wasn't sure how the knowledge he gained translated back at the lab with his own bucket system but at least the doc seemed to be thinking from a different perspective.

"Really coming down, isn't it?" Dr. Heaton said as he stood by the window in the salon.

"What do you mean it's already done?" John pressed.

Dr. Heaton sat and dropped two sugar cubes into his tea mug.

"I booked the three of us on a medical transport to Belfast. It was to be my Chrissy prezzie to you, lad, but the weather wouldn't cooperate. Still, it'll only delay us a day or two."

John stopped listening. The whole salon seemed to dissolve away in his mind when Dr. Heaton delivered the words *I booked us transport to Belfast*. He was going home! He looked out the window to see the snow coming down harder. And even if he missed Christmas day with them all back at the compound, he'd see his mom soon and she'd forget how sad she was today.

A big grin spread across his face. This had just turned into the best Christmas *ever*.

The rest of Christmas Eve was quiet as the three of them enjoyed a roast beef dinner with Yorkshire pudding and fruitcake with real whipped cream. As they sat in the salon in front of the fire, John saw movement from a group of people outside and felt himself tense up. Although he hadn't felt the need to be on guard since he was in Oxford, a baseline wariness never left him. *Be ready.*

"There's someone outside," he said to Dr. Heaton.

"Aye. I should think so," Dr. Heaton replied. He poured a tot of brandy into his coffee.

"It's the carolers!" Gilly said, hopping up. "Come on, John. You'll want to see them."

He followed her into the foyer and she pulled open the front door. Five people stood out front stamping their feet, bundled up against the cold, their cheeks rosy and chapped by the wind.

"Happy Christmas!" they called out in unison.

"Happy Christmas," Gilly said. She pulled her coat off its hook and slipped into it but stayed inside the foyer.

Sandra Lynch was one of the carolers. John also recognized Dr. Davis, one of the other researchers from the lab. They sang *Jingle Bells* and then *Good King Wenceslas* and finished with *Noel*. John draped an arm around Gilly although he'd never done anything like that before. The combination of Dr. Heaton's brandy and the familiarity of the music gave him a warm happy feeling that called for sharing. He knew she wouldn't mind.

Dr. Heaton appeared behind them just as the group was finishing. After an energetic round of applause, he invited them all in for drinks. Only Dr. Lynch took him up on it. As they waved the rest of the carolers off, she joined them in the foyer, kicking snow off her boots and rubbing her hands together.

"We'll soon get you warmed up, my dear," Dr. Heaton said, taking her coat and ushering her into the salon.

John wondered if Dr. Lynch could possibly have joined the carolers for the express purpose of being invited into Dr. Heaton's home for Christmas Eve drinkies. He thought it extremely likely. Dr. Lynch sat down with them in front of the fire and Dr. Heaton poured drinks for everyone.

"To Christmas," Dr. Heaton said raising his glass. As soon as they all drank, John heard a sound that he'd heard every day of his life for ten years and then never again. The distinct sound of a cellphone vibrating against a hard surface. At first he couldn't place it, but Dr. Heaton jumped up and hurried to the console in the adjoining dining room where he picked up the cellphone and spoke into it.

"Daniel?" he said into the phone. "Happy Christmas, old son!"

John looked at Gilly. How had he not known they had working cellphones? She smiled at him with a slightly confused look on her face. Her eyes were dreamy in a way that reminded him that he'd held her in a one-armed hug not fifteen minutes earlier. Clearly *she* hadn't forgotten.

"I didn't know you had cellphones. Why didn't you tell me?"

"Were you going to call someone?" Dr. Lynch asked dryly her eyes watching Dr. Heaton talking on the phone.

"Not everyone does these days," Gilly said, glancing over at her father. His face was animated in a big grin as he listened to his brother at the other end of the line. "But because of his government work, naturally, Dad needs to be reachable. He doesn't carry it."

"Do you…is it possible I might make a phone call later?"

Gilly frowned. "I thought you said your mom didn't have phones where she is?"

"She doesn't. But my grandmother in the States does."

*****

John would always remember the sound of his grandmother shrieking with delight to hear his voice. It nearly made up for not being with his mom on Christmas. He spoke to his grandfather too and heard him choke up with emotion as he wished him a Merry Christmas over and over again. As their only grandchild, John knew the sacrifice they had made to let him go the year before. John couldn't wait to tell his mom that they were well and sounded great.

Dr. Lynch left around eleven o'clock and Dr. Heaton went up to bed a few minutes later with admonishments that Father Christmas would bypass the house if two naughty children were still up and awake. John and Gilly sat in front of the fire with mugs of cocoa. John's mind was in a whirl from everything that had happened that night and it was impossible for him to even think of sleep. He imagined his mother smiling and laughing. He prayed Gavin had made it back home safe. He imagined how wonderful it was going to be to put the whole awful episode behind them. As soon as his mind formed the thought, his heart clenched at the idea of losing Gilly and the doc.

"You know Dr. Lynch is in love with him," Gilly said.

"You think so?" But John had already figured that out.

"Oh, definitely. But she's really plain, don't you think? I mean, I know she's smart and all."

"She's in your dad's lab all the time."

"See? What did I tell you? She's practically stalking him."

"Yeah, but I'm not sure she's there for that reason."

"What do you mean?"

"I'm probably wrong."

"Tell me."

"Well, it's like she's always asking what he's working on and how much he's done and has he found anything new."

"You think...she wants to steal his cure?"

"I don't know. It just doesn't feel very...collaborative, you know? It's more nosy than that."

"I don't trust her one bit."

"I don't think I do either. She's really hard to like."

They sat quietly for a moment staring into the fire, listening to it pop and crackle as the flames devoured the sweet scented applewood.

"I can't believe Dad bribed you to stay because of me," Gilly said.

John looked at her in surprise. She was still staring into the fire.

"What?"

"I'm not a basket case, you know. I guess that's what he thinks of me."

"Parents worry, is all. About everything. My mom's the same way. And maybe that's the reason I stayed in the beginning but it's not the reason now."

She looked at him, her eyes glowing in the reflection of the fire. Her long dark hair tumbled luxuriantly around her shoulders. "Truly?"

"Yeah, definitely. I mean, I'm excited to see my mom and everyone again but I hate the thought of leaving you and your dad."

"Maybe you could just go back for a visit and then come back to Oxford."

"I wish it were that easy."

"Why isn't it?"

"Because…listen, come with me and your dad to the commune sometime and you'll see for yourself. Living like that —which is a lot like the compound in Ireland—everyone has to pull their weight or everyone else feels it. They need me." He turned back to the fire and sighed. "I knew that when I left but I thought finding Gavin was more important. It's a hardship me not being there and not just because my mom's worried about me."

"You're lucky," Gilly said sipping her cocoa and watching him, "to be needed like that."

"Jeez, Gilly, you're needed. The doc needs you big time. And you single-handedly brought me back from death's door."

"All I did was give you broth and hold your hand."

John reached out and took her hand. "That was the best part."

She squeezed his hand and it seemed that both of them held their breath for a moment.

"I really want you to meet my mom," John said softly. "She'd love you."

Like I think I do, he wanted to say, but for now it was enough that he thought it.

"I'd like that," Gilly said, as she leaned into him.

John leaned toward her and kissed her on the mouth. She smelled like lilacs and lemons and chocolate. A tendril of her long hair tickled his nose. She kissed him back.

*****

The next morning—Christmas morning—John watched the dazzling sparkle of the frozen River Cherwell as he and Dr. Heaton walked across the High Bridge. There was not a building or a tree to mar the pristine blank canvas of the river caught in midwinter.

"That's the University Park just there," Dr. Heaton said, pointing to the west bank of the river. "In summer it's paradise. I wish you could see it."

"It's pretty gorgeous right now."

"Aye, but in summer there are picnics and boating and cricket. It's lovely just to walk through."

Gilly had made them a hearty English breakfast before she curled up in front of the fire with the new books she'd gotten for Christmas. John wasn't entirely sure how things had changed between them after last night's Christmas Eve kiss but he knew he liked whatever it was. Hesitant but sure; tentative but secure. He had come downstairs before she did and when he heard her steps on the stairs, butterflies had kicked off in his stomach in a very pleasurable way.

"So John, lad, are ye excited about going home?"

"I am, sir. I can't wait to see everyone. I only wish you and Gilly could come with me to the compound. I'd love for you to meet my family."

"Well, another time we will for certain. As soon as we've got this disease on the run, Ireland will open its doors again. You'll see."

"I sure hope so. Was that your brother on the phone last night?"

"Oh, aye. That was Daniel. I'm sorry you won't have a chance to meet him."

"He's in Parliament, right?"

"Aye, that he is. And doing a smash up job, too. It's no secret he's the reason I got the lead on the work for the cure. Can't let him down."

The doc got quiet after that and it crossed John's mind that his brother might be giving him a hard time about not coming up with a cure yet. He hoped the guy hadn't said anything to spoil the doc's Christmas. When they got to the lab, not surprisingly, they were the only ones in the building. John wasn't entirely sure why the doc wanted to come in this morning but he suspected that his buckets had become a sort of touchstone for Dr. Heaton.

Why doesn't he just bring 'em home? It's not like they're sterilized or special in any way. But the doc was secretive about his work—with everyone but John. John assumed this was because he wasn't threatened by a kid. The way the other jerks in the department and the lab spoke to Dr. Heaton made a pretty good case against ever bringing anyone into your confidence.

In the lab, Heaton flipped on the overhead fluorescent lights and John went immediately to the workspace he'd carved out for himself weeks ago. In the corner of the lab near one of the sinks and under a glass-fronted cabinet was a narrow zinc-topped bench with a stool pushed up to it. On the table John kept his textbooks and a series of notebooks he'd begun writing in. Part of his notes had to do with things he found interesting either in the lab or in Oxford itself. He wanted to be able to tell his mother in detail about his experience here.

The doc's work surface took up most of the main workbench in the center of the room. On it was an assortment of high-powered microscopes, test tubes, a series of immunoassay analyzers and a microplane reader. In the middle of the state-of-the-art immunology equipment sat two white plastic buckets. Dr. Heaton went to the buckets immediately and began inspecting them.

John pulled out his stool to sit when he noticed that one of his notebooks was on the floor. He froze. He knew without a doubt that he'd left all this books and notebooks stacked neatly and lined up parallel to the edge of the table. There was no way he would've unknowingly knocked one of his books on the floor before he left the lab yesterday. He looked at the doc who was humming and pulling a mesh filter out of the lid of one of the buckets. There was also no way that the doc ever came over to John's area and even if he did, he wouldn't mess with John's notebooks.

John reached down and picked up the notebook and flipped through it. Had somebody come into the lab after he and the doc had left yesterday? He knew the doc always locked up but that meant less than nothing. These old locks could be sprung with a paperclip. He stopped turning pages when he came to the place where one page had been torn out, leaving only a remnant clinging to the metal spiral.

A vibration began in his fingers as he realized he was holding proof that someone had gone through his notebooks and taken a page from them. He flipped to the page before and suddenly remembered the missing page held his personal notes about Dr. Heaton's progress in the lab.

21

Finlay tried to remember what late December had been like in his childhood. Cold to be sure. Young John and Gilly were sitting in front of the fire with a pile of good books and more hot chocolate than was good for them. He smiled at the picture.

Nothing in Oxford came close to the bone-chilling walk home from school with Daniel each day when they were boys. Over the moor and two miles across the pasture—or *civilization* as Daniel liked to call it. Finlay grinned as he let himself into the lab. Two days after Christmas, still a holiday weekend and the halls were empty. Finlay preferred it this way. One didn't have to nod greetings or affect a mindfulness that didn't exist. Didn't everyone have way too much to do with their own work to care a toss about what anyone else was doing?

But he knew the lab wasn't that way, had never been that way and likely never would be. Mostly, his colleagues tried to be congenial, even if their efforts were insincere.

All but one. He moved to his lab bench and dumped his briefcase and coat on the chair, frowning as the thought and image of Ethan White came to mind. Ethan hated him. Even Finlay could see that. Ethan never missed an opportunity to sneer or roll his eyes at Finlay, or to cut him as they passed in the hall.

Ethan had been his first friend in Oxford, and his first lab mate. They'd gone to conferences together, and holidayed together with their families. Finlay rubbed a tiredness from the bridge of his nose. Little Ben and Gilly had been natural playmates. Poor little sod.

He turned and walked to the small kitchenette in the corner of the lab.

How many summer holidays had they spent together as families? How many Christmases, for that matter? Jenny and Cynthia weren't quite as natural a pairing as the husbands and kiddies had been, but they enjoyed each other, Finlay was pretty sure.

Well, at least until the Queen's Birthday five years ago.

He filled the electric kettle from the bottom bucket in the water filtration system sitting on the counter next to the sink. He pulled a small teapot down from the open shelf and jammed in four tea bags before walking over to his desk. He booted up the computer. Most people had very limited Internet access these days but for what Finlay needed, limited would do fine. He sat down and typed into the search engine window, *plague effects city or country?*

The news sites were going full force on the trajectory of the plague and making a big deal of the fact that it wasn't in Ireland yet. Huh. The plague and snakes. Wonder what poor ol' Ireland is doing right?

He found a couple bloggers debating about whether or not the disease was worse in the countryside or the city. While history wasn't his strong suit, he seemed to remember that the black plague had hit the cities the hardest. After a few minutes, he got up to stop the screaming teakettle.

How could the general consensus be that the plague's effects were no better in the country? Was that true? Was there a reliable news source that could corroborate that? Because if it was no better in the country than in the city…if that were true… it would mean that whatever Geordie's commune was doing to ward off the effects of the disease had nothing to do with *where* they were. He poured the boiling water in the teapot and watched the tea bags bob to the top before resettling the lid.

If country folk are every bit as affected by the disease as anyone else then is there something about the commune itself? He glanced over at his workbench. He had three sets of buckets. Two of them were from the commune. He'd swapped buckets with them and completely disassembled them.

As he waited for the tea to steep, he took down a large mug and rummaged in a drawer for sugar. He'd have to drink it black. He'd forgotten to bring milk. His wife Cynthia used to drink it black. He remembered his old Scottish auntie admonishing Cynthia about it once, calling it "that filthy Russian habit." Probably no surprise that Cynthia never wanted to go back to visit.

Gilly was ten years old the June they went to London for the Queen's birthday celebration. He could still remember Gilly standing with little Ben at the barricade and watching the spectacular Trooping the Color parade out of Buckingham Palace. After a long and exhausting day, it was that night at dinner that a drunken Jenny had informed the table—children included—that Ethan and Cynthia had been "doing the dirty" for months behind everyone's backs. Finlay never did hear the story of how Jenny found out. It didn't matter in the end. One parade five years ago had terminated two friendships and one marriage. Jenny moved out as soon as they got back to Oxford. Finlay heard she moved back to her parents' home in Dundee with Ben. Three years later they'd both succumbed to the plague.

As for Finlay and Cynthia things weren't so straightforward. He loved her and Gilly needed her. He knew if there was a way to get past Cynthia's infidelity, he needed to find it. He blew on his tea and stared out into the winter sky. It was midday but already it was darkening.

Cynthia said she wanted the marriage to work. She insisted the affair had not been her idea. And because Finlay so needed to believe her, and because he couldn't go back in time and change the facts of what had happened, he chose to do the only thing he could do to right the situation—for Gilly's sake if no one else's.

He changed *himself.* He accepted the crime, forgave it, and pushed it from his mind.

His glance fell upon the three plastic buckets. His hands began to tremble slightly. Something was happening. Something was forming in his mind. An idea had been burrowed deep in his brain and was finally making itself known.

He walked over to the buckets, and set his tea mug down next to them on the counter.

What if I don't alter the water? What if I alter me?

He looked at the dark tea water. And suddenly the answer was *right there.*

It's the tea. The dandelion tea.

He looked out the window and then at the door as if he needed to run, as if he couldn't decide what to do next. His hand went to the mug of tea and then stopped and he turned and ran to his desk and his computer.

Of course! It's the fecking tea. It's whatever chemical is in the damn dandelions. They all drink it. It's not what they do to the water before they drink it. Bloody hell. It's what they do to their bodies as they're ingesting it.

He laughed out loud for the first time in five years.

*****

For John, the two week Christmas holiday was going to be a time to explore Oxford, to read a stack of books in the doc's library, and to fine tune his notes for his mom about life in the UK. John decided to spend most of his two weeks away from the lab because the doc seemed to be obsessed with some new idea that had to do with his buckets—at least John thought they had to do with the buckets.

He and Gilly took long walks together where they developed alternative scenarios in which she either came to the compound to live with him—which was easily the less attractive fantasy as far as *she* was concerned—or where John remained with her and her father all the way through his graduate education. It was a fun daydream and whenever John forced himself to really open his eyes and see, he had to admit that the present was more stimulating than anything he'd experienced in the past four years. And, given the past four years, that was saying a lot.

Bad weather had again forced them to postpone the medic transport to Belfast. The next scheduled one that Dr. Heaton could get all three of them on was later in the month. John found he didn't mind. He'd get home soon enough. He knew that now.

One morning before the Christmas holidays were over as the doc was putting together his briefcase and getting ready to leave for the day, Gilly came bounding downstairs to say her friend Amelia had invited her on a family picnic to Stratford-upon-Avon. John knew that the numbers of infected people in Oxford proper had continued to drop, and healthy people were getting back to normal social activities. The pubs, for example, were doing a booming business. It amazed John that here in Oxford life was almost back to business as usual, when just three hours to the south crazy Mr. Quig was serving a desperate clientele whatever swill he could scrape off the walls and floors to sell them.

"Want some company?" he asked the doc after Gilly ran back upstairs to get ready for her day. "I haven't been to the lab in awhile."

"I would thoroughly enjoy that, John my lad," Dr. Heaton said jovially. He'd been very enthusiastic lately and while he'd been spending longer hours at the lab, he'd come home tired but happy. John pulled the collar of his wool jacket up against his neck to ward off the biting cold as he and Dr. Heaton walked down the street.

"Seen Dr. Lynch lately?" John asked. He and Gilly had been talking about how Dr. Lynch hadn't come by since Christmas. John's theory was that if her interest really was romantic, she'd come to the house. Otherwise, if it wasn't, if it was something more sinister...then it made sense she only showed up at work

"No, no. Nobody in the lab over Christmas," Dr. Heaton said cheerfully. "Everyone has families to be with."

So do you, John wanted to say, but he knew it didn't matter. Dr. Heaton had an important task. A world-shattering important task.

"So are you having more luck with the buckets?" John prodded. "Were the commune buckets significantly different from anyone else's?"

Dr. Heaton stopped walking and John paused to look up at him.

"Can I tell you something, John?"

"Sure." John grinned. It definitely sounded like the doc had an inside track on a new idea and John couldn't be happier. He had hated the thought of leaving Oxford before a breakthrough happened. He knew it would happen. It was only a matter of time. And it sure would be awesome if he could be around for it.

The doc looked at him appraisingly for a moment and then glanced over his shoulder but no one was anywhere near them. He leaned over and whispered in John's ear. "I think I've found the key to the problem."

John felt a thrill run through him like an electric shock. Had the answer been in the bucket filtration system all along? John tried to imagine a more perfect response to all the naysayers and jealous coworkers if it turned out that Dr. Heaton's buckets really had been the answer.

"That's awesome, sir. What is it?"

175

"Well, first, let me ask you. What do you think the commune does differently in treating their water?"

The commune? John's heart began to race. Had the doc found his new idea from visits to the commune?

"Beyond boiling and filtering it? I don't know."

"Well, that was a trick question," Heaton said, chuckling. "Because the answer has nothing to do with how they treat their water, different or otherwise."

"What do you mean?"

"It has to do with their way of life."

"Living outdoors?"

"More like the adjustments they've made to adapt to the new world order after the bomb dropped."

John was silent for a moment. "You mean them using herbs when they get sick."

"And one herb in particular."

"The Dandy tea?"

Heaton stopped and looked at him, his brows drawn into a frown. "How did you know?"

"Just a guess. It's the one thing they all drink. So you think it's the tea?"

"I think it might be a chemical that's in the tea." Dr. Heaton began to walk again with John at his side.

"But Geordie says some of their people have gotten sick. Some even died."

"I believe the way it's prepared—as a brewed drink—is not as strong as it needs to be effective."

"Is it a cure, do you think?"

"I think it's everything."

"Does this mean you're going to tell the whole country to go boil dandelion leaves?"

"No, if what I think is correct, I should be able to find the curative ingredient so that it can be administered in concentrated form."

"Geordie's grandma says that's what got us into this situation in the first place."

"I have immense respect for Mrs. Bancroft. But I also believe science can enhance what nature has given us."

"So you'll create a chemical compound from the herb to be used as a final stage purification? Instead of chlorine?"

"Nay, lad. Didn't I say? The herb doesn't kill the virus in the water. It fights it in the body."

"Wow." John grinned at him. "It figures the Brits would find a way where tea is the answer to everything."

Heaton laughed. "Too right, me boy!" They hurried up the stone walkway and through the archway toward the laboratory. Heaton was so excited about getting back to work on his new theory that he practically jogged down the halls. When they arrived at the lab, he fumbled with his keys to unlock the lab door and swung it open.

At first, John thought they'd opened the wrong door. He couldn't immediately process what he was seeing.

The lab tables were all tipped over, chairs and stools broken or on their sides. Papers were littered everywhere. Beakers, pipettes and test tubes were cracked and scattered across the floor like a carpet of broken glass. The buckets were disemboweled and flung across the room, all the cabinet doors and drawers were open, their contents thrown on the floor. John stepped through the door behind Dr. Heaton who stood with his briefcase in his hand.

He stood over a pile of mangled dandelions ground into the linoleum.

Susan Kiernan-Lewis

22

If someone had told John five years ago that there would come a time when he missed being in school he would flat not have believed them. The two-week school holiday after Christmas, while great in theory, was eventually way more than he needed or wanted. So he was thrilled when Gilly finally agreed to walk out to Geordie's commune with him—even though it looked like more snow coming. What was not so thrilling was the break-in yesterday at the doc's lab—and the fact that the doc asked him to keep it quiet.

Why didn't he want to tell people? John could understand not telling Gilly. She worried about everything there was to worry about. She even outworried his mom and that was saying something. But he also made John promise not to mention it to Dr. Lynch or any of the other researchers in the lab. Since John was pretty sure the sabotage was the work of one of those other doctors, keeping it quiet didn't make sense either.

All of the doc's notes had been taken and while most of the test tubes were smashed, the larger equipment, the mixers and analyzers hadn't been touched.

Almost as if someone expected to need them in future and wanted them in working order.

Although John didn't understand why the doc wanted him to keep it all quiet, what he did know as well as he knew anything was that he should have said something the week before when his notebook had been messed with. If he'd said something then, would it have changed anything? The doc could hardly lock the lab any tighter than he had. Maybe they could have asked for a guard to be posted?

No, even John knew there was little chance of that happening no matter who the doc knew in high places. There wasn't likely to be stronger security even after a break-in. After Dr. Heaton reported the incident to the university security staff, he just went about sweeping up the mess. When John asked him later if anything sensitive might have been taken, Finlay just tapped his head grimly and said: "Not unless they can get in here."

*****

"Hey, Earth to John!" Geordie yelled, giving John a poke in the ribs. Gilly, John and he were sitting on the top slat of the fence that corralled the commune's herd of goats. "I hope you're thinking of a new way to milk a goat. The old way's practically got my fingers worn to a nub."

"Ha ha," John said. It was a cold January day but the sun was shining and creating mesmerizing diamond effects on the fallen snow.

"So you're not vegan?" Gilly asked Geordie. She hadn't complained once about the long walk to the commune and John was grateful since the walk back always seemed twice as long and he didn't have much hope she wouldn't comment on it to him—over and over again before they were home.

"Oh, hell no. We have pigs and sheep. We'd do beef if it wasn't so much work. But we trade out services and milk and stuff for that."

"And not free love either," John said nudging Geordie.

"Crikey no," Geordie said. "Nor drugs. Although I'm pretty sure some of the older kids smoke weed."

"But what's the point?" Gilly asked. "I mean I can see why John's family has to do it in Ireland because they don't have their infrastructure any more, but here? We've got cars and electricity and pretty much everything we had before."

"The elders in the commune—our parents and aunts and uncles—believe that living like this is better for us because it's more natural. They think this plague is the direct result of some of the scientific messing about that's been done with our medicines and our food."

"So you're one of those who's never been vaccinated?"

"No, we've most of us been vaccinated. I don't know about the ones born this year but we're not crackpots. We just want a more honest way of life."

"The way I live isn't honest?"

"I'm not trying to hurt your feelings."

"But that's what you think?"

Geordie looked at John who shrugged.

"I'm not judging how anybody else chooses to live," Geordie said. "I just know what works for me."

Mollified, Gilly looked at the paddock of goats.

"Do you go to school?"

"It's not my thing."

"How is it you two are friends then?"

"Oh, you mean because eggheads should only hang out with eggheads?" John said, arching an eyebrow. "Thanks a lot, Gilly."

"I was just teasing."

"Besides, we got a couple kids here who are keen for school and so they go." Geordie shrugged. "We're not anti education. We're just *pro* personal learning styles."

"That is actually pretty cool," Gilly said.

John beamed with pride in her and it struck him that this was a new feeling. Was it possible he had a girlfriend?

*****

Two weeks.

It had been two full weeks since he, Finlay, had figured out the key to the damnable disease. Two weeks since the flash of brilliance had struck him. How many times had he thought about exactly where he was standing when the notion hit him? The media would want to know. The Nobel prize judges would ask. How deliciously agonizing it was to say nothing to Sandra and Daniel about what he'd found. They looked at him as if he were just ordinary or worse. And yet, he'd done it. He'd found the thing nobody else could find. Nobody in the whole world.

Except he hadn't.

How was it possible that it wasn't the tea? It had to be! And how many times in the last two weeks had he uttered those words? First mildly but confidently and finally in frustration and desperation.

It had to be the tea.

Only it wasn't.

He looked at his hands as he sat at his lab bench in front of one of the heavy duty lab mixers. It wouldn't do to throw the damn thing across the room—as if he could lift it. Even the bastards who'd trashed his lab had been respectful of the size and cost of the thing. How could it *not* be the dandelion tea? What possible sense did it make? He'd had no trouble extracting key compounds from the dandelions and making super strength concentrated tea. He'd done the tests a hundred times. But the tea had zero effect on the virus.

It wasn't the buckets they used at the commune.

It wasn't anything in the tea they drank.

His mobile phone buzzed and he saw it was Daniel again. This time a text: *Answer your damn phone, Finlay, or I'm coming down there.* Heaton sighed. Not now. Not now of all times. When was the last time he'd spoken to Daniel? Wasn't it right after he'd gotten the idea about the dandelions? Just putting it into words made him cringe. Thank God he hadn't said anything. It truly sounded as idiotic as it turned out it was.

He picked up the phone and punched in his brother's private number.

"*Finally,*" Daniel growled. "What the hell, Finlay? I do have to answer to people, you know."

"I know, Dan. So sorry, old chap. Beastly busy and all that."

"Last time we talked you were hinting at a breakthrough. That was two weeks ago. Well?"

"Well, as it turns out, not as breaking as I'd hoped."

"So nothing?"

"Well, not nothing. Every setback in research pushes you a little further ahead of where—"

"Yes, yes, Finlay. Spare me the encouraging mumbo-jumbo. Bottom line, no joy, is that right?"

"I fear so."

"No worries, old stick. These things take time. Pecker up, forge ahead and all that."

"You're being bloody decent, Dan, I have to say."

"Not at all. So is it the buckets?"

"I'm sorry?"

"The buckets. Are you still working on an improved bucket filtration system?"

"I…" Had he told Dan about the buckets? "Yes. That's right."

"Well, carry on then. And keep me informed. No rush but the higher ups need status reports. You understand."

"Sure, Dan. I understand," Finlay said before disconnecting and staring at the phone.

I understand. How jolly that meanwhile people were *not* dying by the hundreds. Children were *not* going to bed sick and then not waking up in the morning. No rush, Finlay. These things take time.

He put his head in his hands and lowered it to his workbench feeling the wash of defeat and despair wash over him like a tsunami of pummeling pain.

*****

Ethan White sat in the pub and watched his hands resting on the side of a glass of lager. He'd started coming here more and more in the last few months. At first it had been a balm. The noise of the place, even just a background murmur of voices, was soothing in a way. Nobody here knew him. It was too far from the college. Most of the others in the department went to the Portingon Inn. Close by. One pint. Usually just a half. Then home to the wife and kiddies. Ethan's heart pinched painfully at the thought.

Even after all this time? *I guess the pain really is forever when you screw up your life to the extent I did. God isn't content with just ruining your marriage and murdering your wife and child. He has to make sure you suffer every breath of every minute for the rest of your life.*

He brought the beer to his lips and drained it, setting the glass back on the wooden table with a satisfying thud.

So the bastard thinks he's found something.

The rumor was it wasn't just magic buckets this time, although Heaton was doing everything he could to make them all think he was still working on a better water filtration system. How's that for collegial sharing? Even with Heaton's own wife dead of the plague and the bastard still can't bring himself to collaborate for the greater good.

The memory of Cynthia slid into Ethan's mind like an invasive worm. Quiet, unobtrusive. But ready to suck all the pleasure out of life. He watched his fingers tighten around the empty glass.

What pleasure? A fucking beer alone in a pub? While Heaton prances about pretending to be near a cure.

Ethan fingered the hilt on his knife. He wore it in a leather sheath on his belt. Little Ben had made it for him as some sort of scout project. Ethan withdrew his hand and saw he was perspiring. What would the people in this pub think if they knew he worked with the killer plague virus every single day? Like all the other scientists in the lab, Ethan had the virus in a test tube on a shelf in his office. How else to find an answer to it? There were countless tests to be run. How else to prove that the millionth approach didn't work? Yet again?

But also how best to prove once and for all and to everyone that Heaton had precisely bollocks for the cure? Ethan looked across the pub and watched the fire in the hearth.

It's the stuff of every sappy Disney movie ever made, he thought with wonder. *The distraught doctor comes up with a cure just in time to save the life of his beloved daughter who was stricken with the disease...*

The tension in his hands eased around the glass and he felt an easing in his shoulders for the first time in months.

Wonder how frisky the bastard would feel then?

23

Something had happened. John didn't know what but it wasn't good.

After weeks of good moods and enthusiasm, now the doc came home lackluster and dragging his feet. Worse, now he brought the buckets home too. One night when the doc had gone up to bed just before dinnertime—something he'd started doing —John picked up a bucket left on the kitchen counter and saw that the doc had put a new mesh filter in it.

Like that was going to work! The doc had told John a thousand times how small the virus was. There was no way a mesh was going to catch it. Was this just a process that might lead to another way of thinking?

Or was it as desperate as it looked?

John had been so sure it was the dandelion tea. He couldn't believe all of the doc's tests came back negative. He'd been so sure! He'd tried on several occasions to engage the doc in questions about the failed dandelions.

"If it's not the tea then why is the commune healthier than the rest of the country? Why aren't they getting sick the same way?" But the doc was done talking about dandelion tea and the commune, too.

It was so frustrating. But as bad as it was for John it was worse for Gilly.

"It's just you and me again tonight," she said to him as she put two plates down on the table. "Dad's gone to bed. Says he doesn't feel well."

"He'll snap out of it. It's just...a terrible disappointment."

"He didn't act like this when Mum died. I've never seen him like this."

"It's just that he was so sure he had it." John should know. He was still reeling from the disappointment himself.

"What if he *doesn't* snap out of it?"

"He will."

"You don't know that. What if he doesn't?"

"I don't know, Gilly. Should you call your uncle in London?"

Her eyes widened and she glanced upward in the direction of her father's bedroom.

"Not yet," she said. "He'd kill me if I did. But if he gets much worse, I will."

She'd made beans on toast with slivers of pork roast. It was a favorite of John's—and of the doc's too. John felt guilty for enjoying it so much. He had three helpings.

The new date for his crossing to Ireland was in two days, the day after the first day back to school. There didn't seem to be much reason to wait and while John was excited about seeing his mother and Mike again, a bigger part of him was sorry not to be continuing on with school. He looked at Gilly as she cleared the table. This was probably a super bad time to be leaving her, he thought. *The doc's a basket case and with me gone she has nobody but him.*

Should he stay? How about if he went over just long enough to tell his mom he was fine and then came right back? Was that crazy? In the last few weeks he'd thought about every possible scenario and most of them came down to the fact that leaving didn't feel right. Not just yet. On the other hand, if he had any hope of ever getting back to Ireland, Dr. Heaton and his medical transport were probably it. Even the doc said things were heating up and the transport might not be an option in another couple of weeks.

When Gilly came back to the table, he put a hand on her arm as she reached for their silverware.

"I'll never be able to thank you enough for all you've done for me, Gilly. Both you and your dad."

She sat down hard in the seat opposite him and her eyes filled with tears.

"It's me who should be thanking you," she said. "I was so lonely here with just Dad. You've seen him. Even when he's not depressed, he doesn't talk to me."

John frowned. "That's not true."

"He thinks girls are useless."

"Now I *know* that's not true. He's always saying how clever Dr. Lynch is. And you too."

"Good try." Gilly wiped her eyes and gave him a tremulous smile. "But that's okay. It's just how he is. He's very paternalistic. It would never occur to him to talk to me. Not about important stuff like he tells you."

"He doesn't tell me stuff."

"No, it's all right, John. He's got you and I'm glad." She squeezed his hand. "But most of all, I'm glad because I've got you, too."

*****

Two days later when John woke up, he saw it was steadily snowing again. He sat at the kitchen table watching Gilly's back as she silently prepared his breakfast. The truth was, her silence was easier to take than the manic and fake cheerfulness she'd been trying for the last few days. More honest anyway.

She turned and thumped a bowl of steel cut oatmeal in front of him and then one at her place setting. She went back to the kitchen counter for a tray and brought it back, transferring a creamer, a pot of honey, and a bowl of toasted nuts to the table.

"Sorry no Sultanas," she said as she sat down and picked up a spoon.

"Sorry?"

She frowned. "You call them raisins?"

"Oh. No problem. This looks great." He poured the cream and honey over his oatmeal and smiled too broadly at her.

Damn. Now who's being obnoxiously cheerful? Afraid she'd get the idea he was happy to be leaving, he leaned across the table toward her. "It's not forever, Gilly."

"I know. Do eat your porridge John while it's hot."

You'll make a great mother, John thought but wisely did not say.

A book fell in the living room where Dr. Heaton was sitting. Because they were travelling today he wasn't going into the lab. In fact he hadn't gone into the lab for the last two days.

Nothing had improved on that front. Meanwhile he barely spoke to them.

Is this really the best time for me to be leaving her? he thought for the millionth time.

"There's oatmeal, Dad," Gilly called to her father. "But no brown sugar." She looked at John and gave a half-smile. "Dad and I both love brown sugar on our porridge. Have you ever had it that way?"

John nodded as he ate his breakfast. "Yeah, brown sugar is great."

Dr. Heaton walked into the kitchen and poured himself another mug of hot tea. He stood staring out the kitchen window for a moment seemingly oblivious to the fact that both John and Gilly were sitting in the room having breakfast.

Gilly cleared her throat. "But the honey's pretty good, isn't it, John? I'm not sure I don't like it better."

John looked at Gilly and then at Dr. Heaton. She was trying so hard and the guy just really could give a shit about honey or brown sugar or the price of rutabagas in China.

"I like it better," John said encouragingly to her. "Did you get this from Geordie?"

"I did. I didn't even know they made honey until you and I went out there last week. It's lovely."

The sound of the mug shattering against the tiled kitchen floor made both Gilly and John jump.

"Dad! Are you okay?" Gilly said, her voice shrill.

Dr. Heaton stood with his back to them staring out the window. John could see the doc's hands were gripping the counter so hard his knuckles were white. He turned around slowly and gazed over their heads with his mouth open.

"Dr. Heaton?" John said, wondering if the doc was having a stroke.

"Dad!" Gilly jumped up and grabbed her father by the arm. He seemed to snap out of it then and drew her into a hug. He smiled at John over her shoulder.

"It's the honey," Dr. Heaton said.

An hour later, after they'd postponed the transport again, they were all three driving back to the commune at Rosemont. The countryside looked like an old-fashioned oil painting of froth-topped cottages with mile after mile of ancient fieldstone walls crisscrossing the snowy pastures.

Only Dr. Heaton was more excited than John, who not only got to stay on in Oxford, but was likely going to be in on the big discovery.

Of course! The honey. It not only went in all the tea the commune drank, it went on just about everything else too. Not everybody drank the Dandy tea—no matter what Geordie's Granny said—but everybody in one way or another ate the honey.

It continued to snow as they drove to the commune and in spite of slower going due to icy roads, they made good time. Geordie had obviously seen the SUV coming down the long driveway. He was standing on his grandmother's porch pulling on a heavy coat. They jumped out and walked over to him.

"Oy, John! I thought you was gone today!" Geordie called.

"I was supposed to be," John said. "Dr. Heaton was wondering if we could see your beehives."

"What for?"

"It's not the hives so much, lad," Dr. Heaton said, his face flushed with excitement, "but the fields they frequent. The flowers they pollinate."

Geordie shrugged. "Follow me."

He led them to the back of the commune. The snow continued to fall and it occurred to John that they might have trouble getting home. Every hut they passed had a chimney with smoke coming out of it. When he'd first visited the commune there had been a central cookfire but it was cold and unused now and under inches of snow.

"Surprised you'd want a tour on what some would say is the coldest day of the year," Geordie said over his shoulder. "But as Granny says, 'there's no telling with city folk.'"

He led them to the back fence of the commune and opened a gate which they all filed through. Gilly was shivering but John didn't dare suggest she stay in the car or go warm herself at Granny Bancroft's hearth. She was every bit as excited as he was about her dad's theory.

Please let it be the real thing this time.

The little white bee houses were lined in two rows of five huts each. The looked like oversized birdhouses with gabled roofs. The field they were sitting in was brown with no hint of whatever weed or flower must be rampant in it in the spring. Geordie went to the nearest hive and knelt by it. He unlatched the lock and pulled out a bottom board to show where the bees built their brood chambers and stored the honey.

"It's right in there, like," Geordie said, pointing to the frames that slid in and out of the hives. "This isn't my job, mind, but it isn't very tricky. The honey is collected from here. Of course, the bees are all hibernating now."

Dr. Heaton squatted next to Geordie and fingered the frame and then looked past him to the field.

"It's really more the flowers I'm interested in, lad. What the bees make the honey from."

Geordie stood up and looked at the field now covered with snow.

"Well," he said, "there's goldenrod, of course. And tansy. Oh, yeah, and borage. Granny uses that in her medicinal concoctions too. And in salads."

Dr. Heaton shook his head. "No, those aren't any good. Are you sure? Is that all the plants?"

"Well, all the ones the bees are interested in," Geordie said. He looked at John. "What's going on? Why the interest in the bees?"

"It's not the bees," John said. He could see discouragement on the doc's face. "We thought there might be something in the honey that y'all eat. You know, as the reason y'all aren't as badly affected by the disease."

"Oh, I see. I'm sorry, Dr. Heaton."

"Me, too, lad." The doc looked out at the field, the lines of his face drawn downward. They turned to walk back to the commune.

"Are you going to test the honey we have at the house, Dr. Heaton?" John asked.

"Sorry, lad?" Dr. Heaton looked at him wearily. "Oh, yes, of course. It's just that if the honey came from goldenrod or even borage—no offense to your grandmother, Geordie—there's little likelihood it could serve as any sort of herbal prophylaxis."

Geordie turned to Gilly. "Do you have both kinds of honey?"

She frowned. "I didn't know there were two kinds."

"What is it?" John asked. "Blackberry flavored or something?"

"No. Wasp honey. We eat loads of it, too."

"*Wasp* honey?" Gilly said, looking over her shoulder at the bee hives on the other side of the fence. "I didn't know wasps even made honey."

"Oh, yeah, they do. But we don't have hives for wasps because they're such buggers, you know?"

"Well, how do you get their honey?"

"We basically find their nests and steal it from them," Geordie said with a laugh.

Dr. Heaton stopped and put his hand on Geordie's shoulder.

"Are the wasps in the same field as the bees?"

"No, they hang out in the woods. Granny had us move their nests from the woods to the front gate to be more convenient like."

"Also a pretty effective security system," John said with a grin.

"You're not kidding," Geordie said.

"What flowers do the wasps pollinate?" Dr. Heaton asked. The way he asked the question seemed to suck all the oxygen in the air around them. It seemed to take forever before Geordie answered.

"Moonflowers," Geordie said.

The transformation in Dr. Heaton's face was immediate. His eyes widened and the flush returned to his cheeks. "Take me there," he said.

The excitement ran through each of them as they hurried back through the center of the commune. When they reached the front gate, Geordie turned to the right and led them to a thick copse of trees. Only a dusting of snow had reached the ground beneath the trees. The light was dim and it was eerily silent. They walked quietly, listening to their own breathing and the soft crunching of their steps on the brittle needles that carpeted the ground. They soon came upon a small clearing. Geordie went to the center of it.

"Here," he said.

Dr. Heaton walked at once to a dead tree that was broken and hollowed out by animals and weather. Up the side of the tree, nearly invisible against its bark, was a network of brown vines.

"Is that it, Dad?" Gilly whispered. "Is it what we're looking for?"

"It's the moonflowers, aye," Dr. Heaton said. He touched the delicate vines with a finger.

John came closer but there wasn't much to see. The vines held no flowers and no leaves. They looked a little like the morning glory vines his grandmother had in her backyard in Jacksonville.

"So these are better than goldenrod?" John asked.

"For our purposes, aye, lad. It's also called Jimson weed. It's a highly toxic herb."

"Is that good?"

191

"Gran says the moonflowers are bad poisonous," Geordie said. "But she says something happens in the abdomen of the wasp so we don't die when we eat their honey."

"Alchemy, me lad," Heaton said, his eyes bright with revelation. "It's called alchemy."

24

The medical transport was delayed another week. John knew how close Heaton was to a cure now. Sidetracked by the failure of the dandelion herb as the possible key to the cure, the doc was nonetheless further ahead because he'd at least accepted the idea of an herbal solution.

It wasn't the tea. It was the honey the commune used *in* the tea. Honey that had been made by wasps that pollinated the flower called Datura or Jimson weed. While the accidental alchemy of the wasp's honey enabled the little commune to escape the worst effects of the disease, Heaton focused on finding an antidote to the herb's inherent poison while isolating the chemical that killed the virus.

John continued his classes with Gilly at the college and went to meet the doc at his lab in the afternoons. The difference in the man's attitude—the very atmosphere in the lab—was electrifying. Not only had the doc been right about the honey, he was making dramatic strides towards a useable cure derived from it.

Three days after their visit to the Rosemont commune, John was hurrying down the corridor toward the lab. The other docs still loitered about the halls or occasionally pressed their noses at the window of Heaton's lab. They knew something was up. You'd be insensate not to feel it, John thought with building joy as he opened the door to the lab.

Sandra Lynch sat next to Dr. Heaton as he studied a slide through one of the high-powered microscopes. She still had her coat on so either she hadn't been offered a cup of tea and an invitation to hang around, or she didn't expect there to be reason to stay. John nodded politely to her before going to his own little corner of the lab and dumping his textbooks.

When the hell does she have time to do her own research? And if she thinks the doc is such an idiot, why is she always hanging around? The idea that Dr. Lynch fancied the doc seemed less likely the more John got to know her. Besides, was her perennially pinched face and wrinkled brow really the face of someone in love?

"What are you talking about?" Sandra Lynch's voice was nasal and high. John turned to glance at her and the doc.

"We know the disease involves both bacterial and viral elements and which complicates treatment," Dr. Heaton responded. "This twofold agency doesn't respond to any of the normal approaches. But it's the virus component that's had us flummoxed."

"I do know this, Finlay," Dr. Lynch said sourly. "I have my own work, you know."

"The disease's bacteria can be removed and killed by filtering and boiling the water but these purification methods are irrelevant against the virus."

"Well, ineffective anyway."

"No, *irrelevant*. It's not the virus in the water that's the problem. It's the virus once it gets *in the body*."

"I see. What will you tell me next? That water quenches thirst? Or that butter comes from cows?"

"He's saying we need to treat the person drinking the water *not* the water," John said, standing up.

Dr. Lynch turned to look at John as if surprised to see him there. John figured it was entirely possible she hadn't noticed him when he came into the lab.

"Exactly," Dr. Heaton said. "I believe it's a waste of time to look for ways of killing the virus in the water before people drink it. We need to sort it out once the virus is in the body."

"And…you've done that?"

John watched Dr. Heaton pull the test tube stand out from behind a stack of books and he had to grin. Looks like the doc had a little bit of showmanship in him after all.

"I do believe I have."

Dr. Lynch's eyes went to the test tube filled with a pale amber fluid. A strong beam of sunlight from a north facing window illuminated it. No one spoke for a moment. Dr. Lynch seemed unable to stop looking at the test tube. John moved closer to the bench.

"Is the formula...complex?" she asked finally.

"Let's just say I don't believe anyone else will replicate it," Dr. Heaton said firmly. For the first time, John saw a flash of steel and determination in the scientist's face.

"Does it work?" she asked.

"It did on fifty mice and half a dozen chickens."

"Infected with virus-contaminated water?"

"Yes, Sandra. Wouldn't be much of a test otherwise, would it?"

"Are you saying it's a cure *and* a preventative?"

"Taken in heavy doses, my discovery should mitigate the effects of the disease in persons already infected before they receive the compound. I believe most will eventually survive as a result. But—and this is the key thing—the compound blocks the disease-causing agency of the virus in persons who take it *before* the virus gets into their bodies. It prevents the virus from its normal pathological pathways in the human body."

Dr. Lynch straightened up, her thick shaggy eyebrows were brought together in a frown. John figured it was a pretty safe bet she didn't love not being taken into Heaton's confidence over what was in the new cure. But to her credit, she swallowed it down.

"Well done," she said.

"Thank you, my dear." The moment between them was brief and, if you weren't looking for it, virtually nonexistent. But John had seen his mother and Mike play this game for two full years before they finally admitted their mutual attraction. He couldn't read adults that well but he could see Dr. Lynch was all in and Dr. Heaton was at least willing.

"What will you do now?"

"Take it to London where it'll be prepared in quantities for mass distribution."

The two stared at each other as if they were the only ones in the room and John had the awful feeling that one of them was going to lean over and...He cleared his throat.

"You know, sir," John said from across the room. "It's weird that Ireland thinks it's safe from the disease because all it takes is birds drinking the infected water to fly across the channel and end up in someone's lunch to bring the disease to Ireland."

Both Dr. Heaton and Dr. Lynch turned and looked at John, who felt his face flush with embarrassment. Had he said something incredibly stupid?

Dr. Lynch was the first to speak. She didn't take her eyes off John.

"My God, Finlay. Where did you find this boy?"

"He found us," Heaton said with a proud smile. "Clever, isn't he? And you're right, John. It's only a matter of time before Ireland has the sickness too. Which is all the more reason."

Dr. Heaton readjusted his attention to the test tube in front of him but Dr. Lynch continued to stare at John. He'd been taught that staring was impolite and now he knew why. If Dr. Lynch's face revealed anything about what she was feeling, it wasn't very nice.

*****

Dinner was a festive affair that night. Gilly had quite outdone herself, what with her joy over her father's new good mood—and the fact that John was still in Oxford. John knew the doc's discovery was a game changer for him. Not only would his colleagues have to look at him differently now, but the discovery would mean more money and more research opportunities. The doc was even talking about visiting the States. There would be all kinds of invitations now.

After dinner, Gilly and John did the dishes. Gilly planned to spend the evening studying for a geography exam. They were headed to London in the morning and she didn't want to get behind in her studies.

"It wouldn't hurt you to hit the books, too, you know," she said to John.

"Why? I won't be here long enough to get a grade. After London your dad says we're heading straight to Belfast."

"I know."

"Well, there doesn't seem much point in studying."

As they were finishing up with the dishes Dr. Heaton came into the kitchen. He had his coat over his arm.

"Darling, will you be all right if John and I pop down to the Horse and Queen for a quick one?"

"Absolutely," Gilly said, tweaking John's cheek. "Have one for me."

The walk to the pub was a half mile of mostly residential sidewalks with enough salt dumped on them to prevent slipping on yesterday's snowfall. The blast of cold air as they stepped out of the townhouse mixed with the excitement that both of them felt. John had never been to London before and was excited about being there for Dr. Heaton's great triumph when he handed over the details of the cure to his brother and the government authorities.

"Does your brother know why we're coming to London?" John asked as they walked toward Alfred Street. Knowing the doc as he did, it was entirely possible he had told his brother this was just a visit.

"He knows I have a breakthrough."

"Did you tell him it's Moonflower honey?"

"All in due time, John. All in due time." Dr. Heaton smiled, his eyes twinkling as he clapped his gloved hands together in unrestrained delight. John guessed there was more to Dr. Heaton's relationship with his brother than he was letting on. Adult siblings tended to have complex interconnections. Or, as Mike used to say, it wasn't all skittles and beer.

"And you didn't tell Dr. Lynch?"

"Oh, she was keen, wasn't she?" Dr. Heaton laughed. "She wanted to know so badly she could taste it."

"After the break-in a couple weeks ago, I figured she wasn't the only one who wanted to know what you were doing."

"Aye, that was upsetting. Sandra would've had nothing to do with that."

"Maybe not. But the day before the break-in I had some notebooks rearranged and one of the pages ripped out."

"Really." Dr. Heaton didn't appear upset by this information.

"You think Dr. Lynch could've done it?"

"Hmmm. Well, I suppose. You know, John, hyper curiosity is one of the bedrocks of the scientific mind."

John shook his head in frustration. *Was the doc really saying it might've been Lynch and that was okay?*

"Won't be long now, lad," Dr. Heaton said as they waited to cross the street to the pub on the other side. "You'll be home in the bosom of your family. I'll be on my way, well and truly. And the people of the UK and Europe can finally begin to heal."

"How soon until the medication is disseminated to all of them?"

"Well, it will take time to manufacture it in large quantities. But once that's done, I'd say just as soon as Daniel's pushed it through all the red tape."

"You'd think with everybody dying left and right that they'd dispense with the bureaucratic barriers."

"You would, wouldn't you? Don't go into politics, John."

"What made you want to go to the pub tonight?"

"Funny you should ask. When I was a boy, my father used to take me and Daniel to the village pub for a pint on Christmas Day."

"Oh, that's cool"

"It's true we're well past Christmas but the sentiment is the same. And as you'll be leaving us soon and I don't have any sons except yourself..."

John felt a warmth well up inside his chest. He knew the doc was fond of him. But to realize the doc felt toward him almost as if he were his own son...John struggled to contain his emotions.

"Thank you, sir," he said and hoped the doc didn't hear the catch in his throat.

"Call me, Finlay. I should've insisted on it weeks ago."

John thought he detected a similar catch in the doc's throat.

Thirty minutes later, John sat at a scarred wooden table in the Horse and Queen pub while the doc went to the bar to get their drinks. John recognized it as the same pub they'd stopped at on their way to Oxford nearly three months earlier. John stretched his hands out to the fire. Tomorrow this time he'd be in London. And two days later he'd be back in Ireland. Dr. Heaton was working to arrange ground transportation to the south but even if John had to walk the entire way, he'd be home by the beginning of February.

It wasn't goodbye. He'd make sure it wasn't. Some day he'd get back to Oxford and the doc was right, now that the medication was soon to be distributed, Ireland would ease its border restrictions. John thought of traveling back here for next Christmas with his mother, Mike and Gavin. The thought gave him a warm flush of happiness.

It had been an amazing adventure. One he'd never forget. But now it was time to go home. Back where he belonged.

*****

At first Ethan didn't recognize Heaton. He hadn't expected to see him in this pub. Seeing him here felt like such an intense invasion that Ethan actually looked around to see if anybody else felt the same way. But the people around him appeared oblivious to the fact that Heaton was even there.

Heaton went to the bar and began joking with the man behind the counter. Ethan could see the barkeep grinning and nodding like a sort of lower classes ape hoping for a tip to be thrown his way. And Heaton was slapping his hands on the bar and laughing as if this was his bar and he'd been coming here every night for months.

Unbelievable!

Ethan looked around the bar again. *Surely to God people were seeing the fucking injustice of this!* The bastard took Cynthia and then when Ethan had lost his own wife, after she walked out because she couldn't forgive him, Heaton and Cynthia had stayed together. That contradicted the one thing he'd counted on. Heaton would throw Cynthia out and she'd run to Ethan. Only Heaton didn't throw her out. He forgave her and the only one whose life went totally to shit was Ethan White's.

His plan to expose Heaton's incompetence by infecting his daughter never got off the ground. The girl was rarely alone and any attempt he made to approach her had been unsuccessful. She looked at him like he was the fucking bogeyman. Not surprisingly, Heaton had probably told her that her mother's death had been Ethan's fault.

It's what I would've done.

His eye fell on the back of the young teen sitting alone at a table near the fire. It was the American boy who lived with Heaton. The one who spent all his afternoons at the lab. The eyes and ears for Heaton, telling all the news and all the secrets from everyone else in the department. Heaton's spy. And now Heaton steps up into academic glory for a nonexistent cure that nobody believes he really has and he keeps his daughter *and* he gets a brilliant son too?

Is anything about that fair?

Ethan bared his teeth and stood up suddenly, knocking his glass of lager over. All heads turned to look at him. Heaton grimaced from the bar and looked away in disgust.

No. You do not get to feel superior to me. Not after everything I've lost because of you.

The knife was out of its sheath and in his hand. His feet moved. There was no way he could stop this. The rightness of it was absolute. Heaton's back was to him at the bar.

Two steps from him now.

*****

At first John wasn't sure what he was seeing. He turned to check on what was taking so long with the beers and saw Dr. White behind Dr. Heaton, holding a knife high in the air.

"Dr. Heaton!" John shouted.

White slammed the knife down into a solid punch into Dr. Heaton's back. Once. Twice. Two men standing nearby grabbed White's arm. The bartender held up a long truncheon in both hands but the men were already pulling White away. White screamed in frustration.

Dr. Heaton slid down the front of the bar, the two glasses of beer he'd held falling to the wooden floor. John bolted from the table, pushing onlookers aside. White was ranting, screaming that Heaton had ruined his life. The knife, coated with blood, lay next to Heaton's head. John turned to the bartender.

"Call 999!" he yelled. The bartender, his face white and shocked, dropped the bat on the counter and bent to grapple for the phone under the bar.

John put his face to Finlay's ear.

"Hang on," he said. "Please just hang on. Help is coming." But when he pulled back, he saw Dr. Heaton's eyes were open. And unseeing.

25

The memorial service was held at St Andrew's Church in the village of Old Headington, outside Oxford. It had been built in 1160 and to John it looked more like a Norman fortress than a church. The snow had begun to melt and the rolling kirkyard that surrounded the church resembled a muddy motor cross track littered with headstones. All throughout the service and the drive there and back, John felt like he was in a dream.

A really bad dream.

Gilly had lost it. John knew she would. Everything since the moment Ethan White stabbed Finlay Heaton to death in front of fifteen more or less sober witnesses had been a whirl of pain and tears. John's and Gilly's. He listened now to the silence in the townhouse where Dr. Heaton would never come, not looking for his supper, not ready to report his day at the lab.

Not ever again.

The police had arrested White of course. It was amazing how uninterested John or Gilly were in what happened to him. Put him in jail, hang him or let him go. What difference did it make?

Nothing could reanimate Finlay Heaton.

Daniel Heaton, Finlay's brother, had come down from London for the service. John was surprised he didn't come down sooner but Gilly said he was very busy running the country and she hadn't expected him to. Daniel Heaton SMP looked very much like Finlay, John noted. He couldn't remember which one was the older sibling and nobody was talking about that sort of thing. Daniel, John, Gilly and Dr. Lynch drove back to the townhouse together after the memorial service as some of the college wives had gotten together with the neighbors to set out a table with casseroles and roasts and drinks.

Gilly hadn't let go of John's hand almost since the moment he'd delivered the bad news to her. He didn't mind. Right now, he needed her as much as she needed him.

He still couldn't believe the doc was gone. It was impossible to fully gel in his mind that he'd never see him again, that he'd never go back to the lab. That Dr. Heaton was not going to be a part of his life going forward. When he thought of it in terms like that—words that took him step by step though his grief and the future he'd have now without Dr. Heaton—then and only then did he want to take a metal bat to Ethan White.

As soon as they got back from the church, Daniel Heaton could be seen standing by the front door to greet people like a one-man receiving line. Geordie was in the kitchen with two large pies from the commune—and a hug for Gilly. He was in and out in a flash though. John didn't blame him. It was almost harder dealing with the bereaved than being the bereaved.

When he noticed Daniel pull Gilly over to stand beside him, John frowned. Gilly needed taking care of right now, not being forced into service. But she smiled bravely and shook hands with everyone who walked in the door. After a few minutes, John saw that seeing all the people who'd loved Dr. Heaton and were so sad, well, it actually seemed to be helping. Gilly looked like she'd pulled herself together.

"It's a terrible thing," Dr. Lynch said as she stood next to John, a plate in her hand, the two of them watching Gilly and Daniel greet everyone.

"I still can't believe it," John said.

"Well, I can well believe that tosser Ethan White did what he did," Dr. Lynch said, her mouth twisted in a moue of distaste.

"You knew he was capable of this?"

She hesitated and then put her plate down, uneaten. "No," she admitted. "Not this."

"It was you who ripped out the page of my notebook, wasn't it?"

She looked startled. "I don't know what you're talking about," she said, turning to go into the living room where she began talking to one of the teachers at the college. She kept her back to John.

Today was the day John was supposed to be on his way to Ireland. A cold finger of dread traced down his spine as he thought of his mother still having no clue where he was, if he was alive or dead. And now, how would he be able to get back to her after all?

Gilly broke away from Daniel at the door and came to John. Without thinking, he drew her into his arms and they held each other. She smelled like lemons and lilacs. She felt firm and strong in his arms, not like she was about to fall apart and John was reminded of how she was when he first met her. Tough, playful, resilient. She was going to be okay.

She pulled back and kissed him on the cheek.

"Have you eaten?"

"Some. You?"

"I will in a bit. Uncle Dan wants me to come live with him in London."

John nodded. "Makes sense."

"I asked him about getting you back to Ireland. He said he can't help us. Not even medical transports are going across right now. I'm so sorry, John."

"That's okay." But it wasn't. It felt like a block of ice had formed in the pit of his stomach. He was stranded here. After all these months of believing he had a way home, now the truth was he was trapped.

"Uncle Dan asked me a lot of questions about Dad's work," she said. "I told him Dad had a major breakthrough."

"Did you tell him about the wasp honey?"

She shook her head. "I don't know why I didn't."

John looked at Daniel Heaton smiling and talking to two elderly ladies who had just come into the townhouse. He looked like he was campaigning, John thought. When Heaton looked over unexpectedly and caught John looking at him, he gave a curt nod but no smile.

He doesn't want me here.

Gilly tugged on John's arm. "Come on, let's eat something. I will if you will." As John went into the kitchen with Gilly he looked back in time to see Daniel moving into the living room and tapping Dr. Lynch on the shoulder. The pair then quickly moved into the foyer and closed the glass door behind them, their heads were close together in private conversation.

*****

Daniel stepped into the back bedroom alone. The dresser top was clean of all personal effects except a silver framed photo of Finlay and Cynthia. Daniel's lip twisted into a grimace. That was classic proof of his brother's immensely poor decision-making abilities. The woman was a whore who married him because she'd gotten preggers. Because Finlay was too sentimental he wouldn't dream of insisting on a DNA test but now that Daniel and Gilly were the last ones standing, it was probably in order.

He walked over to the bed and sat down. Bloody bad timing although he couldn't blame poor Finlay for that. That stupid wanker White had gone and lost the plot and mucked everything up. The only good news was that—White's paranoia and rampant and unwarranted professional jealously aside— Finlay had still been no where near a cure. Lynch just confirmed that Finlay hadn't found anything. And if anyone would know, she would. Gilly on the other hand said her father had recently made a significant breakthrough. Probably with his buckets. Daniel had been sorely tempted to bury him with one.

His phone rang right on schedule.

"Cheers," he said, answering it. "It is as I believed. There are no breakthroughs, so no worries. There is no cure."

"But don't you have a team working on it?"

"Of course we do. But my brother was the lead."

"Well, what about the others on his team?"

"He wasn't working *on* a team. He had little to no interaction with the supposed members of his team."

"I thought you just said—"

"Look, the point is we're no closer to a cure and isn't that what we all want?" He lowered his voice although there was little chance of being overheard. "I'll have to reassign someone else as lead. Rest assured things move slowly in the world of scientific research. And for God's sake, settle down. I did just lose my brother two days ago, you know."

*****

Daniel and Gilly's goodbye was short if not particularly sweet. Gilly clung to him at the door and Daniel had to eventually pry her fingers from his jacket.

"Now, steady on, darling," he said, his eyes going to Dr. Lynch over Gilly's shoulder as if making a silent request. Dr.

Lynch remained seated in the living room. Everyone else had left and it was just the four of them again. Before Daniel had shrugged into his overcoat he'd taken John aside to tell him without any confusion that he wouldn't be able to stay.

"I don't know what arrangement you had with my brother," he said, raising an eyebrow at John as he prepared to depart back to London. "But it's over. The townhouse will be made ready to sell. You'll need to move along."

Now, as John watched the man physically attempt to disengage himself from Gilly, he couldn't help think how unfair it was that the wrong brother had died.

"Dr. Heaton's brother is kind of a dick," John said as Daniel finally escaped out the front door.

Sandra laughed. "You're not wrong."

Gilly came over and sat down heavily on the couch next to John. He picked up her hand. He'd told himself all day long he wasn't going to ask *are you okay*? Stupidest thing you can ask anyone who has just lost a parent. And he'd heard most of the people today say it over and over again.

"You look done in," Dr. Lynch said. It surprised John to hear it from her. She was the least nurturing person he'd ever met.

"I'm going to bed," Gilly said. "I'm absolutely wrecked. The doc gave me a pill to help me sleep but I don't think I'll need it tonight."

John gave her a hand a squeeze and watched her walk to the stairs. If it were him about to go to bed on the day he buried a beloved parent, she'd probably send him up with a cup of tea or something. He felt at a loss for a moment but the moment passed and she was gone. He looked back at Dr. Lynch. For the first time all day he saw her grief on her face and it startled him. Gilly was right. Dr. Lynch had loved her father. Even if she had a seriously crap way of showing it.

"Is it weird that Dr. Heaton's brother thinks the doc's work was still with a bucket infiltration system?" John asked.

Dr. Lynch's face brightened and she looked at John. "You mean is it weird that Finlay lied to his own brother, the same brother who'd hired him to find the cure in the first place?"

"Why would Dr. Heaton lie to him?"

"Maybe because he didn't trust him?"

"His own brother?"

She shrugged. "Finlay told Daniel he had a breakthrough. Daniel assumed it was with Finlay's *bucket* system. You and I both know the cure has nothing to do with buckets."

"Did you tell Mr. Heaton that?"

"I did not."

"Why not?"

"If Finlay didn't trust him, I sure as hell don't."

"But Mr. Heaton *hired* his brother to find the cure. It makes no sense."

"It does if you understand power. To save people or let them die is not the point. It's the ability to do so or not. Whoever has that power has everything. They're God."

They sat in silence for awhile. The ticking of the mantle clock was loud and John wondered why he'd never heard it before during all the times he'd sat in this room reading or watching the fire.

"He was an amazing man," John said.

"He was."

"I'll never forget him."

"He cared for you very much," Dr. Lynch said. They sat again in silence for a few moments before Dr. Lynch finally spoke again.

"Only three people know Finlay found the cure." She turned to John. "Me, Gilly...and you. And not the specifics of what the cure is either."

John felt a wash of unease creep over his skin like a million ants running up and down his arms.

"Are you sure he didn't share the specifics of his work with...anyone?" he asked.

Sandra narrowed her eyes. "It's one of the reasons he didn't make friends in the lab. Finlay didn't share his work with anyone."

Except me, John thought. *He shared all of it with me.* By the way Dr. Lynch looked at him, he didn't need to say it out loud.

She knew.

He took in a big breath. It doesn't matter. None of this matters. People were dying all over Europe and the United Kingdom. If John's idea about the birds was right, they'd start dying in Ireland before long. This discovery was too important. It couldn't die with Dr. Heaton.

"It was me," Dr. Lynch said in a low voice. John turned to look at her. She was staring at her hands in her lap. "I'd seen you write in that notebook. I don't know what came over me. I just wanted so badly to know what he was doing. I'm sorry."

"I told Dr. Heaton it was you," John said. "He said intense curiosity is the bedrock of a scientific mind."

"Well, that's bollocks. But I love him for it."

Suddenly John knew what he needed to do. John was the only one who knew the specific components of the cure. Dr. Heaton didn't even trust his brother with the truth. So John couldn't trust him either. That meant, if the cure was going to get to the people it was intended for—the people Dr. Heaton intended it for—John needed to take it there himself.

"I have to go to the World Health Organization," he said.

"That's in Brussels," Dr. Lynch said, frowning.

"I keep hearing how small Europe is compared to the States. How far is Brussels from here? Like the same distance from Tampa to Orlando or something?"

"There's water between here and there and the Chunnel hasn't reopened yet."

"How do people get across?"

"With the plague ripping up France, most people don't. Besides, what do you plan on bringing to them exactly? Only Finlay knew the formula."

John paused. "I do too."

Dr. Lynch leaned back in her chair. She closed her eyes as though she'd just finished a long fight and was now depleted. "I thought you might. Do you feel comfortable telling me what it is?"

John hesitated. Dr. Heaton hadn't told Dr. Lynch. And if he hadn't told her it was likely for a good reason. The problem was, while John knew it was the wasp moonflower honey that was the key to the medication, he also knew there was more to it than that. Whatever virus-inhibiting compound the doc had discovered in the honey had gone with him to the grave.

If anybody could recreate his steps in the laboratory, it was Dr. Lynch.

"It's a compound found in moonflower honey," he said.

"You must be kidding." She sat up straight and her eyes bored into his.

"Dr. Heaton was able to isolate the compound in the honey that inhibits the virus's action in the body."

"I'll be damned."

John's gut twisted. He'd just told Dr. Heaton's secret to one of the people Dr. Heaton hadn't trusted. Dr. Lynch looked like her mind was calculating a thousand different formulas in her head. Her eyes were hungry and alive.

She looked like someone who had finally gotten what she wanted.

26

The next morning—the day after John was to have gone to Ireland and five days after Dr. Heaton was murdered—John selected the largest jar of wasp honey in the kitchen cupboard. Dr. Heaton had stored his supply of six moonflower honey jars up high to prevent Gilly from accidentally using one of them for their breakfast. The doc couldn't risk keeping any of the honey at the lab.

While Gilly dressed, John carefully wrapped padding around the jar and slipped it into his backpack. He looked around the kitchen of the townhouse. This had been his home for three months and they had been good months and exciting months. He'd found love and acceptance here. He'd found a sense of where he belonged here.

He glanced at his backpack and fought back a shiver. There was still a major challenge ahead before he could even think of trying to find his way back to Ireland. If Dr. Heaton was right, once the cure began to affect mortality rates on the continent, Ireland would drop its border restrictions. However long that took, John would need to be ready.

A knock at the door brought John out of his thoughts. When he opened the door, Dr. Lynch stood there in jeans and a heavy wool pullover and snow boots that came up to her knees. She wore her hair down under a knit cap which framed her face. John was surprised to realize she wasn't as plain as he'd always thought. With her hair down, you could see her eyes better. She had pretty eyes.

"Morning," she said and moved past John into the house. "Is Gilly up yet?"

The plan was for Dr. Lynch and John to escort Gilly to London. What John had yet to mention to Gilly was that John and Dr. Lynch would then travel on to Dover before taking the ferry to Bruges and on to Brussels. There Dr. Lynch would work on the honey sample to attempt to replicate Dr. Heaton's cure. John hated keeping secrets from Gilly but even he could see she was fragile right now.

After Dr. Lynch left last night, John tried to make himself believe he could trust her. He tried to convince himself that telling her had been the right thing to do. After all, if he couldn't trust Dr. Lynch, they were all screwed.

Gilly came downstairs carrying two valises and went immediately to the teakettle. It was still hot and she poured water into a clean mug. John and Dr. Lynch glanced at each other.

"Morning, Gilly," John said.

"Morning," Gilly said, almost sullenly.

"Ready for our trip today?" Dr. Lynch asked. Gilly didn't answer. John went to pick up her two bags and carried them to the front door where he'd already set his backpack.

"Probably have time for a cup of tea," John said to Dr. Lynch. She nodded and set her own bag down.

Was it just sadness at having to leave? Then why did the air feel like it was jumpy and tense? Why did it feel like there was something not so much sad as *wrong* among the three of them? Confused and insecure, John went to fetch two more clean tea mugs.

****

Daniel picked up his cell phone and tapped in O'Reilly's number. He didn't have a whole lot of hope for a pleasant conversation but he did have an alternate way of handling things depending on O'Reilly's reaction.

"This is Shane Sullivan. Mr. O'Reilly is away from his desk."

"You are answering Mr. O'Reilly's private mobile now?" He heard voices on the end of the line and O'Reilly's unmistakable growl come onto the phone.

"Heaton?"

"Afraid you'll drop your mobile in the loo, Liam?" Daniel said, biting off every word. "Most people carry their mobiles with them. Hence the name." The stupid Mick had no idea about the concept of a clandestine operation.

"Why are you calling? Is it the cure?"

"I'm afraid it is. It appears my brother found something after all. Knock me over with a feather."

There was a pause on the line. "Are ye sure?"

"Yes, Liam. My source is in a unique position to know. She...*he* assures me it is a cure. It has to do with some kind of homeopathic approach."

"Who has it now?"

"That, at any rate, appears to be relatively contained. Only three people besides you and myself know the cure exists."

"And those other three people? Because *nobody* must know of this, Heaton."

"I am aware of that, Liam. I'm taking care of it on my end."

"I'm coming to London."

Daniel stared at his mobile phone. *Did the lout really just hung up on me?*

He tossed his phone down on his cluttered desk before turning and touching a button on his landline. "Get me Homeland Security Terrorist Division. Immediately. This is a Code Red situation."

*****

All John could think of was that Dr. Heaton had been so looking forward to making this trip with them. He'd talked about how he was going to take John to the Natural History Museum and the British Museum. As John watched the snowy pastures of the Cotwolds fly by the window from his train compartment, he was stuck by a keen longing to see his friend again. Gilly was still tense and brittle and John had begun to worry it might be the result of the drugs she'd gotten from her family doctor. He'd never seen her so jumpy and he wasn't sure sadness and tears weren't better.

Dr. Lynch, on the other hand, was oblivious to any tension in the train compartment. She was reading a science magazine and never looked up once, not to glance out the window or to make eye contact with Gilly or John. It occurred to John that ever since he'd told her about the moonflower honey, she had changed. She wasn't as tense or as flat. And while she'd probably never be friendly, she was no longer giving off cold, misanthropic vibes either.

It didn't do any good to second guess himself about whether he should or shouldn't have told her. It was done. They'd spend the afternoon in London with Gilly before taking the train to the coast. A small part of John was aware that if Dr. Lynch wanted to be shed of him for whatever reason—this afternoon would be the best time to do it.

"You excited about seeing London for the first time?" Gilly asked, her eyes glassy, her cheeks flushed.

"Sure," John said. "Wish my mom could see it too, is all." *And your dad.*

"Did you talk to Geordie about whether you can stay with him?"

Out of the corner of his eye he noticed that Dr. Lynch had torn her eyes off her magazine long enough to watch him for his response.

"I did. He's fine with it. I'll stay there until they open up the Irish borders again."

"That could take years," Gilly said. "Or never. God knows how long it'll be for someone else to find a cure."

Now he could definitely tell Lynch was watching them. He tried to keep his face impassive when he answered.

"I'll just hope for the best," he said.

The trip was only an hour long and pretty soon John saw the skyline of the city appear before him. Lynch had told him that London was largely unaffected by the EMP four years ago. He could expect the city to be nearly fully operational with people on the streets with cell phones, fast food restaurants on every corner, and whatever else was normal in a typical twenty-first century capital city. Though the effort to rebuild the infrastructure in outlying areas had mildly sapped London's resources, London would still be the first functioning modern city John had seen since he was nine years old.

Lynch stood up and looked out the window as the train approached the London Waterloo Rail station platform. "We can get the tube from here," she remarked rolling up her magazine and stuffing it into her backpack. "Are we dropping you off at your uncle's flat?" she asked Gilly. "Or his office?"

"Oh, his flat, I think," Gilly said pleasantly, smiling for the first time all morning. Maybe Gilly was the kind of person who doesn't deal well with transition, John thought. He was a little surprised at how cavalier she seemed to be about parting from him. They hadn't even discussed how often they'd take the train back and forth to visit each other.

Dr. Lynch and John both shouldered their backpacks and John grabbed up one of Gilly's suitcases while she took the other and they all disembarked. The platform looked old fashioned to John with large pavers and yellow limestone stonework on the walls with ornate rounded archways over the doors. He could almost imagine British troops going off to war at this station as he assumed they must have during World War II.

They walked toward the terminal and the station began to morph into a modern transportation hub before his eyes with dramatic soaring skylights that spanned the full ceiling like a cathedral of light. Even so, the pillars that held up the massive ceiling looked as decorative as they were functional. He glanced at Gilly. It wasn't terribly crowded but in the spacey mood she was in it wasn't impossible to think she might get separated from them.

"You okay?" he said. She smiled and nodded. It was then that he knew what the difference was. Gilly loved to talk and she'd spoken very little since the day started.

Definitely not normal. But was anything normal about today?

The crowd pushed them toward the inside of the station which looked to John like any major transportation center. His first sighting of a burger joint was nearly his undoing. He and his mom had brought back a small truckload of soft drinks to the compound last year—and then never heard the end of it from Mike—but it had been a long time since John had enjoyed a burger with fries and a shake. A quick glance at Gilly answered that question for him. She was totally focused on getting out of the station and getting to her uncle's—not stopping for a Happy Meal.

With one last look at the fast food restaurant, John told himself he and Dr. Lynch would stop in on their way back when they got their tickets for Dover. He could just see Lynch's dark green plaid jacket ahead of him with her orange backpack. In front of her he saw daylight from the station's main entrance but he knew Lynch was leading them to the departure platform of the Jubilee line tube station. John would have loved to have stepped outside for a moment just to see the city but he'd have his chance when they finally got to Knightsbridge.

Once they were settled in their seats on the underground train they rode two stops before getting off at Green Park station and changing to the Piccadilly line. It had already taken them an hour since they first pulled into London at Waterloo but John's

213

excitement and interest in everything he saw kept him wide-eyed and enthralled. Gilly slipped her hand into his when they switched trains in Green Park and they sat closely together, not speaking and not needing to, until they arrived at Knightsbridge.

"You know where your uncle's flat is?" Dr. Lynch asked Gilly.

"Walking distance," Gilly said cheerfully. "Just around the corner."

All of them were past ready to end this portion of the journey. John was hungry and cursed himself for not eating a bigger breakfast when he had the chance. He thought of the large jar of honey he had in his backpack and smiled to think even for a moment about eating a fingerful.

Guess I can starve a little for science, he thought. *It'll be my contribution.*

The tube station entrance on Sloane Street was packed with commuters and, because the station was so near Harrods, with shoppers too. That and the fact that it was pouring down rain kept the entrance congested with people.

"If you don't want to get wet," Gilly said to Dr. Lynch, "we can grab some brollies across the street there."

John saw a tourist shop with umbrellas sporting gigantic union jacks on them.

"I don't care," Dr. Lynch said. "I won't melt." She pushed out of the opening past the scrum of people and then stopped. John ran into her but instead of moving out of the way, Lynch turned around and grabbed his arm.

"Run!" she said, her face a mask of fear.

"What?" John tried to look around her.

"Run!" Lynch screamed and gave him a hard push that sent him falling into Gilly. Before he could collect his balance, he watched Lynch turn and begin to step off the curb. He heard four sharp reports—like firecrackers. And he saw her stagger and fall to the sidewalk.

John grabbed Gilly's arm and pulled her behind him into the crowd. She didn't resist and because everyone in the crowd was so much taller than both of them, they were instantly swallowed up.

"John! What's happening?" Gilly yelled but she ran with him, banging her suitcase against anyone who got in her way. He heard the pure panic in her voice. She'd heard the shots too. John didn't answer but flung the suitcase he was carrying into an open doorway. Gilly may have heard the shots but she hadn't seen what John had.

Six London police stood in full riot gear with their rifles pointed at the body of Sandra Lynch on the pavement in front of the Knightsbridge tube station.

Susan Kiernan-Lewis

27

John and Gilly wove through streets thronged with lunchtime office workers. John was torn between going back to where Dr. Lynch had fallen to see if this was all a terrible mistake or getting to the outskirts of London and the countryside as fast as possible. He didn't stop to think if that made sense. He just knew they had to keep moving.

Gilly was wild-eyed, her face red from the exertion, her eyes panicked. She looked at him and shook her head as if to say, *what will happen to us?* Deciding a full blown panic attack would slow them down worse than a rest stop, John pulled Gilly into an alleyway past a series of cashmere and jewelry shops.

He could see this was a ritzy shopping area. They probably wouldn't get mugged in the dark alley which was too narrow to accommodate cars. There was a loading dock half way down it and he settled Gilly on it before kneeling beside her. They couldn't be seen from the street here. A quick glance upward confirmed that there were no windows to worry about either.

Gilly was breathing fast. Like she was about to hyperventilate. John didn't dare take his backpack off. He didn't know how quickly they'd need to be on the move again. He squeezed her hands.

"You okay, Gilly? Take a deep breath."

"I didn't know they'd shoot her. I swear I didn't. You have to believe me, John." Her eyes filled with tears and she licked her lips, her eyes pleading. He stared at her, uncomprehending. Gilly *knew* the police would be waiting for them? How was that possible?

"I don't know how things got so messed up. It's all a mistake. You believe me, don't you, John?"

He put a hand to his mouth as if to stop himself from blurting the first thing he thought of.

"John?" Gilly's voice was plaintive.

"How?" he asked. "How did you know they'd be there?"

"I didn't!" Gilly said, wiping tears from her cheeks. "I just called my uncle to say we were coming."

Ice seemed to settle on John's heart. He felt his back stiffen.

"Three dudes with AK-47s weren't called out because you told your uncle we were coming to London," he said. "What else did you tell him?"

"I heard you and Dr. Lynch talking last night about going on to Brussels. I knew Dr. Lynch would try to take all the credit. You are so naïve, John!"

"You told your uncle there really was a cure after all?"

"I didn't know they were going to do this!" Gilly wailed.

John's head was swirling.

Gilly told her uncle about the cure. Her uncle sent a death squad to meet them.

"But why kill Dr. Lynch?" John asked. "She wasn't planning a terrorist act. It's almost like they wanted to silence the source of the cure."

Gilly looked at him with such misery he couldn't help giving her hand another supportive squeeze.

"Did you tell your uncle about the wasp honey?"

Gilly frowned, her eyes focusing on a distant unseen point as she thought. "No," she said finally. "Just that the cure involved an herbal approach."

John's thoughts were racing. What did this mean? Were they just after Dr. Lynch?

Or anyone who knew about the cure?

"We can't stay here forever," Gilly said. She had started to shiver.

"I know."

"We should go to my uncle's."

Was that safe? Would her uncle hurt Gilly?

"You trust me, right, Gilly?"

"With my life."

"I promise your father will get the credit for his discovery but I have to get this cure into the right hands. Can you give your uncle misinformation about where I went?"

"You mean tell him you went west when you really went east?" Her eyes filled again with tears.

"Don't cry, Gilly. I'm doing what your dad would've wanted. You know I am."

"I just can't bear the thought of losing you, too. Will you come back to London?"

"I need to go home, Gilly."

"But you can't. Nobody can go to Ireland."

"I'll go to Geordie's commune and wait until the preventative is everywhere and Ireland opens back up again. Even your dad said that's probably what would happen."

"Meanwhile we can visit each other." She sniffled and wiped her tears off her cheeks with the back of her hand.

"Absolutely." He gave her a hug and felt reluctant to let her go. She was his last friend in a crazy world of betrayal and lies. It was almost unimaginable that a week ago he'd felt so blessed and loved—and the prospect of seeing his mother and Ireland had been just days away—and now he'd lost everything —and was about to walk away from the one person he still had.

"You know," John said, "when Dr. Lynch saw the shooters she pushed us into the crowd and told us to run, like she was afraid *we* were in danger too."

"Who knows what was going on in her head?"

"I know she was odd, Gilly, but she seemed afraid for us." He pulled back to look at her. "Are you sure it's safe for you to go to your uncle's?"

"What are you saying? My uncle isn't the bad guy here!"

"His men just gunned down a renown Oxford scientist! What possible reason could there be except Dr. Lynch knew the cure?"

"That's crazy! Why would people *not* want the cure?"

"Dr. Lynch said it's not about the cure. It's about power."

"Well, she should know."

John looked at Gilly and felt a cold shadow flicker across her face.

"Does your uncle know that *I* know the specific ingredients of the cure too?"

She sighed, her shoulders sagging. "I was upset. I might have vented a little because Dad never shared his work with me. I'm sorry, John."

It didn't matter. What's done was done. John patted her knee and stood up. The only option going forward was to point Gilly in the direction of her uncle's custody and to somehow figure out a way to get to Brussels. Would Mr. Heaton assume John would try to continue on across the channel? Would the train stations be monitored?

Gilly pulled open her shoulder bag and pulled out a tissue which she wiped her tears with. In the opened bag on her lap, John glimpsed something dark and recognized her father's cellphone. John hadn't had a whole lot of experience with cellphones in his life but he knew one thing.

A cell phone meant they were being tracked.

The second the idea came into his head he heard the noise at the opening of the alleyway. He jerked his head to look behind him but the alley was a dead end. By the time John looked back at the entrance, a wall of six armed police with shields were marching steadily down the narrow alley toward them. Gilly saw John's face and stood up, dropping her purse to the ground.

Then she saw the police. And screamed.

28

John could see the river as they rode in the back of the black SUV through Westminster. He and Gilly had been immediately stripped of their bags and frisked but not handcuffed. They sat side by side, holding hands.

"Uncle Dan will sort all this out," Gilly whispered to John.

"No talking!" the guard said from the other side of the iron mesh grill separating the back seat from the drivers.

John squeezed her hand and tried to focus on the scenery outside the car. If he could get free—could he leave her here? What was the point of slipping away, even if he could? It seemed a better use of his time to just pray Daniel Heaton wasn't as big a jerk as he'd seemed at the memorial service.

And that somehow, please God somehow, he'd had nothing to do with the attack on Dr. Lynch.

The SUV drove into an underground parking lot where both John and Gilly were ushered out. The men who met them in the garage were not obviously armed, looking more like Secret Service than policemen, it seemed to John. He tried to take that as an improvement in their situation. Still holding hands, the two got into an elevator with three agents. They rode to the fifth floor where the doors opened. Two of the agents stepped off, then turned and grabbed John roughly by the jacket and wrenched him off the elevator.

Gilly screamed. John tried to see what was happening but the men dragged him down a long carpeted hallway. His mind raced. Why were they being separated? Was Gilly being taken to her uncle? He knew it was useless to ask the agents. As soon as they were sure he wasn't going to try to dash back to the elevator and Gilly, they released him and walked one in front and one behind him until they came to a set of double wooden doors. The first agent knocked on the door and then opened it. The second agent pushed John through.

The only furniture in the room was a small conference table with no chairs around it, a couch, a coffee table, and two straight back chairs in the middle of the room.

Sandra Lynch was zip-tied to one of the chairs. She sat with her head down on her chest, her hair covering her face. Her shoulder was sloppily bandaged and bright red was seeping from the wound and dripping to the floor beneath her. John ran to her and knelt beside the chair. He lifted her hair from her face and saw her lips were swollen and both eyes blackened. A spasm of fear ran through him. He looked around the room but the agents had left. Quickly, he ran his hands down to where her hands were tied behind her, but he had nothing to cut the plastic ties with. She groaned.

"Dr. Lynch, it's me, John."

They had done terrible things to her. But she was still alive. Why? Why shoot her and let her live?

"Wake up, Dr. Lynch. Please."

"Never you mind, lad," a strongly Irish accented voice said. John whipped his head around to see a stocky man with red hair enter the room. Behind him was Gilly's uncle, Dan Heaton.

John jumped up and faced them.

"Let her go," he said fiercely. "She's no threat to you. She's hurt."

"Aye, laddie," Heaton said. "We know. We're the ones who did the hurting. But if we untie her she'll fall over. Those ties are the only things holding her up." Heaton had an amiable smile on his face as if he was walking into a cocktail party. John got a sudden image of him at Gilly's house, smiling and nodding at people. It was only now he saw what a monster had been standing in their living room.

The Irishman put his hands on his hips as if to better survey John and Dr. Lynch. He walked over to them. John was struck by how coldly confidant the man behaved. John had seen this kind of attitude before in bullies. They so disrespect their victims—like say a dumb teenage kid and a woman scientist who's in the process of bleeding to death—that they don't even bother tying up the kid.

"Anything in their belongings?" The Irishman asked, although he was scrutinizing John so closely it was almost as if he were speaking to him.

"Nothing useful," Heaton said. "Clothes. Some food. A few magazines. No notes, no books, no slides."

"And you're sure they know the cure?"

"I am reliably informed, yes."

"The bitch won't talk?"

"As you see."

The redheaded man nodded then pulled his semi-automatic pistol out from a shoulder holster and walked over to John and Sandra.

"Oy! Doc!" he said loudly to Lynch as he held the gun to her temple. "Mind answering a few questions?"

John watched in horror as Dr. Lynch lifted her head from her chest. Her eyes fluttered open and she licked her swollen and bloodied lips.

"She's useless," the Irishman said in disgust. "You've gone too far with her. She's feckin' banjaxed, so she is."

"I told you." Heaton went to lean against the wall to observe. John could pick up nothing in the man's demeanor that indicated he was unhappy with the proceedings in any way.

"Let's try a different approach," the Irishman said turning to John. "Hello, lad. Feel like dying today?"

John stared at him and clenched his fists. He didn't answer.

"D'ya know why you're here, me boyo?"

Out of the corner of John's eye he saw Sandra turn her head slightly in his direction.

"Ye say this kid knows?" the Irishman asked over his shoulder to Heaton.

"Oh, he knows. Don't you, lad? Pretty close with old Finlay, weren't you? Just tell us what ingredients are in the cure and you and Dr. Lynch will be back on your bikes in no time. Sound fair?"

"He lies." The words from Dr. Lynch were rasped out but they were clear enough.

"So you aren't quite dead yet," the Irishman said to Lynch. "No matter. We're done with you." He put the barrel of his gun to her temple and then turned to John. "Tell us what you know or I'll kill her."

John felt a dizziness swirling around his brain at his words. He had no doubt the man meant them.

"John, no," Dr. Lynch said, struggling to lift her head. "They're going to kill us both anyway."

"True enough, Doc," the Irishman said with a vicious laugh, dropping his gun from her head. He fished his cellphone out of his jeans pocket and spoke briefly into it. "Shane. Bring the girl in. Yes, now." He hung up and turned to John. "Perhaps there's someone who means more to you."

Daniel Heaton walked over to the Irishman. His face was flushed with anger. "Look here, O'Reilly, I don't know how you do things in Ireland but this sort of thing won't wash over here."

"You have a better way? Even if they don't know the cure, we can't let them live after all this." O'Reilly waved his hand to encompass the room.

"Well, they *do* know the cure. My niece has assured me."

"Which brings up the topic of that little loose end."

"Are you suggesting I kill my own niece?"

John could see Dr. Lynch's head had collapsed onto her chest again. He didn't know if she was listening or if she'd really fainted.

"Don't bugger with me, Heaton. You don't give two tosses for the girl."

"I know I won't allow you to *murder* her, ye daft Irishman! Besides, what does it matter who knows what? Once you kill these two—off premises, thank you very much—whether they talk or no, the secret will be safe. As far as anybody knows there is no cure."

John nearly choked hearing his words and the cold-blooded way he spoke them. His arms trembled with goose bumps racing up and down them. So Dr. Lynch was right. It wasn't about the cure. It wasn't about sick people or doing what was right. It was all about power. He glanced over at Dr. Lynch. Her eyes flickered open again but she looked woozy.

"It *matters*, Heaton, because I want the cure. *Especially* if nobody else has it."

"Liam, if I didn't know better, I'd think that Ireland had started getting sick. Is that what's happened? Have you discovered your first cases on the Emerald shores?"

"That's none of your business. We had a deal and that's all you need to know."

"Well, this is no longer the same deal. So it *is* my business. You don't just need the cure to permanently go away, now it seems you need the cure, itself. That's different. Very different."

"I don't see how."

"I know you don't, Liam." Heaton turned to look at John and Dr. Lynch. "So what do we do with these two? Beat it out of them and hope they tell us the truth?"

O'Reilly narrowed his eyes and looked at John.

"Would ye lie to us, boyo? Knowing ye could've saved thousands from the disease?"

John nearly laughed in the man's face. Was he really attempting to appeal to John's altruistic nature? "I could if the thousands were related to you," John said.

"We'll see how funny ye are when I'm holding a gun to your little girlfriend's head, me boyo," O'Reilly said with a snarl.

"And how am I to pretend things are normal with my niece after all this?" Heaton said. "Won't she remember she was used to extract information from this lad? A lad who then permanently disappeared? Why exactly did you tell your man to bring her here?"

"Because there's no going back, Heaton," O'Reilly said, holstering his gun and turning on him. "The doc, the Yank, your niece…and you're barking if you think there is."

"I was mad to start this with you. And now for the life of me I can't remember why I did."

"For the ore, Heaton, if I need to remind you. You did it for the feckin' lithium deposits that Ireland has and England wants."

"It occurs to me, O'Reilly, that there's really nothing stopping us from just *taking* the ore." Heaton advanced on O'Reilly. His eyes looked fevered as he warmed to his idea. "We'll tell the world—if they're even interested—that we struck a deal with you. I understand your communications over there is still rubbish so our version will stand."

O'Reilly sputtered, "The United Nations would never let you do that!"

"You're joking, right? The world is upside down with recession, the effects of a fecking atom bomb and a world-class plague. Nobody will give a shite about poor little Ireland playing the bitch to England one more time."

"Got it all worked out, do you, Heaton? But I believe you've forgotten one key thing," O'Reilly said, the veins prominently displayed across his forehead.

"I would be entertained to hear what you think that might be," Heaton said coolly.

225

"Ye forgot what devious bastards we Irish can be," O'Reilly whispered into Heaton's ear as he pulled the man close to him. A knife materialized in his hand.

O'Reilly plunged it into Heaton's chest.

29

O'Reilly held the Scotsman in an embrace before taking a step backward. The knife clattered to the wooden floor. Heaton grasped for O'Reilly as he sagged to the ground. The wound in his chest was a fountain of blood. John gaped at the scene before him when a horror-laced scream pierced the unnatural quiet of the room.

Gilly stood in the doorway, her eyes on her dying uncle on the floor and the crazed man standing over him. O'Reilly swiveled around at Gilly's scream and pulled his handgun out. All John saw was the clear intent on the man's face. John launched himself at O'Reilly, hitting him at chest level just as the gun fired and knocking it to the floor. O'Reilly twisted in John's grip, slamming a palm into his chin, but John jerked his head away and missed the full brunt of it. O'Reilly swore and brought his knee up hard into John's stomach. John lost his breath. He fought not to react to the pain.

O'Reilly was still on the floor and he was reaching for something. It was precious seconds later before John recovered enough to see the knife in O'Reilly's hand. It was poised high in an arc over John and slashing downward. There was no place to go, no time to move out of the way.

The gunshot felt like it ripped through John. The noise filled the room until only echoes of the terrible sound were left vibrating through his head. O'Reilly lay instantly still beside him, a bullet hole in his throat and his eyes staring vacantly at the ceiling.

John scrambled to his feet. "Gilly!" He ran to where she lay in a growing puddle of blood. The hole from O'Reilly's bullet where her left eye should be.

227

"Noooooo. No, Gilly!" He pulled her across his lap, feeling her warmth, the softness of her skin. So still. So completely still. He knew she was gone but he couldn't let go of her. He couldn't help feel like he was keeping her warm, keeping her safe. When none of those things she would ever need again. He was dimly aware that a man was in the room, going first to the bodies of O'Reilly and Heaton and then to Dr. Lynch in her chair.

Finally, he came to where John sat with Gilly's body in his arms. John looked up at him, his face streaked with tears, He didn't even care what happened next.

The man held a gun loosely in his fingers. The same gun that had shot O'Reilly seconds earlier.

"My name is Shane," he said to John in a thick Irish accent. "And I am so sorry, lad," he said as he rechambered the gun.

30

It was cold everywhere in Ireland in February. Sarah liked to remember when she lived in Jacksonville, Florida where February often meant an early taste of spring more than a continuation of winter. Ireland wasn't like that. There'd been no snow for most of January—especially on the coast where she lived now—but it had still been bone cold.

The cottage she and Mike moved into two months earlier had served them well. Although she missed the larders full of stored harvest—corn, beets, and potatoes—that they enjoyed in the compound, she had to admit the steady diet of fresh fish almost made up for it. Every morning she woke up to the chill coming off the channel. There was a window at the front of the cottage that faced the sea and so she began her day with a prayer to God and a greeting to her boy across the water.

Wherever you are, dearest one, she thought as she gazed out the window toward England, *good morning. Take care of yourself today. Be well. Come back to me.*

Mike and Gavin spent their days along the coast fishing from shore or occasionally from small dinghys. The boats made her nervous. The little coastal village they lived in now which had once been the bustling fishing town of Rosslare was full of rumors of boats being sunk when they ventured too far from the shore.

When the men left, Sophia would come over and she and Sarah would bake bread, mend the men's clothes, and salt and store yesterday's fish for trading in the village—although trading fish in a fish town was a hard sell, as Mike would say. Each day, they breaded and fried up the day's catch when the men returned.

They had very little, except what they could trade for wine or whiskey or vegetables but the fellowship with the rest of the people in the town was good and it was warm. Sarah was reminded daily of the inherent goodness in people and that bolstered her hopes that John had found someone kind to look out for him.

During that special time of day when her chores were done and the men weren't back yet and the sun was sinking in the sky, she would walk to the stone kneewall that jutted out from the edge of the water. It was unprotected by trees or any other natural windbreak and so she was always alone when she went there to sit at the edge—the closest she could get to Wales without getting in a boat. And she would feel a sort of communion that gave her the strength to go another day with no news, another day where no boat came.

One day in the first week of February after Mike and Gavin had gone out as usual to fish, Sarah and Sophia walked the quarter mile to the center of town where there was often a market happening. Sophia was good with yarn and they often traded for wool for her to knit. Then they would trade the socks or sweaters that Sophia made. Often, they went just to talk to the other women and to see if there was any news.

This afternoon, Sophia had a pair of thick wool socks she'd made and Sarah hoped they would find produce to buy. She was closing in on seven months pregnant and any bit of greenery was precious to her. She craved anything fresh and worried the day would come when she couldn't stomach one more fish filet.

Sophia was always good company and Sarah had grown to love her. The girl worked hard, stayed generally cheerful, and adored Gavin. Mike was pretty crazy about her too.

"You think I am getting much for these?" Sophia asked holding up the socks as they walked to town. The small stump where the girl's pinky finger should have been never ceased to anger Sarah when she saw it.

"It is almost spring. Perhaps people will not want?" Sophia asked.

"Are you kidding?" Sarah said smiling. "It's freezing out. Trust me, they'll want."

She could see activity up ahead in the town center and felt a surge of relief that there was a market going on today. Just the thought of trading for some greens made her quicken her pace.

"*Merda!*" Sophia said with a gasp. "What is this thing?"

Sarah slowed when she saw what Sophia was pointing at on the beach. It looked like the metal grey of a tank or maybe a huge truck. Was it the Garda? Why were they here? As she moved closer, she realized it wasn't a tank or truck but a helicopter.

She began to run toward it.

The military helicopter had an insignia on the side that for Sarah was second only to an American flag—it was the British Union Jack. A helicopter from the UK? Did this mean the travel ban was lifted? As she got closer, Sarah saw that a small crowd had gathered around the helicopter. And since it didn't look like anyone was being arrested, she pushed through the crowd to get closer. Two young men in British military uniforms were standing by the enormous aircraft. One had a small notebook and was talking to an old lady from the village, while the other soldier seemed to be standing guard.

Sarah came upon a woman she knew from the village who was watching the soldiers. "Why are they here?" Sarah asked. "Does anybody know?"

A look of recognition passed across the woman's face and she immediately started waving her arms to the men by the helicopter and shouting. "Oy! Here she is!"

Looking back at Sarah she said, "They're looking for you, love."

Sarah saw the twinkle in the old woman's eye. She turned and walked toward the helicopter as the crowd parted to make a way. She was soon standing before the soldier with the notebook.

"Good morning," he said politely. "May I ask if you are the American Sarah Woodson Donovan?"

Sarah put her hand to her mouth to keep from crying out. "I am," she said hoarsely.

The soldier held a finger up to indicate she should wait a moment and then pulled a cellphone out of a pocket in his jacket, pushed in a number and held the phone to his ear. "Lieutenant," he said. "Tell the lad we found her."

He listened for a moment and then held the phone out to Sarah. "He'll have a word, Missus."

Sarah took the phone in her trembling hand. "Hello?" she said into it.

"Mom?"

Susan Kiernan-Lewis

Epilogue

The day after that phone call, the helicopter returned. This time, Sarah was waiting for it. Waiting with Mike and Gavin and Sophia and the entire village of Rosslare. If she ever had to recount the happiest moments of her life she knew it would have to be every minute and every second after she'd heard John's voice and knew he was alive and well—and coming home. Nothing else mattered and nothing else ever would.

She'd been tested and lived through an emptiness only a mother who has lost a child can ever know. And somehow, against all odds, she'd come out on the other side. The first day that the helicopter had come, she and Sophia went rushing back to their cottage to wait for Mike and Gavin to tell them the good news.

They were going to be a family again. All together. They'd paid no permanent price for their mistakes, their bad choices, their bad luck.

And now they stood and waited, watching the sky, and listening for the sound of the rotors that would herald the coming of the completion of their happiness.

Gavin saw it first.

"There it is!" he cried out. "Coming in at three o'clock. Dya see it?"

At first only a speck in the sky, it was all Sarah could do not to break down just to see the helicopter, growing bigger and coming closer.

"Happy, darlin?" Mike said kissing her cheek. He hadn't stopped grinning—not since he'd arrived home the day before and heard the good news. The miraculous news.

John was coming home.

As the four of them stood watching the speck grow larger in the sky, people from the town walked by and patted her shoulder, shook Mike's hand, and clapped Gavin on the back. They were all so happy for them.

233

Mike slid a warm strong arm around Sarah's waist and held her close. The helicopter was loud now and hovered overhead. Some of the crowd moved back to make room but Sarah knew they weren't standing on the landing spot. And she was never again going to be any further away from her child than she had to be.

Once the helicopter finally touched down, it seemed to take forever before the door opened. John was the first one out and Sarah literally moaned when she saw his familiar form as he jumped to the ground, looked around for her, and then grinned and came running. He flew into her arms. She felt the solid warmth of him and the familiar smell of him. She buried her face in his thick hair, then pulled back to look into his face.

It was him. Not changed. Not scarred. Her boy.

"Whoa, Mom," he said grinning. "Is there something you want to tell me?"

She paused and then realized, he hadn't known she was pregnant!

She laughed and put a hand on her stomach. She wanted to say that if he hadn't left in such a hurry she'd have told him, but she couldn't. She was too full of emotion to quip or do anything but hold him and cry.

"Oy! Can I have him long enough to throttle him?" Gavin said.

Sarah relaxed her grip on him and Gavin grabbed him and hugged him, thumping him on the back then pushing him to Mike who did the same. John looked so happy and now that Sarah was standing back a pace or two she noticed he was thinner and, for all the laughing and great big smiles…sadder.

There would be much for him to tell later. And she would hear it all. But for now, he was back and God was smiling on all of them.

*****

That night after dinner they all sat outside around a roaring fire in a giant black kettle that sat on the ancient stone seawall. John had just finished telling the basic facts of his adventure. Sarah didn't press him for the details she knew he'd left out. They had the rest of their lives for her to hear them.

"I wish you could've met Dr. Heaton and Gilly," John said to Sarah as they listened to the fire crackle in the pot. "I really loved them."

"I'm so grateful you found them and they you. I prayed you'd find people like that."

"So is the travel ban lifted?" Gavin asked with his arm around Sophia.

"It is," John said. "There's been a change of government here in Ireland. I met the new guy in charge." He made a face as if reliving an unpleasant moment. "He's maybe not the friendliest guy you'd ever meet but I think he'll do right by Ireland. At least a lot better than that wanker O'Reilly."

"Oh, my God!" Sarah said. "Liam O'Reilly? We met him. He took all our money."

"It was him that killed Gilly," John said. His voice was steady but Sarah could see how hard it was for him to say the words.

"I am so sorry, John," she said softly, reaching for his hand.

Mike came from around the cottage with an armful of kindling and dumped it by the fire kettle.

"So did I hear the ban's lifted because there's a cure now?" he asked.

"Yes sir," John said. "A cure that everyone has. Every country. Or they will have. It's being manufactured right now. In fact, a good friend of mine is in charge of doing it." He turned to his mother.

"I didn't want to ask you on my first night home and all, but I really want you to meet her, Mom. And if it's okay with you and Mike, I'd like to talk about me going back to Oxford to live with her."

Sarah's mouth fell open. "How...how old is this...is she?"

"No, Mom," John said, rolling his eyes. "It's not like that. She's ancient. At least forty-five. But she's offered to give me a place to stay while I go to school and if you really hate the idea, that's cool. It's just..."

"No, I understand. You're your father's son. Of course you want to go to school. And you should. Yes, we'll talk about it."

She looked at Mike and he smiled sadly. He knew exactly how she felt. She'd just gotten him back and now she needed to let him go again.

"I mean, it would just be for the school year. I'd come home to Ireland for school holidays and for the summer."

"It makes a lot of sense, sweetie. What is her name?"

"Dr. Sandra Lynch. She's leading the work on the cure. Or she will be as soon as she recovers. She…had an accident."

"How soon would you want to leave?"

"No time soon, Mom," he said laughing. "I just got here! Maybe April? Be gone for two months and then home for the summer?"

"That sounds good. That sounds perfect."

As the evening wound down, Sarah snuggled beside Mike and listened to John, Sophia and Gavin talk and laugh together.

"I couldn't be happier," she murmured to Mike. "It's all turning out the way it should."

"Aye, it is. Even with the lad going to school. You've tortured yourself for months wondering if you did the right thing by him."

"I know. And after the shock of the suggestion wore off, I can see it really is the best of all possible worlds."

"The lad's been through some things, though. I'll get him to talk about it bye and bye."

"That's good," Sarah said sleepily, fighting a yawn. "And we'll need to make plans for our trip back to Ameriland."

"That reminds me," Mike said. "Oy, John!"

"Yes sir?" John looked at Mike from across the fire, his face happy and relaxed.

"I'm surprised you didn't go straight to the compound when you went looking for your mum?"

"Well, naturally, I did," John said with a glance at Gavin. "I meant to ask you about that."

"I trust they haven't burned the place to the ground?"

"No sir," John said. "It was totally deserted."

To find out what happens next for Sarah, Mike,
John, Gavin and the rest of them,
sign up for the author's newsletter to be sure
and get notice of when the next installment in The
Irish End Game Series comes out!

ABOUT THE AUTHOR

Susan Kiernan-Lewis lives in Florida and writes mysteries and dystopian adventure. Like many authors, Susan depends on the reviews and word of mouth referrals of her readers. If you enjoyed *Rising Tides*, please consider leaving a review saying so on Amazon.com, Barnesandnoble.com or Goodreads.com.

Check out Susan's blog at susankiernanlewis.com and feel free to contact her at sanmarcopress@me.com.

Susan Kiernan-Lewis

Manufactured by Amazon.ca
Bolton, ON